The Traitors' Trial

ORIGIN STORY BOOK 3

Marc B. DeGeorge

MuseMarc Studio, LLC.

Acknowledgments

A story may be written by one person, but it takes many to turn it into a novel. To that end, I'd like to thank the following for their contribution to turning my typing into reality.

First, my dedicated and awesome reading group, Ben Pick, Salone More, E. Marie Robinson, Tracey Canole, and the awesome J. Logan Rice.

Thank you for your critical commentary, positive support, and friendship. My amazing editors, Savannah Gilbo and Brittany Dory. You have been a huge help in making this book a reality. Thank you.

Also, to my wife and family, for giving me the time to forge this next work, and every single one that follows!

One

"FINALLY!" GRADY SHOUTS. HE grabs the door handle even before the taxi stops and tries to rip it open. He can't, of course. Not even if he had Parrish's strength. Grady knows that the safety lock is keeping him inside and all that does is frustrate him more. I glance at my girlfriend, Kayley, and she returns the concerned look. We're here to support our bud, but we're a little lost for a solution to his misery.

His parents are getting arrested today.

Once it stops, Grady busts out of the taxi, his mop-top of hair flying in all directions. He hits the ground and looks around. When he doesn't find what he's looking for, he digs his hands into his hair and tears some of it out while shouting at the top of his lungs. Two seconds later Afton is out of the vehicle, restraining him.

"Stop messing up that beautiful head of yours," she says as she wrestles with him. Grady throws his arms up and slips from her hold. He backs away, but he listens to her, at least.

When Janek Moreno, Esquire, called last week to hire us, we thought it would be a simple investigation: find out who was threatening Drs. Sugiyama and O'Grady-Davies. We would only need to turn over their latest research and get the truth out there. Something I'd say we're getting fairly skilled at.

But then, two days ago, it turned nasty. Someone—we think it's the same person who made the threat in the first place—dropped a tip to those Anti-Sedition Ministry jerks. At first, Grady's parents were simply told to go home and wait for instructions, so we waited too. Now, this. There might be a way to stop this from happening, but we haven't figured it out yet

"Leave me alone, Surela!" Grady smacks her hand away when she reaches out to comfort him. He stomps towards his front door without even a glance back. Afton wrinkles her nose and folds her arms.

"Well, that's gratitude for you." She glowers after him.

"Go easy on him." Kayley lays a hand on Afton's shoulder as I follow her out of the taxi. "You know he's not good with stress."

Afton shrugs and follows Grady, who's already inside. Kayley and I wait for Parrish to hobble out. His knee has healed almost completely, but he still has some trouble with downhill slopes. Parrish says it's fine because we never went skiing anyway. Not that there's anywhere to do that on Angelcanis. Its two big continents are fairly flat, and unless you want to travel all the way to the poles to freeze your fingers and toes off, you're not going to find much more than a bunny slope.

"Thanks." Parrish wraps his arms around the both of us as he plants his feet on the ground. "It's always something, isn't it?"

"Yeah," I reply, "but this time some government nitwit picked a fight with the wrong people. We're two and oh in the match totals, and we did that with no money!" I grin. "Now, with near unlimited funding from Mr. Moreno, we're going to put this fool right in his place!"

"Or her place," Kayley adds. "Remember, darling, women aren't to be trusted any more than men."

I nod with a bit of vexation. I know exactly who my girlfriend is talking about—Ms. Danny Lecker, hand-hunter extraordinaire and our most recent source of angst. She turned out to be a nice person in the end, but Kayley forbade me to swap Sergo IDs with her. She may have forgotten I already have it, but I'm not going to cross the circuits in our near perfect relationship. I've made both of my dreams a reality—dating Kayley was one of them—and I'm not about to screw things up for myself.

The other is why I'm opening the door to Grady's house right now. Our team fights for the people of Angelcanis, legally or otherwise, and right now two of its most important citizens require our assistance. The only question is how do we help them avoid going to jail, even for a night?

"It's fine, Mom!" Grady says, making a feeble attempt to ward his mother off from squeezing his waist.

"You're not eating enough, Mutsu," Elenora O'Grady-Davies complains. "We left you plenty of automeals in the kitchen. All you had to do is put it in the range and have the steward bring it to you while you're working!"

"I haven't really been home that much..." Grady mumbles.

"And you should be getting outside more too. Photonic emissions from the sun help promote positive body function."

Parrish and I share a knowing grin. We did the right thing in kidnapping Grady to the beach two months ago. It might be a good idea to do it again.

"Mrs. O'Grady, I promise you that we will look after your son," Kayley says, stepping forward with a smile. "Shouldn't we—"

"Doctor," Grady's mom corrects. "It's Doctor O'Grady-Davies, dear. I use my maiden name for everything now. Tadao doesn't mind. And yes, thank you for looking after him. All of you have been good friends...mostly."

All except for me, apparently. Mrs. O'Grady-Davies shoots a wary eye over at me when she says that last part. Sure, Grady and I weren't exactly model students back in school. He didn't pay attention to lectures because he didn't need to. I didn't pay attention because I knew Grady would give me all the answers. In return, I got him through the subjects he absolutely had no interest in—law, history, and his most despised, physical education.

"Doctor O'Grady-Davies," Kayley says after taking a deep breath. "Shouldn't we be speaking with Mr. Moreno? If there's any way to avoid your arrest—"

"Thank you, Kayley," Doctor Tadao Sugiyama says with a smile. "But that won't be necessary. We are not afraid to face a court of law."

"We'll absolutely help Grady with anything," I say, attempting to ease whatever concerns they might have about their son. "He doesn't even need to ask. If it comes down to it, we'll bail you out."

"Grady..." Doctor Sugiyama chuckles. "Rance, I cannot believe you still call my son that. In casual company, I suppose it's fine, but in a professional environment, I would appreciate it if you would at least call him Mutsu, though I'd prefer if you used his full given name."

"Mutsumaji is such a mouthful," Grady whines.

"It was your great-grandfather's name, and he had no trouble with it. What a great man he was, yes? He developed the Empire's Al-Nasir star cruiser class, remember?"

Before Grady can respond, there's a knock at the door. I turn, muscles tightening. Kayley tenses next to me. Are the government agents here already? I thought we'd have more time to figure this out.

"Apologies for my tardiness." Janek Moreno takes his hat and shoes off as he enters the foyer. "I'm glad I arrived before the authorities. How is everyone?"

All this small talk is striking me as odd. Grady's parents—the two most respected ship designers in the entire Empire—are about to go to jail and stay there if we can't find a way to get them out. Yet neither they nor their lawyer are taking it seriously. What's going on?

"Excuse me, Mr. Moreno, but shouldn't we be discussing a strategy to keep them from showing up?" I ask.

"I'm sorry...?" He smiles at me as he pulls a small box from his jacket pocket.

"Rance."

"Ah, yes, young Mr. He'." He flips the box upside down and taps on it twice, sliding out a pair of thin rods. "So you're the leader of your team, correct?"

"Uh." I glance at Kayley, who's just going to let me crash and burn on my own should it come to that. "Actually, Kayley's the leader."

"Ms. Garmonichnyy. Of course. How are you, dear?" He places one of the rods from the box in his mouth. A crunch later, I realize it's a chocolate-covered pretzel. Mr. Moreno offers the second one to Kayley, but she declines.

Why are we not getting on this impending doom that's about to befall Grady's parents? Are they looking forward to some quiet time in a cell? They have no idea what it's like to be locked up. I have been—twice—and I can't say I recommend it. We need to get this conversation moving.

"I'm fine, thank you, Mr. Moreno." Kayley smiles with her best *you're going to do what I say now* gaze. "Could you explain how this is supposed to happen? Is there any way to avoid it?"

"Of course," Mr. Moreno replies, crunching again and then waving the rest of the pretzel around as he talks. "It's all very civilized, so not to worry. First, two agents will show up at the door, and they will escort Doctors Sugiyama and O'Grady-Davies to the courthouse, where the clerk will read the charges, and then they will enter a plea. After that, the judge will decide whether they will await trial at home or to hold them in the prison."

"Could that happen?" Grady asks, his eyes widening. "Could they really not come home?"

"No, likely not," Mr. Moreno replies. "With people as high-profile as your parents and the type of crime they are likely to be charged with, there is no reason for the judge to make a ruling such as that, and to answer your other question, Kayley, now that there's an arrest warrant, I'm afraid we've little choice but to comply."

"That can't just be it," I say, trying to remember some of my law class. "There's got to be a solution. What are they being charged with, anyway?"

"I would suspect the theft of classified materials," his father replies, "but I wouldn't worry about it, Mutsumaji. Your mother and I have the highest level of security approval. Only the Emperor and his highest ministers have anything above that. This is just a misunderstanding, and we'll have it cleared up shortly."

So, that would explain why none of them are taking this seriously. Instead, they think it's just some mixup that will get cleared up by lunchtime. I wonder why he brought us into this, then. Why ask us to investigate when the threat wasn't even a big deal? I need to find out.

"ATTENTION! TADAO SUGIYAMA AND ELENORA O'GRADY-DAVIES! THIS IS AGENT KOPELL FROM THE MINISTRY OF ANTI-SEDITION ACTION. YOU ARE COMPLETELY SURROUNDED! I ADVISE YOU TO EXIT THE BUILDING, UNARMED, WITH YOUR HANDS RAISED! IF YOU DO NOT COMPLY, WE WILL BE FORCED TO ENTER BY ANY MEANS AND APPREHEND YOU!"

"What the heck?" Afton peers out the window. She jumps at what she sees, and now all of us want to know what's happening out there. I lean on her and peer over her shoulder.

"Oh, wow."

If two agents were supposed to show up quietly, no one gave them that memo. There's got to be forty officers out there! They're outfitted like military with plasma rifles and body armor. There's even an armored truck out there, along with five other vehicles. Their lights are all flashing blue-white-blue, and a searchlight powers on and scans the front of the house.

A flurry of questions hits Mr. Moreno all at once. He blinks and throws his hands up as if he can physically block the sound from reaching his ears. Kayley and Grady advance on him, but he does his best to keep his cool.

"Not to worry. Again, this is just some misunderstanding." He turns towards the door. "I'll go out there and calm things down. Everyone just stay here a moment, and I'll get this cleared up."

We all gather at the window and watch as Mr. Moreno descends the steps. Two heavily armed officers run up to meet him. Their guns swing up to take aim at him. He freezes in place, glancing between them and a man with a voice amplifier in his hand.

"On the ground! On the ground!" one of them shouts. Mr. Moreno throws his hands up. I can tell from here that they're shaking like mad. Mine would be, and I've had guns aimed at me before.

One of the officers grabs him around the back of the neck and forces him to the ground. He tries to protect his face from impacting the ground by covering his arms over his head, but it doesn't make much of a difference.

"What is going on?" Grady's mouth drops open as the officers handcuff Mr. Moreno and drag him to one of the patrol vehicles.

"Attention! I won't tell you again! Come out now, or we're coming in for you! You have five seconds to comply!"

"This is highly improper," Dr. Sugiyama states, his face red. "This is not what we agreed to."

"What do we do?" I turn to Kayley, hoping she's got some answer, but she just sighs.

"Can we get out a back way?" Parrish asks. Dr. Sugiyama shakes his head.

The front window shatters as a round projectile smashes through it, followed by another. We're showered in glass fragments before any of us has a chance to react. Grady's mom lets out a yelp. I grab Kayley and pull her down with me.

That's when smoke begins to burst from those round projectiles—smoke bombs! They're really going to come in after us!

Before I can make another move, the heavy oak front door shatters and officers pour in. More come from the back of the house, rifles and lights up and sweeping across the room.

"Down! Down! On the ground!" they shout at us as the rest of our group hits the floor. Only Afton is defiant, and she gets the butt of a gun across her face for it. She goes down with a cry, her hand covering her face. I grit my teeth, anger flooding through me. But there's nothing I can do. I just wrap my arms around Kayley, and she does the same to me.

"Doctors Sugiyama and O'Grady-Davies, you are under arrest for violating Code 41-A-7 of the Anti-Sedition law," Agent Kopell says, standing over them as they stare back in horror. "You will come quietly, or we will use any force necessary to restrain you."

So much for the casual escort.

Two

THE GUARDS LEAD US, no longer handcuffed, into the courtroom. The place is overdone in tradition. An ornate wooden bench for the judge, wooden paneling on the walls, and more than enough flags representing the court, the planet, and the Empire. It's packed with an assortment of reporters, dignitaries, and thrill seekers who think they will raise their stature in society just by being here.

My body is bumped and bruised, and my shoulder muscles are over-stretched from my hands being behind my back for an entire night. My friends are just as bad off, especially Afton, whose face is swollen from that unnecessary aggression by the officer who hit her. Only Grady's parents are unharmed, but not unaffected. They hang their heads, either from exhaustion or shame. None of us got any sleep last night and no one has apologized for our false arrest. If we were citizens of the Empire we'd be making a huge fuss. But we're not, so there's little we can do about it.

I remember my first stint in lockup. It began less violently but ended up with our first success—a full-fledged minister of Parliament! We took him down for starting a war with the Teddys. He's not a minister any longer, but he's also not in jail. He's got too many powerful friends.

"All rise, the Honorable Judge-Superior Hamlin presiding," the court sergeant calls. We never got a chance to sit, so we remain standing until the tall-as-a-tentpole judge walks in and bids us all sit. Since there aren't enough seats at the defendant's table, and since my buds and I are no longer under arrest, we take the first row of seats behind. Grady wanted to sit next to his parents, so they let him.

"This arraignment will come to order." Judge Hamlin taps his gavel and turns to the court clerk. "As duly ordained by His Majesty, the Emperor Joris Regis the Fourteenth, I call on this court to address and name the charges as brought against the accused. Is the clerk ready and able to speak these charges?"

"I am." The clerk, a white-haired pompous type, steps up to the lectern that faces the room. He places a tablet down on the stand and turns to the judge.

"The accused must stand for the reading," Judge Hamlin says, then nods to the clerk. "You may proceed."

"As by the highest authority of this court and by the command of the Emperor, Tadao Sugiyama and Elenora O'Grady-Davies, you are hereby accused of one count of treason, one count unlawful appropriation of Imperial documents, one count intent to conceal said documents, and one count of transgression against a direct order from the Emperor."

The people in the gallery gasp and create enough commotion that the judge has to bang on his gavel until they quiet down. So, it's treason, not a simple issue of theft. That would explain the army that came to arrest them, but it doesn't excuse their rough treatment of us.

"How do the accused plead?"

"Your Honor." Mr. Moreno reaches into his jacket pocket only to come up empty. Then he seems to realize his pretzel box is on the table, crushed and torn from yesterday's mess. "My clients wish to enter a plea of not guilty as per their right to do so. They claim no responsibility for the charges brought forthwith and also wish to enter a statement into the record, if it may please the court."

"Do you have this statement in written form?"

"We do, Your Honor."

"Then hand a copy to the clerk so we can add it to the record."

I'm not really into this stuffy nonsense. There's no reason for this to take longer than a few minutes, but it's going to go way longer than that. I've seen court proceedings before. Not just on cine, but on vid too. There's a lot of proving how important the court procedure is, more than there is about whether someone is guilty of the crime they're being charged with. This isn't even the actual trial yet.

"Counsel for the prosecution, you have heard the plea from the defense. Do you have any reason why I should not release them to await their trial at home?"

"We do, Your Honor."

A chill runs down my spine when I hear the voice that responds to the judge. I know that voice. I know it all too well, even if I haven't heard it in years. I want to look, but I'm afraid to. It's not possible that it could be him, but I know that there can be no other reason for my absolute panic.

"What's wrong?" Kayley asks, picking up on my sudden tension.

"It's..." I steel myself and twist my head towards the table for the prosecution. "It's..."

"Rance, what is it?"

"My dad."

And sure enough, there he is, standing behind the prosecutor's table. He's a little older and a little grayer than I remember him, but his face is unmistakable. I know it because it's almost identical to mine. Eight years ago, that older version of me walked out on us, with no reason and no communication after that. It caused me all sorts of anguish. I was just getting over that. Now he comes back into my life.

This trial just became a complete nightmare for me.

Kayley turns to look at him. She stares for a few moments before I see recognition in her face. Her arms wrap around me, and she presses her head into mine. I press back, grateful for the momentary respite from my dread. My girlfriend has always been good at helping me this way. I just didn't realize how much I needed it until now. I'd really prefer not to be here right now, but I want to support my friend, and holding onto Kayley's hand, tightly, is giving me the strength to do that.

"Thank you, Prosecutor Cavalcante. You may proceed with your presentation."

"Thank you, Judge." My dad steps out from behind the desk and bows to the judge, then he turns towards the table for the defense, scanning it. He knows Grady's parents, though not very well. I'm sure that whatever relationship still exists there will have no bearing on his determination to prosecute them. He gave up his family for the opportunity to lead cases like this. A few acquaintances won't make a difference to him.

"Rance, is that..." Grady turns to me, wide-eyed. When he catches me cringing against Kayley, he gets the answer he was looking for, but not the one he was hoping for. His slumped shoulders and reddening eyes state that without any doubt. I can't help but agree.

We're in big trouble.

"Your Honor, the accused have held a position not just of authority, but of ultimate responsibility. Their knowledge is the catalyst by which our Emperor projects his strength and his authority. Surely the accused know this. Therefore, it is necessary...no, it is *imperative* that the court rule them as a menace to the Empire. We, the prosecution, ask Your Honor that the accused be incarcerated until such time that a free and fair trial may be performed."

As I expected, my father makes an inspired plea to the ultra-royalists in the gallery. People stamp their feet and pound on the backs of the benches. There's a solid majority supporting the prosecution, and they're not afraid to be heard. I hope the jury isn't selected from this group. We'll lose for s ure.

There is one small hope that comes out of this. It's remote, and next to impossible, but if my father has any sort of love left for his son, he might just listen to me. If I beg and plead enough, he may just agree to drop the case against Grady's parents. I don't know if I can, and I'm really unsure whether I can gather up enough courage to even talk to him.

No, I have to help my bud. For his sake, I'll try.

"Thank you, Mr. Prosecutor." Judge Hamlin turns to Mr. Moreno. "Does the defense have any statement contrary to what the prosecution has claimed?"

"We do, Your Honor." Mr. Moreno struggles to stand. He might be doing it for show, but I can guess there's at least a little truth in his agony. Of course, the reporters eat it up. I can hear the cameras whirring and clicking away with every strained motion he makes.

"If it may please the court, I have not one, but two points that I'm sure will refute any statement the prosecution has made." Mr. Moreno straightens up and steps from behind the desk to stride about the space. His bow is both deeper and longer than my father's routine formality. He turns and bows to the gallery, too, and I grin internally. Whatever he says, I know it's going to have an impact.

"The first—I can prove without a hint of doubt the accused's loyalty to the Emperor and the Empire. Doctors Sugiyama and O'Grady-Davies have served in their positions for over twenty Imperial years. During their time, they have developed over fifty new ship designs and advanced the technologies of the Empire more than three hundred times!"

Mr. Moreno swivels between the judge and the gallery, watching for their reactions. I catch several pressed lips and vigorous nods. So, there are a few of their supporters out there. The others stay silent, but I can tell by the redirection of their eyes that they respect the contributions of Grady's parents. No one else could have done so much. If this puts any doubt into my father's brain, I may have a way to reach him.

"Secondly," he continues, "at no time during that twenty plus years have they ever been out of contact with the Minister of Defense, his aides, or any high-ranking official of the military. They have been cooperative with the investigation, even after agents of the Anti-Sedition Ministry forcibly arrested two innocent people who were ready to go without contest!"

A disturbed murmur erupts in the gallery. One man stands and cries out in disgust. Our arrest must have been kept quiet from the media outlets.

"Counsel, that is a serious accusation," the judge says. "Do you have any evidence to submit to support your claim?"

"I do!" To the surprise of everyone, Grady jumps up and thrusts a finger at Afton, who slides down in her seat. "Take a look at my friend's face! That happened yesterday when an officer smashed her with his gun!"

Shouts of outrage combine with yells of "lies!" and "slander!" The gallery turns on itself, and the judge has to pound out a warning before it begins to quiet down.

"Son, this is a criminal court of law," Judge Hamlin says to Grady. "Any accusation that is laid before this court is taken seriously. I will be ordering a full investigation into it."

"Thank you, Your...Your Honor," Grady replies. That's at least something.

"Now, I know who you are, and I understand that you are trying to protect your parents, but I want you to understand that we follow tradition and decorum in this court. Outbursts, like the one you just made, do not fit within our procedures, so I will warn you not to do it again, or I will find you in contempt of court. That means you will be arrested and potentially face a term in jail should I so decide. Do you understand?"

Grady's nod of confirmation is barely visible beyond the front of the courtroom. I think he surprised himself with his explosion. Still, I'm impressed by my introverted friend. Speaking in front of audiences is not anywhere near an enjoyable pastime for him.

"Does the defense have anything else to add?" Judge Hamlin asks as he motions for Grady to sit down again.

"No, Your Honor," Mr. Moreno replies. "I think my statement stands for itself."

"Very well. Would the accused please rise? I will now announce my judgment on whether you will be put under house arrest or whether you will await trial in jail. But before I do, is there anything you want to say on your behalf?"

So this is it. I squeeze Kayley's hand, and she squeezes back. We don't need to speak or even share a look. The sheer anxiety we share is transmitted through our fingers. I'm pressing myself to have confidence. Mr. Moreno made a really strong argument. While my father...

I glance over at the prosecutor's table again. He's discussing something with his colleague as they await the judge's decision. I shouldn't, but I keep staring at him. I'm not sure if I'm falling into shock or if I just can't believe it's him. I never expected to see him again anywhere, much less as the lead prosecutor of Grady's parents. My breathing gets short as I think about having to talk to him. To actually walk up to him and find some way to beg him to stop this nightmare of a trial.

"Rance," Kayley whispers into my ear. "You okay?"

"I...yeah." I don't want to freak Kayley out. "Why?"

"Because you stopped breathing half a minute ago."

Judge Hamlin's gavel pulls me back to reality.

"I have heard both sides," the judge says. "And while the accusations made by the defense are difficult, they do not have a bearing on my decision. The charges put forth by the prosecution are severe and in a great enough number that I must weigh them with the importance they deserve. Therefore, it is my judgment that the accused are to be held without bail until such time that this court can schedule a free and fair trial. Sergeant, please take Doctors Sugiyama and O'Grady-Davies into custody. Counsel, please approach the bench so we may choose a date for the trial."

"No..." Grady gasps. "Mom...Dad..."

"Mutsu." His dad turns to him as the court officers approach. "I don't want you to worry about us. You'll have a great deal of responsibility taking care of the house and accounts. Don't disappoint us, son."

With that, his parents depart, and so does whatever hope I had of turning this around with a conversation. The smug look on my father's face turns my insides out. I can't talk to him like this. I don't even know why I was thinking I could.

I need to get out of here.

Three

As we shuffle from the courtroom, Mr. Moreno attempts to cheer Grady up with whatever appeals or legal maneuvers he can apply to get his parents released to home arrest. Grady just hangs his head while Parrish and Afton help walk him out. They've got their arms around him, but he makes no indication that he notices.

Kayley and I follow behind, hand in hand. I wish I could do something for Grady, but if Kayley, master of words, can't find something supportive to say, then I've got no chance whatsoever to make him feel better. I know that none of us are going to let him be alone tonight, regardless if he agrees or not.

"Rance!"

My leg freezes in place before I take my next step. No, not now—I can't face him now. If I speak one word to my father, the conversation will collapse into a global thermonuclear war.

"Keep going," I whisper to Kayley, but it's not her who's stopped. She turns to look at me, a question on her lips.

"Rance!"

I sigh. It's too late. He's caught up with us. I don't really want to make a scene in the courtroom, but I have no idea how I'm going to react. I know how I *want* to react, but that would likely get me thrown in jail right next to Grady's parents.

"Go, I'll catch up," I say to the others. Afton glares back at my approaching father, then nods and ushers Grady out.

"I'm staying with you," Kayley says, and I grit my teeth. She's doing exactly what I didn't want her to, but I truly love her for defying my wishes. I'm certain that I would commit some level of violence if she wasn't here.

My father steps up to us, wearing an uncertain smile that might be an attempt at covering up his own discomfort. Good. I hope he's as bothered by this confrontation as I am. Actually, I hope it's worse for him.

"This is unexpected," my dad begins. "Though I suppose it's nice to see you've kept your friendships going for as long as you have. Is this...Kayley?"

"It is," Kayley responds, tightening her grip on my hand. She might be trying to tell me she's got my back, or she might be preparing to keep me from punching him in the face.

"Well, good to see you too. I remember when you were just a toddler. Your mother would bring you over to play with Rance." He glances down at our entwined fingers and raises his eyebrows. "So, you two are dating? How long?"

"What do you want?" I spit through my teeth.

"To talk to my son. Is that alright?"

"If you wanted to talk to me, you could have called anytime in the last eight years."

My father tenses his jaw and ducks his head. I would smirk at my scored point, but my face has petrified into a permanent glare. I'm ready to pound him with several million other points that I've collected over the years. All he has to do is press the right button, and I'm off. There are quite a few buttons too.

"Listen," he says. "I realize this isn't the proper place for this conversation. Why don't we go—"

"I'm not going anywhere with you."

But Kayley tugs on my arm in encouragement. She wants me to have this conversation, even if I don't. She thinks that it'll be good for me, but I have my doubts. Though, it might be good to commit murder. I might feel better for it. Now *that* would be good for me.

"Well," he says, "there's another trial beginning in here shortly, so we can't stay here."

Kayley digs a nail into my palm, forcing a glance in her direction. She brings out that all-powerful smile of hers, and that means I have a choice. Either speak with my dad now or listen to her tell me how I screwed up for the next two weeks.

The lesser of two evils is definitely my dad.

"Fine, where then?"

"There's an atrium on top of the building. I go there to have my lunch sometimes. It should be quiet at this point in the morning."

Silence comes between the three of us as we make our way to the roof. Small talk is a waste of breath. It's good to use when you want to get to know someone or build a relationship. I have no intention of either when it comes to my dad.

The tightness in my chest makes the climb up the stairs difficult. Kayley takes notice of my dragging feet and takes the lead to help me. My father is a few steps ahead and staring forward towards the polycarb enclosure that makes up the atrium roof.

I wonder what might be going through his head right now. I don't really care, but I am curious. What does he expect to accomplish with this talk? There's no way he's going to overcome eight years of hard feelings in a single conversation. It's not like he can just give me some random explanation and then I'll forgive everything. Until he gets on his knees and apologizes to my mom, there's no way I would even consider it.

"I want you to know," my father says, turning his head back to me, "this is not a personal vendetta against the Sugiyamas. The Emperor himself asked me to take charge of this case. I'm sure you understand."

I keep my mouth shut. There's no good reply that I can think of that would result in me agreeing with his assessment. I don't understand. And that lack of comprehension stems from the moment he walked away from his family.

"Why?"

"Why did I choose to obey a direct command from His Majesty?" He sits in a semicircular enclosure that's covered by vines wrapped around a lattice made of twigs. If it weren't for this moment and this conversation, I might enjoy a quiet moment here with Kayley.

"No. Why did you leave?"

He crosses his legs and takes a breath.

"You really want me to explain that?"

"You *owe* it to me to explain it!"

Kayley tugs me down to sit next to her on the side of the bench, facing my father. She's been abstaining from saying a word, and I know that must be hard for her. If she's going to back me this much, I owe it to her to have this conversation.

"I suppose that's fair," my dad says after a considered moment. "And I suppose an apology is due you as well. Rance, I'm sure that it isn't something that you'll accept from me so easily, but I am sorry, my son. I—"

"You don't get to call me that, no matter how sorry you are."

"Whether or not you forgive me, that doesn't change the fact that I am your father, and you are my son." His prosecutor's mask comes down across his face. "Now, will you hear me out or not?"

The wrong words nearly fly from my mouth. I want to tell him to go to hell or that I never want to talk to him again. That he's hurt my mom and me to such a level that he can't ever be forgiven. But I realize I would never get the answers I need to hear if I did that. Not that it will be easy to hear. I don't know what's more painful, to know or not know.

But if I could take something back to my mom, some information that might help cure her own wounds, then I can tolerate listening to him. At least for a few minutes.

"I'll listen."

"Good." He nods, and the sides of his mouth curl up just a bit.

Was he really worried that I'd say no?

"Rance, you may not believe this, but I had an impossible decision to make. Of course, things were going well for me on Angelcanis, and I was looking forward to the day that you graduated so we could start working together." He shifts on his bench and turns away for a moment. "About a week before I left, a member of Parliament approached me. He told me of the chief DA's...indiscretions. I was shocked because I would have never expected Chief Sukebe to be a dishonest man. I mean, he was my mentor. I had learned a lot from him."

"Fine. I get it." I narrow my eyes at him. "Why don't you skip to the part where you just had to leave us?"

Kayley knocks into me gently—more of her non-verbal prodding. This time she's saying, *Shut up and just listen, Rance, before you ruin the opportunity.*

"I'm telling you all of this because I want you to understand, Rance, that my choice was never going to be one where everyone is happy with the results. Especially the chief. I had to testify against him. The man I looked up to. I had to help take him down. Maybe you'd be glad to know that I chose to do so because it followed our mission, son. I was protecting the people of Angelcanis by doing it, and if I could receive a promotion in the process, all the better. Think of it, Rance. The higher I go in authority, the more capability I have for protecting our planet."

"That still doesn't tell me why you left without telling us."

"That wasn't my choice, Rance. The Emperor commanded me to go to Albion, immediately."

"Why would the Emperor command someone to leave their family?"

My father tilts his head and just looks at me. It's a question he's got no answer for. Only the Emperor would have the truth of it, and I won't be talking to him anytime soon. I don't really care. Some man on a throne is not someone I have much respect for. Now that I just learned he took my father from me, I have even less for him.

"Why didn't you at least call and explain after?" There's accusation in my voice.

"I couldn't."

"Then how about a message or a letter?" My tone picks up even more of an edge.

"It wasn't possible, Rance."

"Do you really care for us that little?" I shout. Kayley jumps, but I'm so on fire that I can't stop. "Do you even understand how much you hurt her? Do you? And for what? Whatever did your promotion get us?"

Kayley puts a hand on my arm to restrain me. That's when I notice I'm just about to jump off the bench and launch myself at him. I'm breathing hard now, the edges of my eyes threatening to break out in a torrent of moisture. I'm shooting flames at my father, and he replies with a cool gaze of his own. That burns me even more.

"Alright." My father uncrosses his legs and drops his hands on his lap. "I suppose I was expecting a little too much from this talk. I see how you've been keeping this in for so long, so it's okay that it's coming out like this."

He stands, and I look away. Here he is again, leaving, and I've got no more real answers than I had before. The whole "I did this for you" attempt to explain things has only got me more confused. Is he trying to guilt me into understanding? I've got so much rage built up over him, I can't even consider why he'd do that.

"I want you to know how excited I was to see you this morning." He takes a step towards Kayley and me. "I've heard about your recent accomplishments. Minister Crowley, Deputy Brownrigg...you've really grown into a young man of integrity. You're fighting to protect the people of Angelcanis, and I could not be more proud of you, son."

"I told you not to call me that," I growl.

That pushes him away, and I immediately regret it. My father turns to go but pauses and turns back.

"I'm sure you're going to be around for the trial. You were always good about supporting your friends. No matter what the outcome, I do hope I get to talk to you again."

I shouldn't have seen him like this. I can't believe he's the lead prosecutor in my friend's parents' trial. And then for him to make excuses for running away? It's just too much. The moment he's gone, I drop my head in Kayley's lap and sob.

Four

Parents are difficult, no matter what the situation. I tried to talk with my father, and that didn't go very well. Now here we are, in the visitors' waiting room of the lockup where Grady's parents are being held, and I'm hoping his conversation goes way better than mine did.

It takes him a few minutes to gather himself up and approach the counter where he can fill out the request. Then we will wait. And wait. And at the end of all that waiting, what should happen is he gets to go to a special room where he can have a pleasant chat and see how they're doing. If all goes well, there will be some quality time spent between parents and child, and then there's only the trial to freak out over.

This waiting room is not a great place to center your calm. First of all, it's in the center of a prison. There's no décor. Nothing to read, not even a plant to add some atmosphere. It's just badly painted gray walls with a single blue line running through them at about waist height. The seats—if you can call them that—are hard plastic, and they're bolted into the floor so they can't be used as a weapon. The only distraction to keep you from thinking about why you're in a prison waiting room is a vid screen, safely protected by metal grill. Right now it's playing a repeating program from Angel-1—a forum discussing Grady's parents.

"So, when are they coming?" Afton asks. "Shouldn't they know where their prisoners are?"

"Afton," Kayley chides and pokes her in the arm. "Let's not call them prisoners, okay?"

"What else should we call them?"

"How about we call them Doctors Sugiyama and O'Grady-Davies?"

Afton rolls her eyes, which is her way of acquiescing to Kayley.

"Is there any reason they wouldn't let Grady see them?" I ask. It seems like we've been waiting a long time, though it's difficult to tell. The repeating Angel-1 program doesn't help, and they made us leave our Sergos at the security entrance.

"No," Kayley replies. "He's their son, so he's got every right to." I knew that. The law makes it a requirement of all prisons to allow familial visits, time of day notwithstanding. The only exception is when the facility has an emergency.

With nothing else to do, I slide a little closer to Kayley and turn to watch the program on the vid screen for the third time. They've changed it up a little, adding a live reporter from outside the prison. But she's just repeating the same things they've been talking about for the last infinite number of minutes.

"I can't believe it," Grady moans as he walks up to us, throwing his arms out and sighing. "They won't see me!"

"They won't let you in?" Kayley asks. "But they have to, it's the law."

"No, my parents refused the visit."

Afton, Kayley, and I all share a glance. I'm not sure I understand. Why would they not want to see him? Are they ashamed? No, that can't be it. More likely, they don't want to be a distraction for Grady, which makes sense to me when I think about it. They've always been about Grady's success as a person and an engineer. Sometimes that interest in seeing their son prosper has verged on abusive parenting, but they've always wanted the best for him. Their imprisonment and trial have no place in that plan.

"Should we go, then?" Afton asks. I don't think she's trying to be indifferent, but she's doing a good job of making it look that way.

"No, wait," Kayley says. "Grady, isn't there something else we can do? We shouldn't just leave. That's not what you want, is it?"

Grady hangs his head. It's not what he wants, but I also think he doesn't know what to do. I'd have the same dilemma if my mom was in jail and refused to see me. And just like Grady, I don't have a clue what I would do about it.

The vid program bleeps in that annoying "I want your attention" tone. It always works too. I look up at the screen, which is now showing some kind of special report. It's all special reports and breaking news these days. No one wants to watch the good old-fashioned news anymore.

And I have no interest in watching anything at the moment. Our bud needs us and we've got to help him figure out what he should do next.

"Why don't we go get something to eat and come back?" I suggest. "Maybe then they might be more willing to see you?"

"Come on, dude," Grady replies. "When can you remember my parents changing their mind about anything?"

It's true, they never do, so I've got no idea how to refute that. I also have no idea how to solve his problem. If they won't see him, there's little we can do about it, yet none of us want to just get up and head home.

"Grady, why don't you sit down for a little bit?" Kayley pats the seat next to her and gives him a smile.

"No, thanks." Instead, he crosses his arms and paces in front of us. Afton hums in a dissatisfied tone. She's just verbalizing what we all feel.

A word from the special report catches my ear and I look up. A protest has formed outside the prison. It's all royalists and conspiracy nuts who, without any evidence presented yet, have already decided that Grady's parents are guilty.

Grady's eyes are on the screen too, and I try to distract him the moment I notice. He doesn't need to see this. It'll only make him more upset than he already is.

"Hey, so what about that food, huh?" I glance at Kayley to try to get her to play along.

"Sounds like a good idea," she adds, catching on.

"If you're hungry you two can go, I won't mind." Grady turns and looks back at the clerk's desk.

"But I would," Afton adds. "I'm hungry too."

I try to communicate my entire *that's not what we're going for* message through my eyes at Afton. She either ignores it or takes no notice. Either way, it's not helpful. I wanted all of us to give Grady a little needed buddy-pressure so he would agree to go with us.

"Are you not hungry?" Kayley tries switching to mom mode.

"Not at all."

"But you barely ate any breakfast."

"I think you can understand why."

"Grady." Kayley reaches out for his hand and stops him from pacing. "You may not feel like it, but you know it's not healthy for you to do that. Now why don't you—"

A red light flashes around the room, breaking us from our buddy-saving attempt. We glance around like the rest of the visitors, wondering what's happening. Red flashing lights are standard portents for bad things happening, but when I look over at the clerk at the desk, she hasn't moved at all.

I'm thinking that we need to get up and get out before something goes wrong, but nobody else is moving. Grady's stopped pacing, at least, so that's a plus.

"I'm going to find out what's up," Afton says and goes to speak with the clerk. In the meantime, we're back to our main dilemma.

"Grady, tell us what you're feeling," Kayley says.

"I think you know."

"Sure, but I want to hear it from you."

"I really don't think they're going to change their minds, but…"

"But?"

"I'm not ready to give up."

"Dude," I say. "If we go home, that's not giving up. We're never going to give up on your parents. Maybe we can't see them today, but that doesn't mean we can't see them tomorrow, or the next day."

He mulls that over for a moment, while Afton comes back with a shrug.

"She said it's probably just a drill. If there's no alarm sounding, then it's likely no problem."

That seems to comfort Grady a little. I guess that even if he sees logic in my suggestion, he really doesn't want to leave. I know Grady loves his parents, but they are right about one thing—he needs to be more independent from them. That he's not is mostly their fault. They wanted him to be even more successful than them so badly, they micromanaged his life to guarantee success. Now my bud is not only stuck in a prison waiting room, he's stuck with indecision.

Then the alarm that wasn't supposed to go off does, along with a flashing white light to go on top of the red one. The clerk at the desk stands up, and so do the rest of us. A guard walks in, her pace speedier than the norm. She talks to the clerk in hushed tones, then turns to face all the visitors.

"Ladies and gentlemen, for the safety of our guards and the inmates, we are temporarily securing the main gate. We advise you to stay here and remain calm. Visitations will resume once we reopen."

"Remain calm?" Afton says, looking at all of us. "They just said they're going to lock us in here with inmates and we're supposed to be happy about that?"

Grady's eyes drop and Afton realizes her mistake.

"Sorry, buddy. I didn't mean…"

"S'ok. I have to accept it."

"Can't we leave?" a woman holding a baby in her arms asks. "My baby has a doctor's appointment."

The guard put her hands on her hips and stares at her for a moment. She's considering something. Perhaps weighing the risks of letting a woman and child out the door and what danger they might be in if she does.

"Alright," the guard replies, "if you have to, I can escort you to the employee gate. It's around the side of the building, away from the protest."

Protest? So that's it. They're concerned about it getting out of hand. The vid screen is just replaying their standard program, so there's no update there. I wonder just how bad it has to be out there to make a highly secure facility concerned for their safety.

"Anyone else want to leave?" the guard asks.

"Hey, that's our cue," Afton says, prodding me with her foot. I'm in agreement with her since we're not likely to accomplish much today by sitting around here and waiting.

"Grady?"

My bud turns to me and sighs. I know he recognizes the futility of the situation, but with another glance at the clerk's desk he makes it obvious he still can't make a decision.

So Kayley makes one for him.

"Grady, it's dangerous for you to be here," she says. "Let's go back to your house, and we'll think of a reasonable way to get through to your parents. Besides, being here is doing nothing but causing you pain, and I don't want you to suffer."

Any more than you already have is the part she leaves out. I wouldn't want to remind him of it either.

"Hey, are you four going?" the guard asks. "It's now or never. Things are getting rough out there."

Grady nods twice, a grimace on his face. I feel for my bud. He's got a lifetime of struggle sitting on his shoulders right now.

"Yes," Kayley says. "We're leaving."

Five

"Keep your eyes open," I say to Afton as she, Kayley, and I lead Grady towards the final gate at the entrance to the prison. The guard warned us to be on our toes before getting the all-clear from her colleagues and then shoving us out the door.

Afton replies with a short nod and steps through the gate first. She scans the area, then glances back at us. All good. No sign-wielding nutjobs outside waiting for us. I'm the next out, and I turn back to keep an eye on my girlfriend as she escorts Grady with her arms wrapped around his. I smile at her, grateful for all that she does for our friends and for me. Kayley smiles back and they move through the gate.

The street just outside the gate is deserted. It's surrounded by the pale concrete walls of the industrial park that the prison sits in. If any convict ever thought the Empire wanted to treat them kindly, all they would have to do is take a look outside to know the truth.

"Shoot, we forgot to call a taxi." I look to Kayley for an answer. Her smile and shrug, followed by a nod in my direction, are all the impetus I need to reach into my pocket and grab my Sergo.

"Shoot! We left our stuff inside at the gate!" In our rush to get out, we totally forgot that we checked all of our electronic equipment, including our Sergos, with security at the main entrance. I'm already having withdrawal symptoms just thinking about how I won't be able to scan the latest gossip on the cine forums.

That's when we hear the commotion coming from down the street.

"Oh, what's this, now?" Afton groans.

When we turn to our left, we come face to face with a horde of raging...scientists? I blink because I must be imagining the lab coats and coveralls. But I'm not. A banner that they carry before them reads "Free Tadao and Elenora!"

They let out a series of shouts in coordination and pick up their pace towards us. Some break into a run, bearing down on us. We're nowhere near prepared to bolt. I turn to Kayley. We could really use her leadership skills right now.

"You've got to be kidding," she says. "Guys! Let's move before we—"

Too late. We're swept up with the tide of humans headed in the opposite direction of where we need to go. I find myself turned around and pressed towards the front of the prison—the place we were trying at all costs to avoid.

An impassioned woman dressed like a patent clerk jams herself between Kayley and me, separating us. A stream of lab techs wind their way to the front of the mob, cutting Afton off from the rest of us. I reach an arm out to Grady, but he gets swallowed up by a group of students—from the engineering department, by the uniforms—who mistake him for one of their own. I shout out to my buds, but if they heard me, their replies are overwhelmed by the roar of the protestors.

The mass of people presses us forwards, carrying us down the street towards the inevitable. I have no idea what will happen when the unstoppable force of this group smashes into the immovable object—the royalists out front. There's sure to be some words hurled back and forth, but I certainly hope that's all that gets thrown.

"Can you believe those jerks?" A guy a few years older than me throws an arm around my shoulders and looks me in the eye. "Blaming the Ingeniorum for stealing their own work! They need to update their programs to this millennium!"

"What did you call them?" I shout back.

"Geniuses! Of course! What else would I call them?"

I give him a wan smile, but he wrinkles his nose at me and pushes off. I guess I wasn't enough of a true believer for him to connect with. I'm sure that I'd find humor in all of this somewhere if I weren't panicking over the safety of my friends. It's already strange enough that this multitude of people would find enough common ground on a subject to leave the comfort of their workplaces and form a protest.

That's just how much celebrity Grady's parents have.

As our motley mob turns the corner and spots the royalists, a chant spreads through our group.

"Free the chiefs! They're not thieves! Let them out! There's no doubt! Innocent! Innocent! Innocent! Innocent!"

I try to follow along, but only so I can blend in a little. I'm rotating around, trying to find the others, but so far nothing. I've got to find them before there's more than just shouting going on. Then we have to get out of here. That's another problem. We've got no way to call—

Wait a minute, yes I do!

"Teddy! Teddy! Can you hear me?" I touch the spot on the back of my neck that activates Teddy comm. After our last debacle with it, I had it permanently installed by Doc Elizabeth. She insisted it wouldn't cause any *major* problems. I'm fine with it. I wasn't really using that spot for anything much, anyway.

"Rancid. Tone is perceptible," comes Original Teddy's reply. "Make the requisition."

"Oh, great!" I push my way through the mass of people to get out of the crowd. It wasn't beneficial to be in there, anyway. "Teddy, we need an emergency lift!"

"Conveyance is possible. Shuttle is adjacent. Rendezvous in fifteen."

"Thank you, Teddy!"

One issue solved. Now I need to gather Grady, Kayley, and Afton and meet the Teddy shuttle in fifteen minutes. Possibly less. Teddys don't always count seconds correctly.

There's a pole just on the corner that's high enough for me to get a better vantage point. Once I'm up, it should be easy to spot Kayley's fiery hair. All I have to do is climb it.

My first attempt is pure failure. I jump on only to slide straight down after someone knocks into my arm and loosens my grip. I take a deep breath and jump on the pole again, digging the edges of my boots into the slick metallic surface.

I get a few feet up, and then some guy in coveralls grabs my leg and yanks me back down.

"Hey, whatcha doing?" he asks with a smile. I just stare back at him, thinking this guy might be a few electrons short of a hydrogen atom.

"I'm looking for my friends, which now I can't do since you pulled me down."

"Oh, sorry about that...you want a lift?"

"Sure."

The guy gets me on his shoulders, and it turns out I'm already at a good height to survey the crowd. I should be just a little less hard on him for the help.

The two mobs are as close as they dare to be, which is still closer than I would have expected them to get. Two steps forward and anyone would be in danger of getting a jab to the face. Then it will devolve into pure pandemonium. I don't want my buds to be in the middle of that. Especially Grady. The ladies have likely used their girl radar and found each other already. If so, they're finding a way out of this stormy sea of people.

Grady is shockingly easy to find. Once I cover the front row of scientific supporters, I spot him, dead center.

Chanting and shaking his fist at the royalists.

His side quiets down as he steps up behind the banner. Someone from the royalist side, a middle-aged blonde woman, steps out of her group and matches glares with him as she folds her arms in front of her. I think she might recognize him. Not that he'd be hard to remember. Our entire team has been on Angel live broadcasts more than once. The journalists even tried to interview him as he walked out of the courtroom last time. He didn't say anything, but he didn't need to. He's as famous as his parents.

"My parents aren't traitors! They are totally loyal to the Empire!" Grady shouts.

"Prove it!" the woman spits back.

"I don't have to prove anything to a stupid cow like you!"

Oh, no.

I hop off the guy's shoulders and vault into the crowd, just in time to get shoved to the front as the entire scientific horde surges at the mass of royalists. The racket they make is like one of Grady's engine tests, except the engine only ever ran for a few seconds. This din is continuous.

All I can think of is getting to Grady. If I have to be a bit rude and step on toes or slam someone aside, I'm going to do it. A bruise is a small price to pay to save my friend's life.

I duck down, avoiding the plethora of projectiles that fly from our side and are returned from the other. At this angle, I make good progress towards the front, ever conscious that I'm pressing towards the spot with all the danger.

Both sides blend together in a multigenerational riot. Young students are mixing it up with older executive assistants. A white-coated technician wrestles with a white-haired laborer. The good thing is none of them really know how to fight, so nobody is getting seriously hurt.

"Grady!" I shout as I arrive at the spot I saw him last. The banner is there on the ground, torn and shredded into not much more than an oversize rag. It gets tangled in the feet of the protestors and brings them down as they try to escape it.

There he is!

I spot Grady not far away, just a body's distance inside the royalists' front line. Not that there's much of a front on either side now. He stomps forwards and throws an arm around the blonde woman's neck, putting her into a headlock. I have to blink to make sure I'm seeing what I'm seeing.

"Grady!" I yell again and rush forwards, evading a bespectacled man with a thrust of my arm. He goes down with a grunt, and I smirk at my small act of vengeance against the government.

Grady is still trying to hold or grapple with the large blonde woman. Whatever it is he's doing, he's not trying to choke her, though he may want to. I can't say I blame him, but he can't be seen causing harm to someone else. That'll just make trouble for his parents.

I grab his arms and rip them off the woman, pulling him away. But I get an open hand across my face and a flash of light in my eyes for my trouble. It's the woman, trying to get at Grady from the other side of my arms. I hook a foot behind the woman's knee and pull hard. She topples back, her arms flying up to catch her balance. She falls on top of another royalist, possibly a grocery store clerk, and they both go down together. I'm not proud of it, but I had to save my friend before he really got into trouble. I hope the Goddesses will forgive me.

"Rance!" Grady's eyes are wide, and his hair is sticking to the sweat on his face. He's the perfect picture of a mad scientist. His mom and dad would be proud.

We fight our way back and out of the mob just as the authorities arrive. Grady is shaking, and his knees give out from underneath him. Good thing he doesn't weigh much. I put one arm around his waist and haul him clear of the skirmish.

Kayley and Afton had to have gotten clear by now. I glance back to watch the anti-riot team break through the crowd like they're parting the ocean. Their sirens had already scared the fringes of people away, and now the rest are cluing into the fact that they'll get arrested if they remain. That's exactly what's happening to those who are still fighting.

I catch a black dot in the sky moving towards us. That'd be the Teddys—better find a place for them to land.

"Teddy, this is Rance."

"This is obvious, Rancid. Request location for anchorage."

"Uh." I do a quick search around. "I think the next intersection out from the prison should work."

"Duck soup. Rendezvous is occurring momentarily."

I'm already dragging Grady as fast as I can. He gets his legs back under him and pushes away from me, stumbling along.

"I'm fine now, dude."

"You sure?" I glance at him. "You couldn't walk a moment ago."

The shuttle comes down right where I suggested and right on cue. Afton and Kayley pop out of an inset doorway across the street. Kayley's holding her arm, and that worries me. Whatever happened, I hope it's not bad.

At least we're all safe.

Six

KAYLEY SETTLES INTO ME with a whimper as we try to get comfortable on my living room sofa. She cradles her arm, now bandaged, and drops her head onto my shoulder with a sigh. Her silky hair rubs against my neck, and I sigh too. It's been a while since we spent a quiet moment together. Too bad this one won't last.

Afton had found Kayley fairly easily in the crowd, not by using girly radar but using the same method I was planning to use—her hair. Red hair isn't common on Angelcanis, and Kayley's is fiery with pinkish-orange tones. It's unmistakable in any crowd, even one that's in a full-on brawl.

"Don't worry, darling," Kayley says, taking notice of my attempt to baby her. "Elizabeth says it'll heal quickly."

"So what exactly happened?" Parrish says, walking in from my kitchen, a tray of food in his hand and an apron around his waist. I don't know exactly when I became a guest in my own household, but when he saw Kayley's wound, he insisted on taking over for her as assistant to my mom. My mom needs no help to mix something up for us, but she does like the company.

"Grady picked a fight," Afton says. She's sitting on the floor next to Original Teddy and Blue Buddy, with her back pressed against the smaller sofa. The three of them are playing some game with marbles that she taught them and then purposely changed so she could win more often. It was only fair. Original Teddy and BB were using their Teddy tech to talk so they could gang up on her.

"That's not like him." Parrish places the tray down on a short table and drops himself into the smaller sofa. "Grady's always far away from the action. That's where he likes to be."

"This time, Grady *was* the action." Afton grabs a marble and tosses it into a circle, where it sinks into the fluff of the living room carpet.

"According to Rance, he's the one that lit the fuse. Then he caught him wrestling with a fat lady."

"But he didn't get hurt?"

"Not physically," I say. "But he's a bit of a wreck, even though he insists he's fine." Doc Elizabeth gave him something to help him relax, and it worked well. Too well. Grady's sleeping it off in the guest bedroom. It's quickly becoming his home away from home, and that's fine with me. I'm glad to have him, but we're going to have to go back to his place soon. If only to make sure all the windows that the agents smashed were repaired.

"We have another problem," Kayley says. She squeezes my hand as I get tense. I know what's coming. "The lead prosecutor is Rance's dad."

Afton and Parrish freeze. Even my mother comes out of the kitchen and leans on the wall. She's watching me, her arms folded. My mom knows I've got no love for him, but I still squirm under her gaze. Sometimes I wonder if she wants me to forgive him.

Sometimes I wonder if *I* want to.

"Do you think your dad is really going to try to put Grady's parents in jail?" Parrish squeezes his hands closed.

"He doesn't have a choice. It's his job...he told me—"

"You talked to him?" Afton springs to her knees. "What'd he say?"

I couldn't see it, but Kayley must have shot Afton down with her eyes because she drops to a kneel. Afton pouts like a scolded child and turns her eyes up at me, still waiting for an answer.

"He said the Emperor made him do it. That the charges come directly from the Emperor himself."

"Do you believe that, Rance?" My mom breaks her silence with a question that I am in no way prepared to respond to. Her tone is curious, calm. I'm even more confused. What should I say? What should I think?

"I...I'm not sure. It was hard to be just suddenly talking to him. I wasn't thinking straight about anything. One minute I wanted to know why he had left. The next, I was ready to punch him in the face."

My mom nods and looks away. This has got to be hard for her too. They were together for ten years before I was born. There's a ton of history there that doesn't get erased simply by someone walking out the door.

"I...think," I continue, "he didn't have a choice but to obey. At least, that's the vibe I got from him. It doesn't make it right, and whatever situation he's in, he put himself there. I can't sympathize with that..."

Or can I? Part of me wants to sympathize with his predicament, and another wants to just shake my head and smirk. My father was a great dad for most of my life. It's only been eight years since he's been gone. I've stuffed my outrage deep down for that long, but I just found out how quickly it can come to the surface. No, I'm not over it at all.

"Don't force yourself," Mom says. She turns to go back into the kitchen but looks back at me. "You're going to have a lot to get through before an answer is clear, Rance. Be patient."

"Mom's right," Kayley adds. "We've got a long way to go to get through this trial."

"That's what bothers me." I squeeze Kayley's good hand, more for my comfort than hers.

"What can we do?" Parrish isn't looking at Kayley when he asks, but he definitely wants Kayley to answer.

"That's a great question." Kayley touches her finger to her lower lip and considers.

"Let's do our own investigation," Afton suggests. "That's what Janek was going to hire us for, isn't it? Find some evidence so he can win the case?"

"Why do you get to use his first name?" I ask. Afton's reply is to smirk and wiggle an eyebrow.

"Opportunity is available," Original Teddy says, tapping Afton's leg with a tentacle. She frowns at him but returns to the game.

I could easily support Afton's idea, but a thought occurs to me. If we investigate, we wouldn't just be supporting Mr. Moreno's defense of Grady's parents. We'd be going up against my father, and something about that makes my stomach queasy.

"That's not a bad idea," Parrish says and nods. "I'm sure he could use our help. What do you think, Rance?"

"Well…" I must have distorted my face into a painful frown because Parrish gets concerned.

"Parry, realize that you're asking him to fight his father," Kayley says, coming to my rescue. "The Emperor could consider a failure as a personal insult, and nobody insults the Emperor."

"Yeah, I get that, but his da…Mr. He'—"

"That's his mom's last name," Afton corrects, her eyes never leaving Teddy and BB as they take their turn. "It's Mr. Cavalcante."

"Right." Parrish shifts up on the sofa and clears his throat. "But no way Grady's parents are traitors. If we don't have the evidence now to prove that, then we go find it."

I need to join this conversation, but I don't know where to get in. There's no way I'd want his mom and dad to go to jail. Not only don't they deserve it, but they've been really good to me. When my dad left, they unofficially adopted me as second and third parents.

But as much as I hate my dad, I don't want him to go to jail either. Or worse. Who knows what the Emperor would do just to save face? He may deserve my resentment, but he doesn't deserve to die for doing his job.

Now that I've thought a little bit more about it, and now that I had the chance to shout in his face and let him know how he's hurt me, I think I might want to try to build a relationship there again. Maybe.

"What is it?" Kayley looks at me when she hears my long sigh. Parrish also takes note and tilts his head.

"What do I do, KayKay?" I must look like a hurt puppy to her because she wraps her one good arm around me and gives me a squeeze.

"He'll be fine, dude," Parrish says. "Let's concentrate on Grady and his parents."

"He might not be fine," Kayley shoots back. "Do you really want that hanging over your head?"

"Hey, I don't want the guy to be executed! But Mr. Sugiyama and his wife very well could be. Do *you* want that hanging over *your* head?"

"Come on, guys, don't fight. We've got enough troubles as it is," I plead to them.

"Discord is detrimental," Original Teddy says out of the blue. I agree. We should be more like Teddy society and try to solve this together.

"What do you think?" I ask Afton, who's in the middle of counting marbles. Her head pops up, and she glances around until she finds me staring at her.

"Who? Me?"

"Yes, you." I soften my glare. "I'd appreciate the help...Afton."

She returns the gentle look, pressing her lips together and curving one side of her mouth up. We've been through some tough spots, Afton and I. In some ways, I think I'm closer to her than I am to Kayley. My girlfriend has known me my whole life, sure, but Afton and I have seen the dark side of bad together.

"We investigate," Afton says, her eyes locked with mine.

"Wait a minute!" Kayley shoots forward on the sofa. She starts to speak again, but Afton holds up a hand.

"We investigate," she says again, "while Rance convinces his father to drop the case. Doesn't matter how, but if it helps to keep him in the

Emperor's good graces, we'll share our findings so he can come up with the best way out."

"Whoa." Parrish turns to his fellow athlete, eyes wide. "That's pretty good."

"It is," Kayley agrees, if a bit begrudgingly. She turns back to get my attention. "Are you up for that? It's a lot to ask of you, darling, I know."

"I'll do it...I mean, I'll try. I have no idea if it'll be possible."

"But at least we'll be trying to help him." Kayley touches my cheek and smiles. I do too. At her, at Afton, and at Parrish. There's no real plan yet, but this feels right. It feels like something I want to accomplish.

"So, you guys ready for seconds?" Mom is smiling at us from the edge of the kitchen. How long has she been there? Did she hear what we just decided? If she approves, then I do too.

Seven

THE SECOND MOON IS up and nearly full as I walk with Parrish and Afton down the path that leads to her house. The path is also gently lit by spherical lights that hang from their own power lines, spaced every few steps. If Afton weren't so tense, I might be enjoying the jaunt more.

We're here to grab some clothes and other stuff so she can stay with Grady at his house. As much as we insisted he didn't need to stay there, Grady kept going on about his responsibilities and how his parents expected him to keep the house in good order for the anticipation of their return.

I offered to stay with him but Afton volunteered and told me to focus on my father. Parrish wanted to stay too, but he's worried about leaving his mom for long. She's not been healthy as of late, and he wanted to be there to keep an eye on her.

"Just let us know what you want us to do, and we'll get everything done in a few minutes," Parrish says.

"Don't worry about it, just grab the bags when I hand them to you...and say nothing to her but hello or goodbye." Afton is speaking with a tight jaw. She's getting close to putting holes in the ground with the way she's stomping forward. I'm unsure of what's got her so wound up. I'd ask, but I don't think she's interested in discussing it.

Once we enter her house, it all becomes clear.

"Where have you been?" Her mother blocks the hallway, hands on hips. "Did you think to call to let me know you'd be late? How about some consideration for me, yes?"

Afton brushes past her mother and leaves us standing face to face with a woman who doesn't appear too happy to see us.

"Good evening, Mrs. Jee. Nice to see you," Parrish says, his voice leaning on the meek end of its deep basso.

"Good evening, yourself," she replies, staring at us. "Well? What are you waiting for? Come in. You can have a seat in the den."

Mrs. Jee is not a mean person, but even my mom says she can be a bit...abrupt. Mom also says that's what happens when you try to raise more than one boy at a time. Since Afton's got two brothers—currently out on a long-range mission with their dad—I can see how she might have had to adapt.

Afton hasn't made it easy for her either. I guess Mrs. Jee really wanted a more feminine daughter, one that played with dolls and wanted to be a princess. Afton's got her moments, but I could never picture her in a frilly pastel dress like Kayley wears from time to time. Not that I see any problem with that. Afton is comfortable in her skin. Nobody has the right to criticize that. Not even her mom.

"Gee, I hope everything is cool between them," Parrish says, glancing around. The den is the first room in the front of the house. It's got a set of sofas and a low table in between them. Unlike Kayley's family den, this one is cozier...and darker. Not just because the light is off. The color selection here is much more utilitarian. That might have something to do with Mr. Jee, military man that he is. There's a hutch with a bunch of pictures on it. A few are of the family, some together, some individual, but the one that catches my eye is a photo of Mr. Jee standing next to a woman wearing all yellow. That's not a very common color for a business suit, so I stare at it for a while. Whoever the woman is, she was bold to wear such a bright hue.

"Do you think they've been arguing? I mean, before Afton came with us to court?" I ask.

Parrish looks at the hallway, likely checking to ensure Mrs. Jee and her daughter are not in earshot. It's not a secret that they don't get along well, but nobody wants to see their friend fighting with their parent.

"Maybe." Parrish shrugs. "She hasn't said anything to me, but we haven't been training like we usually do. That's when we talk about stuff."

I overhear Mrs. Jee shout something, but she's too far back in the house for me to understand what she said. If I'm going on tone alone, I'd say it wasn't something friendly.

"Have you?" I glance at him as I ask.

"Been training?" He shakes his head. "Honestly, my leg hasn't felt up to it...but I'm still doing all the rehab exercises they taught me. My old coach also had some suggestions on how to get back up to speed."

I hope that's the case. Parrish isn't planning to go into professional sports, but he has mentioned a few times that he wants to keep playing something. Should he change his mind, though, I bet any team would be glad to have him.

"Why are you staring at that photo for so long?" Parrish asks.

"Just weird to see Afton's dad with his arm around another woman, that's all."

"Huh?" Parrish comes over to me, but before I can elaborate, Afton's voice comes echoing down the hallway.

"I said I don't want it!" A moment later, she shows up with a bag and drops it near the front door.

"Ready to go?" I ask.

"Not yet. I think I need more stuff. I'm not coming back here until my dad returns."

With that, she darts back into the house. Parrish and I share a look as their raised voices turn edgy. There are a few volleys back and forth, then a crash.

"Should we…" I curl my lip and grip the armrest of the sofa.

"Afton can take care of herself."

"That's what I'm worried about."

She'd never purposely hurt her own mother, but—

Another crash and I jump off the sofa, dashing down the hallway towards the sound. The Goddesses might need a small prayer or two from me to make sure nobody's hurt, so I do that as I run.

I come on them in the kitchen. It's a veritable standoff between mother and daughter. Afton glances at me as I enter but goes right back to staring her mother down. Mrs. Jee waves a finger at her.

"You have responsibilities in this house! You cannot just pick up and go any time you feel like it!"

"Everything alright? We heard something crash," Parrish asks, coming up behind me.

Mrs. Jee turns around to look Parrish and me over as if she's wondering why we're in her house. I look to Afton for an explanation, and she provides an unexpected one.

"The cat knocked over a plant." Afton nods to the broken pottery mingled with soil and the remains of a ginger plant. There's no cat to be found, and I don't remember seeing one when I was here before. That isn't all that often, so I turn to Parrish for confirmation. He looks away, tugging on his ear.

"You may excuse us," Mrs. Jee says. "We are having a private discussion. Return to the den. I will bring you something."

"You don't need to. I'm almost done."

"No! You are not done until we discuss you taking along your saree!" Mrs. Jee holds up what looks like a bolt of shiny red-and-gold cloth. The moment Afton sees it she shakes her head.

"I am *not* taking that!"

"But of course you should! What are you going to wear if you go somewhere formal?"

"We're going to be in a courthouse!"

"Exactly! You need to present yourself well."

"I'll get a suit."

"A suit is for men!"

"I'll get one with a skirt, then!" Afton sighs and picks up the pieces of the broken pot. I want to move to help her, but I don't want to disturb the uneasy impasse between Afton and her mother.

"Leave that. I will clean it." Her mother looks down on her. "Didn't you say you were leaving?"

Afton shoots an angry glance up at her mom but continues to pick up the pieces. Her mother folds the saree into a smaller square, unzips Afton's bag, and stuffs the saree in as if the whole disagreement over it didn't just take place.

"You'll need the jewelry...and a good pair of shoes." Mrs. Jee turns and heads towards the back of the house. "You have none, I know, so I will let you borrow a pair of mine."

Once Mrs. Jee is out of the kitchen, Parrish and I drop to help Afton clean up the mess. I grab a few pieces, and he scoops up some of the soil in his hand. He looks around and asks where the trash bin is, but Afton just waves us off.

"Guys, thanks, but I got it. Just grab the bag on the table and wait for me at the front door. I'll be there in a minute."

"Are you okay?"

"Never better. How about you?" Afton's sarcastic tone is enough to tell me not to reply. I won't press her. Not while we're still in the middle of a war zone. "Go...I'll be right there."

Parrish rinses off his hands, and I grab the bag. It's better if I don't mention that her mom stuffed the saree—I'm guessing it's kind of a dress—into her bag. That'd only cause more conflict, and Afton has had enough for the evening.

It's not long before Afton shows up in the hallway, a small backpack slung over her shoulder. She gives Parrish and me a small curl of her mouth, trying to put us at ease.

"Don't worry, guys, this is the way it always is."

"Even when your dad is home?" I ask, my thoughts going back the photo in the den. I'll have to ask Afton about that one. Now doesn't seem like the best time for that kind of question.

"No, my brothers give my mom enough to complain about when they're all around." Afton drops her eyes and shrugs. "I don't have to be the target of her frustration then."

"Should we go?"

"Wait!" Her mother comes around the corner into the hallway, carrying a pair of heeled strappy things and a multi-stringed necklace. "You forgot these!"

Afton sighs and slides the backpack off her shoulder before she turns to see what her mom has.

"I don't need that stuff," she says.

"Yes, you do!" Her mom shakes the stuff in her hands at her, her eyes widening. "They go with the saree!"

"I'm not getting married!"

"These are not for marriage. You don't have any nice shoes, and the Matha Patti will get you respect. Just have Kayley make your hair nice. That girl knows how to make herself beautiful, at least."

"How many times do I have to tell you I *don't fit in your shoes*? You can't even call those shoes! They're a pair of spiky platforms with some straps on them, and I'm not putting that thing on my head."

"Why don't you ever respect me, Surela? I am trying to teach you how to be a proper lady, but you insist on...on..."

"On what?" Afton leans into her mother's face, daring her to say whatever it is she's reluctant to say. "Face it, you don't really care what I do, do you? It's always 'Aakesh is so wonderful,' and 'Ji-Min did this or that today!' When did you ever praise me?"

"You are a woman, so that is different! You only need to be proper, and if you'd learn that, then perhaps you would have something to praise!"

"I really hate you," Afton growls.

"How dare you say that to your mother!" Mrs. Jee winds up and hurls the necklace thing at her, but it flies wide. Parrish's hand shoots up and catches it. As he glances at me sideways, he stuffs it into the bag he's carrying.

Afton stands still, glaring at her mother with such intensity that I'm starting to believe she really does hate her mother.

"I'm leaving."

Eight

My father wanted to meet me for lunch, but that would have been too much for me to handle. We agreed on a talk in the park instead. Kayley pressed to go with me, but I asked her to let me try meeting him on my own. She wasn't happy, but she agreed to let me go by myself.

As I made my way to our meeting spot, I kept trying to find excuses to get out of it: Mom's sick, I'm sick, Kayley's sick, my pet's sick...basically anyone or anything being sick. I didn't think he'd believe any of it if I tried. My father is a very perceptive man. He can read the moment and take the appropriate action. It's part of the reason he moved up so quickly.

I don't know why I agreed to meet him at all. I guess somewhere in the back of my head is this dream where he's exactly the same as before he left. Maybe it's the little boy in me wanting his dad back. Maybe it's just me wanting to see my mom happy. I know it's nonsense, but here I am, holding on to that delusion.

The park is in the center of town, close to the office he has here on Angelcanis. It's not the biggest park in our capital of Bradbury, but it is the swankiest. Cherry blossoms, genetically modified to blossom for half the year, line the promenade at the entrance. Behind them are rows of cedar and pine, diminutive so they'd fit inside the boundaries. Everything surrounds a fountain in the center. In the middle of that is a statue of Joris Regis the Fourteenth, our current Emperor. All of this is an alleged gift from him. I think of it more as a reminder to the people of Angelcanis who's really in control.

My father is standing right near the fountain, and I consider that positioning as I approach him. His hands are in his pockets as he watches me arrive. His posture is strangely similar to the statue's. It's a bit too coincidental for my brain...kind of like the statue is saying, "He's mine now, and you can't have him back."

"Hi, Rance," my father says, holding out an arm as if to embrace me. "Glad you could make it."

"Hey." I stuff my own hands into my pockets, making it clear to him that nothing of the sort is coming.

"Let's get a seat, okay?" His arm lowers so he can usher me to a bench near the corner of the plaza. I act the dutiful son and do as he suggests.

He takes a corner of the bench, sitting at an angle so that he can look directly at me. I, on the other hand, sit flat against the back and stare out at the fountain, so I don't have to do the same. My father remains silent about my choice of seating position. That doesn't mean he approves. It could just mean it doesn't bother him.

"It turned out to be a nice day, didn't it?" My father's attempt to break the ice between us. I think it's an acceptable try, so I answer him.

"Yeah, this time of year isn't usually too bad in Bradbury. It starts to get toasty down by our...the house."

I almost gave him part ownership of the house I sleep in. No matter what he may think, the moment he stepped out the front door, that house and everything inside it stopped being his.

"I remember. We used to take you down to the beach. You couldn't have been more than—"

"Can we not do the reminiscing thing?"

"Okay." He releases a long breath. "I understand. It's just I haven't thought about memories like that for a long time."

"Not helping."

"You're right." He holds his hands up. "I'm sorry."

So far, this conversation has gone from shaky to heading towards disaster. I didn't expect that it would be otherwise. This is the second conversation I've had with him after eight years. The first one didn't end so well, and I expect this will crash just the same. Still, I'm here, so I might as well make an effort. I might never get another chance.

"Forget it," I say. "What did you want to talk to me about?"

"Well, I—"

A woman screams, drawing our attention to the edge of the plaza. I find her pointing up at a nearby building. My eyes follow, and there at the top, at the edge of the eightieth-something floor, a man is hanging from what looks like the pole of a collapsed shelter. He's in real danger of becoming a rice pancake if he can't hold on.

"Goddesses." My father jumps up, and his hand flies up to shade his face from the sun. "Rance...call emergency services."

"Already on it." I pound the notification into my Sergo, but I'm sure the other thousand people who heard the scream have already done the same thing.

Another scream makes me look up again—uh-oh—the man's slipped down the pole to the near edge, and there's no other place to grab a handhold. If he slips again, he's coming down for sure.

"Rance, we need to go help him," my father says, turning to me, his eyes full of resolution. He holds my gaze for a moment, then spins and sprints towards the building.

If I were seven years younger, I'd be running right next to him, my head filled with delusions of grandeur. I'd become the hero, the champion of the people, just like my father and I had dreamed about. Now, well, I'm not so ready to follow someone who's given me so much to be angry about.

Despite that, I don't want to see anyone fall to their death, and I still have my agenda in life to promote. My team could honestly use some positive coverage as of late. Being connected to the trial like we are has generated some negative feelings towards us on the net. We need something to pull us out of that muck, or we could wind up drowning in it.

I sigh and race after my father, who, for a middle-aged guy, moves unexpectedly fast. He's already entering the front door of the building while I'm just about to cross the street. It doesn't take me long to get there, but he's already getting into the elevator by the time I hit the lobby.

"Rance, come on!" My father jams on the door hold and waits for me to scramble in. A moment later, we're on the express ride up to the roof, making every attempt to catch our breath.

As we wait impatiently for the doors to open, we share a brief look. My father gives me a grin. I can't help but smile a little too.

"We always wanted to do this kind of thing together, didn't we?"

I don't know how to answer. He's right, of course. We had always planned on doing something like this together, although perhaps not such a physical version of it. Our idea of saving lives was more from a legal angle.

I'm saved from answering by the door chime, followed by the elevator opening directly to the roof. There's already a small crowd of people there. Most are just watching while a few try to secure the shelter's poles so the man doesn't drag the entire contraption over the side of the building.

Except it's not a shelter. As we get closer, I see it's an air glider of some sort; a triangular construction of tubes and a big white aerofoil sail to keep its passengers aloft. The craft is getting crushed by the forces pressing on it in ways it was never designed to handle. In its current state, it won't do anything but plummet to the ground.

"Stand aside!" my father yells. Those who are acting as mere spectators follow his direction, and we're able to make a direct line to the edge of the building. Some must recognize him because there's a sense of awe about them as they move aside. I'm not about to question it because it gets us right where we need to be.

I peer over the side, and the man is there, desperately hanging on with both hands to the crossbar. The thing is bent in half, and it doesn't look like it's going to last much longer. He doesn't either. That pole is a thin little thing to grip on, and I doubt he's got much strength left in his hands. We better do something fast.

"Dad, let's get someone down there to tie a line around him, and then we can pull him and the whole thing up."

"Good, Rance!" My father glances around for a rope or some cable. He doesn't have to look for long. Someone produces a length of cable and hands it over to me.

"Okay, son, we'll get you down, and you can get the line around him. You ready?"

"Ready? Me?" I take a quick glance at the man below and the ground, much farther below. "Shouldn't we use someone lighter?"

"Why?" He takes a quick guestimation of my weight. "You should be light enough."

"Should be," I mutter back. He's so quick to sacrifice me. That part of him hasn't changed.

He wraps me in a few cable rotations and secures it by making a bowline knot with the end. That's about as secure as I'm going to get without some real hardware, so I'll have to trust it. If the Goddesses want me, then there's very little I can do about it.

One man he's roped into helping hands me another cable as I step to the edge. I'll have to make the same knot that my father just did, except I'll need to do it while suspended eighty floors up. And that's only if I remember how.

"I can't hold on much longer!" the man cries. I glance down at him and give him a thumbs-up. Really, I don't know what else to do to comfort him. We should just be standing aside and letting the professionals handle this. If only they were here now.

I place my feet on the side of the building, making half an attempt at a rappel while my father and the others lower me as gently as they can. The cable digs into my sides, and I focus on breathing so that I can push the pain away. It's hard, but I'm managing for the moment.

"Please!" the man cries as his wide eyes look at me.

"Don't worry, you're going to be okay!" That might be a bit of a lie, but what else am I to say?

I make sure I'm secure against the side of the building so I don't go spinning around. Then I wrap the cord about him, the entire time thinking about the possibility that my father made me get down here and save the man so he could look good. I wonder what he'd answer if I put the question to him.

The man cries out as he slips. One of his hands slides off the pole, and he can't secure himself again.

"Calm down!" His erratic movement complicates my attempt to secure the cable around him. "I've got to tie this up, or you can't get pulled up!"

He nods, squeezing the pole as tight as he can. That won't hold him for much longer. I've got to get this secure now. Let's see...make a loop...then pull the end through...pull the end through...shoot! What comes next? Why haven't I practiced this more often?

Oh! I remember! Pull the end through, loop it around the mainline, then pull that back through the loop, and pull it tight. Done!

"He's secure! Pull him up!" I look at the man. "Listen, when you feel them begin to pull you up, you've got to let go of the pole. Do you think you can do that?"

"Okay! I think I can...yes...I will!" His answer seems to be more for his own confidence than it is to confirm my query. I don't care either way. As long as they pull him up quick, so then they can pull me up right after that.

I grip my cable as I watch him get hoisted up. It's slow going, but the team above is making constant progress, likely directed by my father.

"No!" the man drops as the cable relieves some slack in its line. It's only a brief fall, but it's enough to scare the pants off all of us. I breathe deep and press my head against my line. Perhaps I should have made my knot tighter. I'm very glad Kayley isn't here to witness this...she might just see it on tonight's news broadcast, though.

My cable inches up the second after the man's feet are over the edge. It's not long before I'm up and safe. Everyone cheers and congratulates me. I smile and nod, but the feeling of accomplishment is secondary to my focus on my father.

Of course, he's in the middle of it, shaking hands and patting shoulders. As I pull the cable off me, he takes his time to revel in his success. Only when he's talked to everyone does he approach me.

"Not bad, son, not bad at all," he says. "Looks like you've been working on our dream all along."

I give him a slight upward curve of my mouth. I do feel some level of happiness to be recognized by him, but it's tainted by all the other negative thoughts running through my head. Sure, we accomplished something great just now, and we did it together, but so many years of anger from him *not even calling me once* doesn't go away so easily. I'll take the moment, but if I had any hope that he'd be different, that he'd be better, that's already gone.

Still, Grady needs my help, and if that means I have to smile at a man I can barely think of as my father, I'll do it.

Nine

THE AIR IN THE courtroom is stifling. I know the ventilation system is on, but it must be maxed out by the number of people in the galley. Every bench is packed, and the two side aisles are stuffed with at least one journalist from each of the major media outlets across the Empire.

Grady wasn't allowed to sit next to his parents this time, as they've been placed in the official defendant's box, opposite of the jury and surrounded by court officers. Instead, he's in the front row, jammed in between Parrish and me. Only Mr. Moreno and his assistant are up at the defense table. They look so lonely up there compared to the team of people my father has surrounding him.

"All rise."

There's a massive rumble as the sports arena's worth of humans stand as the judge enters. It's the same one as last time. I don't know how to feel about that. He did his job as any judge should, but he wasn't lenient when he blocked Grady's parents from waiting at home for the trial to start. If that means he's got it out for them, this trial is already over.

I look over at Mr. Sugiyama and his wife. Their time behind bars so far has already made them shrunken and weary. I worry that if they are sentenced to jail, they won't survive for very long. My two days in lockup plus Afton's and my experience getting locked in a cell in Exodus was enough for me. I don't ever want to repeat it.

"You may be seated," the Honorable Judge-Superior Hamlin says and stamps his gavel. "This courtroom will come to order. Today we will hear the opening statements from both sides. The prosecution, are you prepared to make your opening statement today?"

"Yes, Your Honor." That's from my father. He gives a quick glance over to our side, looking for me, likely. If he spotted me, there's no reaction on his face. I'm disappointed, but I don't understand why. It's not like I wanted him to see me, did I?

"Defense, are you prepared to make an opening statement today?"

"No, Your Honor," Mr. Moreno says to the surprise of us all. He leans back in his seat, rubbing a bit of chocolate from his cheek. Then he grabs another pretzel rod and munches down. I shake my head, doubt flooding into my head about his ability to handle this case.

"What's he doing?" Grady hisses loud enough that the assistant turns around. Grady leans forward to fire words back and forth with her. The assistant shakes her head and waves a finger at him, but that only irritates him more. He pounds on the railing separating us from them, drawing not a few curious looks.

"Does that mean, Mr. Moreno, that you are not prepared or that you do not wish to make an opening statement?"

"Yes, that's correct, Your Honor," Mr. Moreno answers, licking a finger. Judge Hamlin only furrows his brow and tilts his head. I don't get it either, and likely everyone else in the court doesn't either.

"Mr. Moreno...please give me a more specific reply than that. I still don't understand what you want to do."

"Your Honor, as I said, the defense is—"

Grady flails an arm out and strikes Mr. Moreno on the back, knocking his crunchy snack out of his hand. The lawyer jumps and spins around, his eyes wide.

"What's your answer, Mr. Moreno?" The judge's jaw is getting tight.

"Your Honor, may I have a moment to confer with my client?"

"Very well, but make it quick."

Kayley gets up and gets into a huddle with Grady. So now I need to do the same. She likely has some good advice to share with Grady, and I'm curious to know what it is.

"And so we don't want to get trapped into refuting a theory that the prosecution isn't going for," Mr. Moreno is explaining. "The jury is going to base their decision on whether we did a good enough job breaking down the prosecution's case. To do that, we need to know what their plan is. I couldn't have just called up Mr. Cavalcante and asked him what he was planning to do because he wouldn't have told me. He's got no reason to do so. We've got to wait for their opening statement."

"But you can't just keep silent today!" Grady tightens his grip on the railing. If it weren't made from strong wood that's been hardened with a shiny finish, he might be putting dents in it.

"I understand your concern, Mutsumaji. These are your parents, and you want to do as much as you can for them. Please trust me. This is the best strategy. Here, have a pretzel rod, it'll make you feel better."

"Defense? Are you finished?"

"Tell him no!" Grady spits between clenched teeth. Mr. Moreno gives him a wistful glance and turns around.

"No!" Grady cries.

"Your Honor, the defense yields. The prosecution may begin their statement." Mr. Moreno sits, and I grab Grady and pull him down with me. We've got to trust that Mr. Moreno has a plan and that he's good at what he does.

Judge Hamlin raises an eyebrow, but then sighs and turns to my father. That's when I realize I just gave my dad an easy target to spot. If he was looking over here, and likely he was, he now knows exactly where I am, which means if he wants to talk to me after, he knows exactly where to go.

"He's gonna screw this up!" Grady mutters.

"Mr. Moreno is the best lawyer that your parents' money can buy, dude," I say, "and I think you know your parents have a lot. Give him a chance."

My father begins his statement, giving the jury—and the media—a preview of how he intends to convince them that Doctors Sugiyama and O'Grady-Davies are the worst people the Empire has ever known and trusted. My stomach twists listening to him speak. Not just because he's stating how he's going to make sure Grady's parents get committed to hell, but because the sound of his voice is all too familiar to me. My body aches with every word he uses to explain how he will prove my buddy's parents are traitors to the Empire. This is a man I looked up to and respected greatly. Someone I trusted and loved. All this leaves me gasping for air.

"And so, ladies and gentlemen of the jury, we the prosecution will seek to portray for you how the defendants sought a prospective buyer of the Empire's technology, stripped it from the Emperor's hands, and planned to sell it for their own profit. We will prove, beyond *any* reasonable doubt, that the defendants' intentions were malignant, deviant, and completely selfish."

"Hey, are you okay?" Kayley whispers, rubbing my arm.

"I don't know." I lean over, trying to catch my breath. What makes this worse is that I know Grady is suffering a thousand times more than I am. I've already lost my father. Grady will lose both his parents if we don't win this case.

"Talk to me...what's wrong?" Kayley slides off the bench and gets down, so her head is at the same level as mine. She tries to soothe me by putting a hand on my back, stroking back and forth as if she's petting an animal. In some ways, she is.

I take a deep breath, trying to calm my body into something that'll allow me to answer her clearly. My father has already completed his statement, but his voice still echoes around my brain, building in intensity with every word.

"KayKay...do you think Mr. Moreno is doing the right thing?" I ask, turning my head away from Grady. I don't want him to hear. I don't want to fill him with any more doubt than he already has about his parents' future.

"Honestly, that's a tough one." Kayley shakes her head slowly. "I don't know enough about court proceedings to even guess at that."

"But you understand the strategy, right?"

"Sure, but we don't have the experience to know whether it's the right one or not, Rance."

"He should at least say *something*."

I'm drawing a blank on what that something could be. Like Kayley said, we're no experts. We're not even beginners. There are a few things I remember that my father taught me, but refraining from an opening statement wasn't one of them. And what's with the pretzels in the middle of a courtroom?

"Thank you, Mr. Cavalcante." Judge Hamlin turns to give Mr. Moreno a troubled look. His face scrunches up as he decides what to say. It's unnecessary. Mr. Moreno stands and prepares to give him an answer to the question he didn't answer before.

"Your Honor, the defense—"

"Mr. Moreno!" I hiss. It's loud enough for the judge to hear. I know I've just lost a bunch of points with the judge, but I have to at least try to get our lawyer to reconsider. If only for Grady's fragile state of mind.

"Apologies, Your Honor, just a minute."

"Your Honor." My father's voice is gritty with irritation. "Haven't we had enough attempts to delay from the defense already?"

"We have," Judge Hamlin replies. "So this will be the very last time I'm going to allow one, and if you're not ready to give your statement, then we are going to recess for today and move to calling witnesses tomorrow."

"Thank you, Your Honor." Mr. Moreno bows to the judge and turns on us. There's a purposeful pause when he realizes it's not Grady interrupting him. He bends down and motions Kayley and me to get close. "What is it? We're already on thin ice with the judge, so I hope this is worthwhile."

"You've heard the prosecution's opening statement?" I ask.

"We all did."

"What do you think?"

"This is hardly the time for a strategy discussion."

"I mean, shouldn't you reconsider declining an opening statement?"

Mr. Moreno squeezes his lips together and puffs his cheeks. I get it—I wouldn't want some dumb kid casting doubt on my decisions either. The fact that he's even thinking about it is a testament to his character. This has got to be difficult for him as it is. He doesn't need pressure from anywhere else.

"Alright, I'll say something, but since it's not planned, it's not going to be great."

"Mr. Moreno, you have exactly three seconds before I bang my gavel, and we end our session."

"Once again, apologies, Your Honor. I will make a brief statement." He reaches into his pocket and grabs another pretzel. I close my eyes and hang my head. I just can't believe Grady's parents hired this guy.

"Very well, go ahead."

"Ladies and gentlemen of the jury, you've just heard the prosecution speak." Mr. Moreno steps out from his table and walks towards the jury box. "What Mr. Cavalcante claims he can accomplish is a huge challenge for him. We, the defense, on the other hand, have no need for such out-landish claims. We will easily show you how the prosecution's case is full of holes and riddled with exaggerations, and possibly contains a few mis-truths. I intend to let my clients' records speak for themselves, and you will see, by the end of this trial, there will be no reason to convict them."

"That's it?" Grady glances between Parrish and me. We don't reply, so hopefully he gets his answer. It's not the one he might have hoped for, but our silence is for the best. Words would only do damage at this point.

As Judge Hamlin closes the day, I share a moment of disappointment with Kayley, hiding my face from Grady as best as I can. I don't want him to see the look of defeat there. We may have pushed Mr. Moreno into a corner, and he only tried to make us happy. We should have kept quiet and let the professional do the job he was hired to do.

Now he looks like an amateur too.

Ten

"Mr. Cavalcante, you may call your first witness."

Judge Hamlin motions to my father, who clears his throat and rises. He adjusts his jacket and takes a breath. It's so silent in the courtroom I can hear the air pass in and out of his mouth from our spot in the first row, on the opposite side of the room.

"Thank you, Your Honor. The prosecution calls Ms. Cecelia Nilsson-Lim, chairperson of Jinse Shaloo Technology."

A side door opens, and a woman steps in. She's wearing a golden-yellow business suit and a yellow Eugenie hat with a single gigantic feather sticking off of it. She wears it tilted to one side like the empress they named it after.

It's the woman in the picture with Afton's dad! Now I've really got to find out from Afton what this woman's connection is to her dad. It may be a clue, and I'd be happy to find fault with her. I can tell that I'm not going to like her just by the way she saunters to the witness box, smiling to herself, as if she's become the star of the show.

"Dude, do you know who that is?" I whisper to Grady. He side-eyes me and frowns.

"Dude, didn't you just hear her name? That's Cecelia Nilsson-Lim, chairperson—"

"I know *that*, dude. What's her connection to all of this?"

"She's done some business with my parents. Weapons and parts supplier, mostly. She has these big parties that my parents used to go to. I've heard they're pretty over-the-top. My parents always came home with these big smiles on their faces."

So, someone who's gotten rich off the work done by Grady's parents? That would explain the photo. She'd be visiting military ships all the time, which is where she'd run into Mr. Jee. Maybe I'm wrong about her. She wouldn't have any reason to want them to go to jail. If she has no client, her

company can't make money. I'll hold my judgment on Ms. Golden Canary fo
r now.

"Chairperson Nilsson-Lim, thank you for—"

"Please, it's just Cecelia for the court. I'm here to do my duty as a citizen of the Empire. We can forego the titles for today."

"Thank you. Now...Cecelia, as we already have your name and profession on record, please share with the court your relationship to Doctors O'Grady-Davies and Sugiyama."

"Well, you could say our relationship is mostly professional. My company supplies parts for the Sugiyama drive, as well as some other equipment for the fleet." Cecelia smiles. It's just like Kayley's, only I know my girlfriend's is honest. I don't know what to think of this woman's yet.

"Of course," she goes on, "they have attended most of my receptions...sometimes even as the guests of honor!"

"I see." My father nods, pacing from the witness to the jury box. "And what is your professional opinion of the accused?"

"That should be obvious, given the amount of business we do together. I think they're both truly gifted designers and engineers. I wish they were working directly for me."

"Thank you. Let's get to some of the specifics of the case. Thirty-seven days ago, that would be May the nineteenth. Do you remember having contact with the defendants on that date?"

"Yes, we were meeting over lunch."

"And could you share with us the topic of what was discussed at this meeting?"

"I'm sorry, no, I can't."

"Why not?"

"Because the topic is highly classified."

"I see. Could you tell us what the mood of the accused was on that day?"

"Yes, well...at first they were their usual selves, but then they turned angry. I asked them if it was something I said, and they said no, it was what the Emperor had commanded them to do with their new designs. They were upset they were going to be used in a way they didn't approve of."

"What way was that?"

"I'm sorry, I can't reveal that. It's classified."

That's a convenient way to not answer a question. I wonder what other questions she's going to answer that way. At least she hasn't said anything yet that's damaging to Grady's parents.

"Doctors O'Grady-Davies and Sugiyama are accused of stealing information from the Emperor. Designs which, as you have already reminded us, are highly classified. Can you think of any reason they would be motivated to do such a thing?"

"Objection, speculation!" Mr. Moreno says.

"Your Honor, this goes to motive," my father says.

"Very well, I'll allow it."

"I think..." Cecelia Nilsson-Lim furrows her brow and chews on her lower lip for a few seconds, her eyes darting upwards. "If anyone were to do something like that, it would be because the designs are highly valuable and they wanted to make money off the sale of them."

"The accused are very well paid already." My father turns to look at the defendant's box. "Why would they want to risk their entire careers on getting more in this way?"

"I have no idea."

"I do." My father turns back to the witness stand. "Did the accused borrow money from you?"

Cecelia's eyes go wide, her hands squeezing her clutch purse until her knuckles turn white. I glance at Grady, but his face is a mess of confusion. If this is true, he had no idea.

"Answer the question, please." Judge Hamlin leans towards her and stares.

"Yes...yes, they did."

"How much money did they borrow from you?"

"Ten million jorins."

Gasps spread through the gallery like rocket fuel igniting. I turn to see Grady snap his head towards his parents. They're not looking anywhere but down. That's an instant admission of guilt if I ever saw one. I want to withhold my opinion here, but...why would they need that much money?

"You could buy three of Grady's house for that much," Afton whispers, leaning into Kayley. I overhear only because her whisper verges on shouting.

"Did the accused tell you what they needed that significant quantity of funds for?" My father is doing a good job of pretending to be shocked. It fills me with anger, but I never said he wasn't good at his job. After all, it's his job that made him leave my mom and me.

"They said they were trying to fund a side project," Cecelia replies, shifting in her chair and dropping her gaze.

"Did they tell you what this side project was?"

"It had something to do with a new engine design."

"Thank you, no further questions."

"Defense, your turn to cross-examine," says the judge.

I really hope that Mr. Moreno can provide some valid reasoning for all of this. Grady's parents are looking terrible, otherwise. If the jury is making connections between the stealing of the plans and the money, they'll almost certainly think that they're trying to build the engine away from the eyes of the Emperor. And if they believe that, it's all too easy to believe they're guilty.

Mr. Moreno approaches her as if he's not in any hurry to get there. "Good morning, Ms....may I also call you Cecelia?" He offers her a pretzel, but she declines.

"Of course." Ms. Nilsson-Lim's reply is flat, and her smile is about the same.

"So in your professional opinion of my clients, you've stated you hold them in high regard."

"That's correct."

"And what about your non-professional opinion?"

Cecelia freezes, her mouth opening slightly. I check her hands just to see if her knuckles are turning ghost-white again—they're not, but Mr. Moreno caught her off guard. I grin at Grady, but he's not as confident of his lawyer's tactic.

"I'm sorry, I don't understand. What is it you want me to tell you?"

"Well, you said they've attended several of your parties and were even guests of honor at a few of them, so surely you know them in both a casual environment and a professional one."

"Objection!" My father shoots up. "Relevance!"

"I think it's well relevant, Mr. Cavalcante. Overruled. State your question, counsel."

"Thank you." Mr. Moreno bows to the judge and turns back to his witness. "Please tell us your *personal* opinion of Doctors O'Grady-Davies and Sugiyama."

"Like I said, they were the guests of honor at my parties."

"Yes, but that doesn't really tell us if you personally liked them, does it?"

Grady leans forward in his seat, an air of expectation about him. I nudge Kayley and motion towards him so she can see for herself. She smiles and presses her shoulder against me.

"Does it?" Mr. Moreno repeats, rolling a pretzel rod around in his mouth.

"No."

"Then please explain your personal feelings towards my clients."

"I..." Cecelia shrugs. "I guess I like them fine."

"Did you like them when you lost the bid on the recent launch project?" He points the remainder of the pretzel at her. "One that could have netted your company a very large profit?"

Murmurs come from the gallery. Grady drops his hands on the railing and flexes his fingers. I think I'm forming a better opinion of Mr. Moreno today than I had yesterday. He might just be worth the money he was paid after all. Maybe I won't mind the pretzels so much.

"Bids and contracts like that come and go." Ms. Nilsson-Lim waves a dismissive hand. "It's expected that the Emperor's own people are going to win bids more often. We benefit by becoming a subcontractor, anyway."

"Thank you. Now, this loan that you gave them. Would you truly categorize this as a loan...or an investment?"

"What do you mean?"

"I shouldn't need to explain the difference to a chairperson of a major company."

"Objection!" My father jumps up again. "Your Honor, counsel is badgering the witness."

"I would agree, Mr. Cavalcante. Counsel, ask your questions or rest...but do not do that again."

Mr. Moreno paces and turns back, unhurried. His little misstep hasn't ruffled him at all. Either that or it was his plan. If so, I think some points are due to our lawyer. I'm looking forward to seeing where he goes with thi s.

"Understood, Your Honor. Now, Cecelia, could you answer the question?"

"What was it?"

"Was the money you gave my clients a loan or an investment?"

"A loan."

"A loan. So then, they gave you some type of asset as collateral?"

"No."

"No?" Mr. Moreno raises an eyebrow and makes a show of it to the jury. Some of them are frowning, and I like where this is going. "So you gave them ten million jorins with no collateral or guarantee they'd pay it back? And this was for two people you just said you liked fine. Not that you liked a great deal, but who were...fine."

He waits to speak the last word until he's facing the jury fully. I can't see his face but I bet he's doing his best to not grin.

"One last question…Cecelia."

My father is sitting in a similar position as Grady, although he looks as though he's about to rocket off his seat to protect his witness. Mr. Moreno is going to shoot one last hole in her testimony, and that will create some solid doubt in the jury. At least, I think it will, and that's exactly where we want to be.

"Could it be that the money you gave them wasn't a loan at all, but an investment into the development of a technology that you would control, as sole investor?"

"Objection! Ms. Nilsson-Lim isn't the one on trial!"

And with that, shouts fly from the gallery. A few men stand, either to throw insults at our lawyer or praise him for his brilliance. Grady's also on his feet, pumping his fist and cheering. Afton and Parrish both get in on the act. After a minute, I realize I'm missing out on the fun and join in as wel l.

Judge Hamlin pounds on his gavel in sheer annoyance until everyone quiets down. He takes an extra minute to glare at everyone who dared to disturb his courtroom. His eyes end on Grady, but he can't single my bud out for something that half the courtroom just did.

We all wait for him to rule on my father's objection, unsure of which way he'll go. Up to this point he's been fair to both sides, so the anticipation is really building up. Kayley lays a hand on my arm and grips it. It's not her usual death grip, but it's enough to show she's as anxious as the rest of us.

"Mr. Cavalcante, I agree that your witness is not on trial, but if it goes to the credibility of your witness, defense counsel has a right to ask." He turns to the witness box. "Ms. Nilsson-Lim—"

"Cecelia, please, Your Honor." She smiles at him as she corrects the judge in his own courtroom. That's mighty brave of her.

"Cecelia." The judge smiles back. "Please answer the question…and re-member, you're under oath."

The smile disappears as if it was never there to begin with, and the muscles of her jaw tighten. Then she shifts again, a hand going to her chest, and her respiration increases.

"No…" Cecelia shakes her head, her breathing getting faster and faster. "No! It's a loan! Just like I said before! My loan isn't personal…it's just business! I've always respected them!"

"No further questions, Your Honor."

After her testimony, I can't say I have any worse feelings for Ms. Nilsson-Lim, but I am definitely adding her to the top of the list of people that we should investigate.

Eleven

As I press the buzzer on Grady's door the next morning, I glance up at the sky and smile. There's not one cloud, and I'll take that as a sign that things are headed in a positive direction. Mr. Moreno really showed his talents yesterday, and now I've got strong confidence he'll be able to get an acquittal. Grady's parents will be home in no time!

"What do you want?" Afton stares at me as she opens the door. I stare back because it takes me a moment to remember she's staying here. Of course she is. Grady doesn't want to be alone, and Afton can't stand to be at home. They're perfect for each other.

"Uh, *you* are at *my* friend's house. Does that make it clear enough for you?"

Afton stares some more, to the point that I tilt my head in confusion. She turns around and walks back into the house.

"Close the door after you're in. Some idiot with a camera tried to sneak in yesterday. I had to threaten to break his legs."

"Did that stop him?" I step in, and of course, close the door.

"No."

"So what did you do?"

"What do you think?"

I give her the Kayley eye roll. I wouldn't put it past Afton to scare the life out of a jerk like that, but break his legs? Unlikely...I hope.

"Where's Grady?

Afton points straight up and walks to the kitchen in the back. Before I can ask her what that means, I hear the crooning of a rich tenor wafting down from upstairs. It's a curious but familiar voice, so I go to investigate.

It's Grady, singing in some archaic language I've never heard before. I'd forgotten that he practices singing. To be honest, I'm a little envious of my bud. He's not half bad.

"What are you doing, dude?" I ask, hitting the top step that leads to his mezzanine bedroom space.

He finishes the line with a lilting tone that ends kinda sad. It's a moment before he sighs and closes the music folder he was holding, and puts it down.

"There's a singing contest that my mom and I enter every year. It's always around this time, about a month from now," he says, turning to face me.

"Oh, cool. So you were going to enter it?" I ask, praying my question doesn't throw Grady into a bad mood. His parents *could* be home in a month, but that doesn't leave them much time to rehearse.

"Well," Grady says and looks back at the folder, "I was kinda hoping…"

Yeah, I understand what he means. If there was any way I could get his parents back here faster, I would. Grady is more than a little lost without them. It's not his fault, really. Even when they were off-planet on a project, they would check on him daily to make sure he was following orders. Now with no contact and no directions from them, he's got no idea which way to go.

"Hey," Afton calls up from downstairs. "Your food's here!"

I motion to him, and we go down together to find Parrish standing in the foyer with a covered tray in his hands. He grins at the two of us and shows us the tray.

"That's a lot of noodles, dude," Grady says, peering closer. "What's the red stuff all over them?"

"It's a sauce made from tomatoes."

"Dude, you put tomatoes on noodles?" Grady narrows his eyes and shakes his head at Parrish.

"Yeah. My mom showed me how to make it." Parrish grins. "Trust me, you're going to like it."

"If you say so." Grady shrugs and takes the tray from Parrish to put in the kitchen, where Afton divvies it up and drops it on some plates. We all wind up at the dining room table, some of us more eager to try Parrish's cooking than others.

"Good day in court yesterday," Parrish says, attempting to lighten up the mood. I try to be supportive by nodding and giving him a thumbs-up. Grady's handing out the chopsticks while Afton fills some cups with something that I hope will be potentially drinkable.

"Yeah, Mr. Moreno is getting into his stride," I say. Grady continues to play the wall, and we keep trying to talk to it. After I use up all my peppy attitude, I'm ready for some straight truth.

"Dude, why the glum act?"

Grady looks at me, his mouth turning down. He grabs the chair at the head of the table—his mom's—and slouches deeply into it. Parrish and I share a concerned glance, but we're patient for his reply.

"I'm just not all that hopeful this is going to turn out well."

"What do you mean?" Parrish asks.

"I just have this feeling they're never coming home."

"You've gotta keep your head up, buddy." Afton puts a cup in front of him and kisses his head. "I never gave up hope about my dad coming home, and look what happened."

"Yeah, you ran away from home," Grady mutters. Afton doesn't let her buttons get pressed. Instead, she takes the seat at the other end of the table—Dr. Sugiyama's seat.

We've all got sympathy for him, but if he won't take the usual happy boost from his friends, then we've got to go deeper. We had agreed to try and do some investigation to help Mr. Moreno. I'm not sure if that applies any longer, but the other part of that—convincing my dad—will be far from possible if he thinks he's winning the case. Still, we could at least talk about the first part. That might get Grady's spirits up.

"Hey." I pick up my chopsticks and fit them in between my fingers. "Why don't we talk about our investigation?"

"Investigation of what?" Grady pushes one of his chopsticks away. "It's not like we have any leads to go on."

"True," Parrish says, "but if we put our heads together, we could figure it out, couldn't we?" He glances between us, seeking confirmation. He gets a non-committal shrug from Grady and a sour face from Afton. At least Grady didn't discount it outright.

"It's possible," I say. "We've done it plenty of times before."

"I've got an idea." Afton grins and sits up in her, or rather Dr. Sugiyama's, chair. "Why don't we go grab one of those media slugs outside and strip them for whatever they know."

"Hey, get serious, or I'm going to start pulling out the Surela."

"I was serious," Afton pouts. "No need to get nasty."

The buzzer rings, and Afton pops up, happy for the distraction. If it's another one of those sneaky journalist types, she'll gladly give them a black eye or two, just for the fun of it.

Wait...that's not a good thing.

I jump up and dash to the door, just behind her. I'm not going to be able to stop Afton's arm from swinging, but I could at least delay her long enough for the poor soul to get away.

"Hey, darling...Afton." It's not a media type—it's Kayley. We were expecting her. She smiles at both of us as she steps in, planting a kiss on both our cheeks.

"Why am I second? I opened the door."

"Salutations, Rancid...Afton." Original Teddy came with her. We weren't expecting him, but I'm glad to have him. He touches my cheek with a tentacle and goes to do the same to Afton, but she backs away.

"Don't you dare."

"Oh, were you guys eating?" Kayley goes to inspect our plates in the dining room. "What is it?"

"Noodles and tomatoes," Grady answers. "Parrish made it."

"Any good?"

"We...haven't tried it yet, actually."

Kayley blinks and turns to me for an answer. I've got the feeling that I'm on the hook for something that isn't even my fault. I was about to eat, but I didn't get the chance yet.

"We were talking about the case," I explain. "And about potentially investigating, er...something."

"Investigating?"

Afton takes my girlfriend by the shoulders and sits her down in the chair next to mine, and goes to make up a plate of Parrish's concoction for her. Kayley's gaze never leaves me for a moment, but her stare turns into a scowl.

"That reminds me," Kayley says, shooting up off her seat. "Did you guys see the interview this morning with that Cecelia lady?"

All eyes swivel onto me, and I take a step back. Do they think I should know something about this when I don't? What would lead them to make a conclusion like that?

Oh, I'm dumb.

"Kayley was at home this morning...her own," I say, and all eyes slide back to her. Save for Original Teddy, who's gone into the kitchen to get himself a plate.

"Well, she couldn't stop talking about how mean Mr. Moreno was to her and how innocent she is of all the things he accused her of...how her company was an honest business that fully supported the Empire."

"Did she say anything about my parents?" Grady's hopeful gaze must be blinding Kayley in its expectation because she squints and looks away.

"She did."

"Well?"

"Well." Kayley sighs. "Honestly, Grady...even though she swore up and down that she loved them more than life, she also kind of insinuated that they're guilty."

Grady nods and looks down. I'd hoped that she'd turn out to be on his parents' side, but, just like my dad, I was too hopeful too soon. She could want them in jail...for business reasons.

"There!" Afton pounds Kayley's cup on the table, sending its liquid flying across the table. "You want someone to investigate, investigate that back-stabber!"

"Boy, you're really on fire lately," I comment.

"That's right, buddy, and don't you forget it." Afton points a finger at me as she walks to her seat.

Kayley sits too, rubbing a finger on her lower lip. Her silence draws all our attention. When she's like that, we know she's running the options through her head like any grand commander would do. There's a strong chance that whatever she says next will have implications for all of us. Even Original Teddy pauses and turns to her.

"Okay," Kayley says, nodding.

"Okay?" I ask.

"Let's come up with a plan."

"To do what?"

"We're going to look into Cecelia Nilsson-Lim and Jinse Shaloo Technology."

"Why?"

"Because it's our only lead, and I agree with Afton...she's a total back-stabber." Kayley dips her chopsticks into her noodles and slurps up a sizeable amount.

"Okay." I smile at her, then share my optimism with the rest of the team. They grin and beam back, and now we're feeling like a team with a purpose, once again. At least I am. My dad coming into this mess really threw me. I'm glad that our little team is going to be contributing to—

"Wow, Parry!" Kayley cries out. We all spin our heads to see her grinning, a big red smudge of tomato on her cheek. "This is *fantastic*!"

Twelve

"What's his name?" Afton asks as she, Parrish, Kayley, and I head down a back alley next to a Jinse Shaloo office in downtown Bradbury. We're inviting trouble being here, but that's pretty much why we're here. If we wanted to be safe, we would have stayed home.

"Mr. Kesh-Kaeo," Kayley responds.

"Cash-Cow?" Afton asks, an eyebrow raised.

"No, Kesh-*Kaeo*. Pronounce all the vowels. He's the managing director of the office here."

"And you're sure he's going to be open to us asking him a few questions?" Parrish asks.

Kayley only looks at him, keeping her lips pressed together. She's got her doubts, as do we all. No one who wants to keep their job would willingly conspire against their boss. We'll have to be especially careful with our questions. Not that careful has ever been our specialty.

"And where's Teddy?" Afton asks, glancing around. "I thought he was going to be here?"

"He's coming," I reply. "They can't just sparkle the shuttle to the other side of the planet. The shuttle doesn't even have a sparkle drive."

"Whatever, let's get this over with."

The reason for the back alley approach is that going in through the front door would get us nowhere. Too many obstacles, like secretaries and guards and getting recognized, blocking us from our target. Someone would stop us long before we even saw the inside of Mr. Kesh-Kaeo's office.

With a little help from Captain—formerly Lieutenant—Cortell, we were able to find out that Mr. Managing Director leaves from a side door that exits into the alley. He then goes to his personal vehicle waiting for him at the back of the building. We don't want him to get that far, so we're going to position Teddy at the end of the alley so he can popsicle the man in case he tries to get away. Only Original Teddy isn't here yet, and it's almost quitting time for Mr. Kesh-Kaeo.

"Okay," Kayley says, checking the time on her Sergo. "If Teddy's not here in five minutes then Parrish will be blocker."

"Usually I'm the forward position, but I can play that spot too," Parrish says.

"Dude, you can play any spot."

"He has," Afton adds.

A click comes from down the alley, and Kayley and I share an open-mouthed look. Is our timing off? She motions for the four of us to drop and get against the wall. We inch forward towards the exit, holding our breath. If he's leaving already, we've lost our chance to get information.

The door opens, swinging wide to block our view of the person coming out. The four of us go still, waiting for the person exiting to show themselves. I feel my neck get tight as I squeeze my hands together. I hope it's not him.

It's not him.

Four sighs of equal length spill from us as a man exits with a wave towards someone still inside. He's too young to be our managing director, and his full head of hair also negates him as our target. Adding to our luck for the moment, he turns towards the back of the building and strolls away.

"Keep moving up," Kayley says. "We don't want to be caught off guard like that again. Parrish, get around the other side."

We get into position and stand up, attempting to appear casual. We're going to attract some level of suspicion just hanging around here. Better that we don't add to it by squatting and making ourselves seem even more odd.

As we wait, two more employees exit and head towards the back of the building. Only one of them even notices us, and her glance is more of confusion than suspicion. She quickly moves away when Afton snarls at her.

"Maybe this exit is more popular than we thought," Afton says after the woman has gone.

A second later, the man we've been waiting for comes out. Mr. Kesh-Kaeo is the shining characterization of an executive. He's round and balding, with miserly eyes, and the crown of his head is sweaty. He pauses when he notices us, his hand coming up as if to stop us from approaching. There are definite signs of suspicion all over his face, and he looks ready to bolt.

"Hi there, Mr. Kesh-Kaeo," Kayley says with a smile as she approaches him. "We're junior reporters from the local college, and we wanted to ask you a few questions about your job. Do you have a minute?"

"For you?" Mr. Kesh-Kaeo looks between us again, taking specific notice of Parrish. He starts to pant a bit, and I tense. I know KayKay can pull this off. She's just got to take it easy.

"Yes." Kayley keeps up her secret-weapon smile. "It will only take a moment. If you'd just come with us—"

"No!" he shouts and charges at her. Kayley's eyes go wide. She only got a microsecond to jump out of the way. Otherwise this rampaging bull of an executive would have bowled her over.

"Shoot! After him!" Afton cries and takes off. He heads towards the street, not the back. Parrish did his job, but we didn't expect he'd just go the opposite way.

He dives into a side alley. I didn't notice it before. Now we have to double back. Afton's gaining on him, but even she's had to overcorrect.

The alley is dark, and a few seconds later we lose our target. He's bound to know the area better than we do and likely has a hiding place or two for a situation such as this.

"Cover both ends," Kayley says, breathless. "We can't let him get to the street. Rance, take that side of the alley, and I'll take the other."

She's right—if Mr. Kesh-Kaeo gets into a public space, we've lost. We can't be seen trying to question him, or we could be in trouble with the court for trying to influence the outcome of the case. Then we might get thrown in jail ourselves, and that would be of absolutely no help to Grady and his parents.

"Do you think he recognized us?" I ask as I check the rusty door of a storage area.

"Of course," Afton replies. "Why else would he run?"

"Maybe it's better to let him go," Parrish suggests. "If he's recognized us, then he'll tell his boss and then our snooping is over. Better we're not on the hook for anything."

"We're not snooping," Afton says. "We're investigating."

"What's the difference?"

"Hush," Kayley says. "Less talking, more looking."

As I peer and peek at every nook and cranny that I can find, I wonder about Parrish's statement. Right now, there's nothing that Mr. Kesh-Kaeo can tell his boss, Cecelia Nilsson-Lim. We only tried to ask him a question, and there's nothing illegal about that. Of course, she might still turn around and try to complain about it, but it won't go anywhere. If we push him, however, he will have something on us, and that could be a problem.

"Anything?" Kayley whispers to me.

"No..."

But we need to find out about the Jinse Shaloo CEO and what she's really up to. Pretending to be friends with Grady's parents is an obvious sham. She must want to put them away for some reason. What that might be is unknown. If we could find out, then Grady's parents might just get released.

There's a strange rattling from a container two steps away from Kayley and me. We share an unspoken communication and motion Parrish and Afton to get closer. No telling if it's him, but even the largest rodents don't make sounds like that.

We tiptoe closer, trying to remain as quiet as we can. Another rattle rings out, and now I know he's got to be hiding there. Only I don't know what I'm going to do if I find him there.

A large mass bursts from out of the container—it's him! Mr. Kesh-Kaeo evades my reach and charges towards Parrish, but changes his mind and spins to try his chances with Afton. Afton sizes him up and drops into position. She's planning to stop him with a spinning kick to his face.

"Afton, wait!" I shout. I don't want her to hurt him. That'd make things really complicated.

Afton stares at me for one microsecond too long, and Mr. Kesh-Kaeo pulls off a surprisingly agile evasion. He pivots around her and sprints back down the alley towards the street. Afton glares at me, then goes after him.

All I can do is clench my jaw and follow. I may have just messed this one up. It might have been for good reason, but if Grady's parents get convicted, I'll have this little moment on my conscience for eternity.

Afton slips as she turns the corner and slides down on her side with a curse. She's out of the chase. Kayley and I hop over her and continue, but we won't be much help taking down a man that likely weighs the same as both of us combined.

Parrish is gaining, but he was far away when Mr. Kesh-Kaeo jumped out. I don't know if he'll make it before the man hits the street. I let out a cry of despair as Mr. Kesh-Kaeo makes his last steps out to safety. He hears me and turns back to grin at us.

"That'll teach you kids not to meddle with Jinse Shaloo! Now go home and play with your toys!"

He rotates and aims for the alley exit, but pauses. I keep running, hoping he's reconsidered talking to us. That's unlikely, given what he just said.

It's strange, though. He must hear us catching up to him. Yet it's like he's frozen. He's as unmoving as a dormant volcano. He just needs to take a few more steps, and he's free. Why doesn't he move?

Frozen? Wait a minute...

"Teddy?"

Original Teddy rounds the corner and waddles towards us, his tentacles waving in the air in his usual welcome. The four of us come to a halt and try to catch our breath.

"Felicitations," Original Teddy says. "Teddy is fashionably tardy."

"No, Teddy," I reply with a smile. "You're right on time."

Thirteen

WE DRAG THE POPSICLED Mr. Kesh-Kaeo back into the side alley and prop him up against the rusted wall of a storage room we found open. There's just a bit of light streaming through a dirty window, enough to see where we are but not enough to let others see. In terms of a place to hide, it's as ideal as we're going to get.

Mr. Kesh-Kaeo's body is as lifeless as a mannequin, but there's activity behind his eyes. His muscles may not be working for him, but I bet his brain is functioning just fine.

"So, what should we ask him?" I say, continuing to stare at the tubby body before me.

"Who said we were going to ask him anything?" Afton replies. "I say we just pummel him until he spills everything."

"We're not going to do that," Kayley says, taking Afton by the arm and pulling her back from the paralyzed man. Afton scoffs, but she knows better than to go against Kayley. Afton might be the toughest physically, but she's no match for KayKay's willpower.

As if he knew we were talking about him, Mr. Kesh-Kaeo blinks, his body coming back to life. He groans and rubs his head. I guess getting popsicled gives you a serious hangover. I've never had the pleasure of it happening to me, but if I really wanted to know, I could just ask my three buds here. They'd give me the answer and then make sure I felt extremely guilty for causing it to happen to them.

"Can you hear me, Mr. Kesh-Kaeo?" Kayley leans over him. His eyes rotate to look at her, then he coughs and tries to sit up.

"What the hell did you do to me?" he asks in a groggy voice while he rubs his head.

"Us? Nothing," Kayley replies.

"Yeah, not a thing," I add.

"Not that I didn't want to," Afton says.

Mr. Kesh-Kaeo shakes his head, then gags. Kayley goes to help him, but he pushes her hand away. She backs up a step, wary of any attempt from him to attack her and gain an advantage. I'm not concerned about that. We've got Original Teddy here, even though he's hiding at the moment.

"You definitely did, and I'm going to consider it assault. But if you let me go now, I won't go to the authorities."

"Sir." Kayley smiles sweetly at him. "You have absolutely no proof that we did anything to you. We haven't laid a finger on you. We haven't attacked you with any weapon...basically, you've got nothing on us."

Mr. Kesh-Kaeo narrows his eyes at her. He knows she's right, and his threat attempt goes down the drain.

"So what do you want from me, then?"

"The same thing I said before. We just want you to answer a few questions for us."

"About what?"

"About your boss, and her intentions," Afton says. Her outburst earns her a glare from Kayley, and Afton steps back. Mr. Kesh-Kaeo lets out a quick grunt and shakes his head.

"If you think I'm going to give up confidential company information, you've got a lot to learn about how things work, girl."

"We don't care about what kind of poison your company makes," I say, stepping up. "We want to know what she really thinks about those scientists on trial for treason."

I don't mention their names, just in case he hasn't realized our connection to Grady and his parents. It's a weak hope, but if we can avoid that problem sprouting up from the dirt, then we might just get what we want and stay clear of causing Grady any trouble.

"What do I care about traitors?" Mr. Kesh-Kaeo snorts. "If they went against the Emperor for their own greed, then they deserve whatever they get."

"I didn't ask you what you thought." I fold my arms, getting closer.

"Well, I don't read minds, boy. If you want to know what my boss thinks, you should ask her."

"I doubt she'd be willing to speak to us."

"What makes you think I am?"

He has a point. We're not intimidating him at all. We'll need to figure out a better way if we want any information from him. There's got to be a way to appeal to his greedy side. We just have to find out how.

"Because if you don't I am going to cause you some severe hurt," Afton growls. Mr. Kesh-Kaeo looks up at her. He's weighing the truth of Afton's words, likely thinking she's bluffing. That would be a wrong assumption on his part. Afton's not overly violent, but she is highly protective of her friends. There's a good chance she would do a lot more than use harsh language at him if we gave her the chance. We're not at the point where we need to consider physical means, and I hope we never get there. Mr. Kesh-Kaeo isn't making it easy, though.

"Look," Kayley says, trying to play the good side, "we just want to know what Ms. Nilsson-Lim really thinks of Doctors Sugiyama and O'Grady-Davies. That's all. That's not a trade secret. Tell us what you know and we'll let you go home."

"Sorry, girl. I'm not even going to tell you my shoe size."

Kayley turns away from him, her hands on her hips. It's becoming clear that we aren't going to get anywhere being polite. I'm not so sure we'd get any further by threatening him with violence either, but one thing's for sure. Right now we're not getting anywhere at all.

"Let's huddle up," Kayley says, motioning us over. "Parrish, would you keep an eye on him, please?"

"Why me?"

"Because I know you won't bash him unless you have to."

Parrish shrugs and nods in agreement. I couldn't find any argument there. Parrish wouldn't step on a flower if it was in his path, but he plays some rough-and-tumble sports and isn't afraid to dive in when needed. I don't think he even knows just how strong he really is.

"What's up, KayKay?" I ask as she, Afton, and I gather in the corner.

"Well, clearly we're not getting anywhere, so we need to come up with a new plan. Any suggestions?"

Afton jumps right in. "Sure. Let me break his little finger, and that way he'll get how serious we are."

"No," Kayley flatly replies. "How about an actual idea?"

"Well, we could try pretending we know some top-secret thing about his company and threaten to release it to the public unless he talks," I suggest.

Kayley puts a finger on her lower lip and looks down. She's thinking that through, and I get a jolt of excitement coursing through my body. It's not common for her to approve of my ideas, as hard as she tries to support them. Just one of the million reasons I love her. Though, I might just love her a teeny bit more if she approves my idea.

"What kind of top-secret thing?"

"Companies like these always have something to hide. Tax evasion, environmental destruction...you name it, they've likely done it."

"Yeah, but we'll need to be specific," Afton counters, "or he'll know we're bluffing."

"But not too specific or he'll know right away if we're just making it up."

"That might not matter," Kayley says. "If he believes we have actual evidence of something, he might just work with us."

"So then, like what?" Afton asks.

"It shouldn't be too difficult to find evidence of pollution on Magnarapax or Sordibus Prime is chock-full of environmental violations," I reply. "We could Sergo something up and twist it to make it sound like it's tied to Jinse Shaloo."

"I like it." Kayley nods, pulling her Sergo from her pocket. In two seconds she's already pulled up an Angel-4 article about some company using the pristine grasslands of the colony planet Sordibus Prime to dump their manufacturing waste. She summarizes it for us and says, "It's a real situation and we could make the case that Jinse Shaloo dumped it there."

Wow, KayKay's going with my idea. I glance over at Afton, who's trying not to find ways to crush the idea into micro pancakes. I'm guessing she doesn't hate the plan entirely. It's just that she thinks that fists and feet will get us what we want faster.

"Alright, Mr. Kesh-Kaeo," Kayley says, turning to stroll up to him. "We didn't want to do this, but we know Jinse Shaloo is involved in this mess on Sordibus Prime, and we've got the evidence to prove it. If you don't start answering some questions, we're going to the Ministry of the Environment and telling them everything we know."

He blinks up at her, his lips parted just slightly so he can run his tongue across them. I get hopeful as he takes a deep breath and lets it out slowly—Kayley's threat is affecting him! I feel my heart pick up its pace. We're finally getting somewhere.

"What do you think you know, exactly?" Mr. Kesh-Kaeo asks.

"We can trace that dump of iron silicate compounds to a manufacturing process that your company uses. I even have a way to spectra-analyze samples of the material so the Ministry can see it's an exact match."

"Well." He blows a breath out, his shoulders sinking. Kayley grins. We've got him now! All we have to do is get our questions out.

Then Mr. Kesh-Kaeo breaks into a laugh that emanates from his belly and bursts out of his mouth as he slaps a hand on his abdomen. Kayley takes a step back, her eyebrows coming together. Even Afton is uncertain about the sudden change in his disposition. She tightens her jaw and narrows her eyes. She's ready to stomp her boot right into his face, and we are getting close to a serious problem.

"You kids really thought you had me, didn't you?" He bursts into another round of laughter. "That wasn't us by a long shot! Go ahead and try to pin that on us, you'll get nowhere."

"That's it!" Afton shouts as she charges him, fists raised over her head. I break from my position to cut her off, but even though I'm heavier, Afton is stronger, and she blows right past me.

"Afton, no!" Kayley shouts, and bolts after her—too late. She couldn't stop a runaway Afton if she wanted to. I'm a fraction of a second behind. I reach out but I can't catch her. Afton's going to do him some real hurt, and we'll be guilty of assault.

Sorry, Grady. We tried to help.

Out of nowhere, Original Teddy drops from his hiding spot, directly in front of Afton. She has to skid to stop to avoid smashing into him, and barely keeps her balance. He glances at her as if he's surprised that she wasn't expecting him, but I'm just applying human attributes to an alien race again.

"What the hell?" Mr. Kesh-Kaeo shouts, his eyes wide. "What's that thing doing here?"

It's clear that he's genuinely afraid of our fuzzy friend. That's good, and it hits me that this is the only leverage we needed this whole time.

Kayley's face turns sly, and she approaches him with renewed confidence. She knows exactly how to use our extra advantage and she's going right in for the kill.

"We thought you might not believe us, Mr. Kesh-Kaeo," she says with a snarl, "so now we're going to feed you to our friend here. He just so happens to eat animal flesh."

"Fresh is best," Teddy says, opening his maw to reveal his double row of razor-sharp teeth. Mr. Kesh-Kaeo presses his back against the wall, his hands going up to protect him. Original Teddy chomps his teeth together and does his best monster imitation. It's too easy to dismiss our fuzzy friends as less than genius by the way they speak Empire Common, but I know they're way more intelligent than any human in the Empire. Even G rady.

"Okay, okay!" Mr. Kesh-Kaeo cries. "I'll talk! I'll tell you what you want to know! Just keep that monster away from me!"

"Very good," Kayley says, taking a quick high-five from Afton. "Tell us what Ms. Nilsson-Lim's intentions are."

"That's it?" He shrugs but keeps his wide eyes on Original Teddy. "That's not really a secret, you know. Ask anyone in the industry, and they'll tell you the same. Jinse Shaloo wants to have all the Empire's military business. My boss is just trying to make that happen."

The four of us share a look. Then a sigh. All this effort for that bit of information. It's useful, of course, but as usual, we totally overdid it. If only we tried the easy way.

Fourteen

I REALLY DON'T UNDERSTAND why Original Teddy and Doc Elizabeth wanted to watch a court proceeding. It's dull and slow and is full of as much anti-logical procedure as you could cram into the storage memory of a tablet. That's like 597,000 copies of my favorite book, *Holden Unleashed*. They made a great cine out of that story, but I still wouldn't watch it that many times.

Teddys are still a curiosity around the Empire, but they're fairly commonplace here on Angelcanis. Original Teddy barely gets a few glances. He's not the show people have come to see. Our spectacle-loving citizens want to see some real courtroom drama happen today. We have little of it on this planet—courtroom drama, that is. Nobody has much of an interest in breaking the law.

"This looks much like I remember a courtroom on Earth to be," Doc Elizabeth says, glancing around. Now here's a spectacle, if anyone really wanted to see one. A human, living with the Teddys on their ship for who knows how long, claiming to come from a long-lost human planet.

"Were you ever on trial?" Kayley asks her.

"Hopefully not."

After Judge Hamlin asks my father to call his first witness, my dad stands, adjusting his jacket and clearing his throat. I think it's a nervous habit he's got. Either that or it's like one of those stupid rituals that sports teams do to ensure their victory. As if it ever works.

"Your Honor, the prosecution calls Dr. Tipiwai Cooper-Wake."

Grady's mom gasps. I spin my head to the defendant's box and see her hand cover her mouth. Even Dr. Sugiyama looks shocked, but no sound comes from his open mouth. I don't know what they were thinking. The prosecution can call whomever they want, whether that person wants to testify or not.

Grady is faring better than his parents. Hopefully, that's because he's among his buds, and he knows we're not about to let anything happen to him. That extends to his parents too, but that's still a work in progress.

Dr. Cooper-Wake is a mouse of a woman. She's got white hair and keeps her hands tucked close to her chest as she walks. The rapid darting of her eyes completes the image of a small animal looking out for large predators.

"Oh, the poor woman," Doc Elizabeth says. "She's frightened to death of this place."

"Maybe," Afton says. "But she's got three doctorate degrees, so she's not gonna go down that easily."

"How do you know that?" Kayley asks. Afton only winks and grins.

When the good doctor swears to the Goddesses that she will speak only the truth, her voice is timid and squeaky. Her posture when she sits down is uncomfortable and anxious. It's like someone uncovered her hiding spot, and now she has nowhere to run.

"Thank you for agreeing to testify today, Doctor." My father walks up to her, trying to put as much charm on as he can. Grady's mom's associate isn't falling for it. She glances both ways as if to say *are you talking to me?*

"Uh, I was given an unconditional summons to be here."

"Well." My father smiles. "You did still come, so we appreciate it. Now, if you would please, for the record, state your relationship to the defendants."

"Uh, I work with Dr. O'Grady-Davies on a currently classified project."

"Thank you. Now, on the night of May the twenty-first, you were working late with Dr. O'Grady-Davies on that particular project, yes?"

Dr. Cooper-Wake nods.

"Please confirm verbally for the record, Doctor."

"Yes, I was."

"How did she seem to you that evening? Was she nervous? Or relaxed?"

"Objection, leading the witness!" Mr. Moreno stands up, a pretzel stick in the air.

"Sustained. We don't need multiple choice here, counsel."

My father bows once to the judge and makes a leisurely circuit across the floor, coming back only after he's figured out a new way to phrase the question. I know that's what he's doing because I do the same thing every time Kayley stymies me with her own form of judicial policy. My skin is crawling with the simple idea that he and I are alike in any way. I know he's my father, but that doesn't mean I enjoy the fact.

"So, once again, please describe the emotional state of Dr. O'Grady-Davies that evening."

"She seemed fine to me." Dr. Cooper-Wake shrugs and shakes her head.

"Seemed?"

"I wasn't there to observe my colleague. I was there to…work on something classified."

"Yet you're an expert in observation, aren't you?"

"Yes."

"So you're telling me an expert in observation didn't observe her colleague at all?"

"I…I don't usually…"

"So then, you did notice something."

We all shift on the bench, rocking it under us. We've seen enough of this case now to know when a cross-examination is about to slam into the atmosphere on reentry. It gets bumpy at first, and then friction caused by air resistance burns things to shreds.

"No, not really."

"Doctor, are you being truthful with this court?"

"Of…of course."

"Then tell us, please, what you observed in your colleague."

"Well…she was a bit distracted that evening."

"Distracted how?"

"I guess she had something personal on her mind, but we didn't discuss it."

"Fine, now on that same evening, did Dr. O'Grady-Davies ask you to take something for her?"

"Like what?"

"Yes or no, please, Doctor."

"Well…yes, she did."

My father strolls back to his table and picks up a data chip, and holds it up. He makes an effort to show all the jurors before he walks back to the witness stand with it. He holds it directly in front of Dr. Cooper-Wake's face.

"Doctor, is this the memory chip that Dr. O'Grady-Davies gave you?"

"Objection!" Mr. Moreno makes a show of being disgusted. "Your Honor, that's just a standard memory chip. How could anyone—"

"But it's not just a standard data chip, is it, Doctor?"

"Well…it could be."

"Take a closer look, please."

"Uh." Dr. Cooper-Wake leans forward and peers at it. He presses the chip into her face so close that she jerks back and stares at him, eyes wide.

"You recognize it, don't you?"

"Yes...no...well...I think..."

"Answer the question, please."

"Yes."

"Good, now please tell the court what is so special about it."

"Um...I'm not sure I should. It's...uh...."

"Doctor, you must answer the question."

"It's coded specifically to my colleague."

"Please state for the record who that colleague is."

"Elenora O'Grady-Davies."

I didn't think it possible, but Grady's mom's colleague shrinks in the chair even more. My father has something he's about to reveal and it's not boding well for Grady's mom. There must be something on that chip that condemns her.

"Your Honor, I would like to submit this chip into evidence as exhibit 42.1-A. I request that in a closed hearing, we review the contents of this device so we can prove, without a doubt, that Dr. O'Grady-Davies gave secret documents to her colleague."

"Wait...no, that's not true!" Dr. Cooper-Wake shouts. When my father turns on her, she pulls back as if she even surprised herself with her outburst.

"What's not true?"

"I didn't receive any secret documents!"

"Did you not state that on the night of May twenty-first, Dr. O'Grady-Davies gave you this chip?"

"Well, yes...but..."

"Doctor, did you not just say this belonged to your colleague?"

"Well, I think it does...but I'm not sure."

"What are you not sure about? Did you just not say this chip is coded specifically to Dr. O'Grady-Davies? How could you be so sure just a second ago and now you're not? Aren't you an expert at observation, or are you trying to protect your friend?"

"Objection! Badgering the witness!"

"Overruled."

"I would like the record to state that Dr. Cooper-Wake is an uncooperative witness, and as such, she may bias her answers in favor of the defense. I also submit that she may withhold evidence."

"Duly noted," Judge Hamlin says and turns to his left. "Clerk of the court, you may add that note into the record."

"Thank you, Your Honor. No further questions."

"Well, that could have gone better," Doc Elizabeth says. I'm in full agreement. Grady's mom's colleague is exhausted and beaten. She might be a force to be reckoned with in the lab, but in the court, she is at the mercy of my father's rough style of questioning.

I check on Grady, two spots down from me on the bench, with Doc Elizabeth and Original Teddy in between us. Our fuzzy friend has said little this entire time, so I decide to ask him what he thinks of the trial.

"Proceeding is abnormal" is his reply.

"How so, Teddy?"

"Teddy does not commit torment. It is unwholesome. Teddy has no requirement for persecution."

"I hear that," Parrish says from the opposite side of Grady. I think Original Teddy means there's no need for court trials because no Teddy has ever stolen anything. Mostly because no Teddy owns anything, so stealing is not a thing in their society. Plus, when they have a problem, they just conclave and figure it out. Group harmony is paramount, as he would say. I wish humans could figure that out too.

"Defense counsel, your witness."

"Thank you, Your Honor."

"Objection!" my father says and jumps up. Mr. Moreno side-eyes him and cracks his knuckles.

"On what grounds, counsel?"

"Your Honor, stating code 12.1-A16.2, 'no testimony by a witness found to be biased may be entered into the court record,' I move that the defense be barred from cross-examining Dr. Cooper-Wake because the jury must be forbidden to consider any of the defense's testimony."

"Oh, that's just pushing it!" Mr. Moreno throws his hands up in a grand gesture, playing the part for the jury and the media people in the gallery. But when he catches Judge Hamlin's pensive look, he just shakes his head. "Oh, come on, Your Honor, you can't actually be considering this!"

"I am," the judge replies. "You might want to come up with a counter-argument, counsel."

"Well." Mr. Moreno sighs and taps on his box of pretzels to pull out another one. "Firstly, Your Honor, Dr. Cooper-Wise has not been found to be biased about anything! That's just speculation on the prosecution's part. And let the court not forget that Mr. Cavalcante is also biased in his own right. He's got the pride of the Emperor weighing on his shoulders."

"Did you just accuse me of running an unethical case?" My father puts on an indignant face.

"I did no such thing," Mr. Moreno replies. "I merely state that you are stretching the meaning of code 12.1-A16.2 to suit your own needs!"

"Why you!"

Judge Hamlin bangs his gavel as the debate collapses into name-calling and personal accusations. A few members of the gallery get into it as well, but the somber mood in the air keeps the majority from causing a ruckus. I hang my head and glance at Kayley next to me. Her lips are pressed tight, and her hands are flat on her legs. I reach out to touch her hand, and she takes mine in both of hers as our eyes connect. Her face remains impassive, but I know my Kayley, and I can see the storm building behind her mask.

"Is everyone done? Can we return to acting in the proper decorum of the court again, please?" Judge Hamlin stares down Mr. Moreno and my father until they acquiesce and bow to him. "Thank you so much. Now, I think we can all agree that the witness will testify to contradict everything on the current record when the defense questions her. So, to expedite our due process, I will dismiss the witness."

"Your Honor!" Mr. Moreno approaches the bench. "Shouldn't we hear what Dr. Cooper-Wise actually has to say and not just assume it?"

"We will let the record speak for itself." Judge Hamlin bangs his gavel. "The witness is dismissed."

Oh, boy. My father really is going in for the kill, former relationships be damned. If I was hoping for a new way to reconnect with him, I don't think that's on the table any longer. Still, as much as I want to, I can't find it in me to hate him now. Parents are so complicated.

Fifteen

THE TWIN MOONS SHINE down on the seven of us as we stroll along the boardwalk of White Orchid Beach. We're the largest group of humans—and one Teddy—around. Only a handful of couples and a late-night pet walker pass us by. They divert their eyes or pretend not to notice us. Ever since our arrest was blasted across all the Angel channels, few are interested in autographs or even a simple greeting. Oh, how we've fallen.

We're out here in the near-midnight hour because Doc Elizabeth was concerned Grady would expire from worry sitting at home. Seeing as how Grady loved the beach the last time we brought him here, she prescribed a little ocean air for all of us. We didn't need it, but the doc didn't want to single him out as that would only make him feel worse.

"It's a beautiful night, isn't it?" Doc Elizabeth asks, glancing up at the stars. I would expect she would have had enough of stargazing after her time on the Teddy ship. The sand and the surf should be more interesting to her.

"Yes, it is." Kayley slides her fingers in between mine, adjusting our more practical hand-holding into something more romantic. It's welcome because, just like the others, we're both searching for ways to cheer ourselves up after a hard day in court.

"What do you think?" Afton throws an arm about Grady's shoulders and tilts her head down towards his face. Since she moved in, the two of them have gotten closer. Kayley told me how Afton has done the work of a Goddess caring for Grady. We've all done our bit, but Afton's there around the clock and has taken on the role of proxy mom. She gets him up in the morning, makes him breakfast—Parrish has been coming by and cooking lunch and dinner—and caters to his needs like he's a toddler. I think Grady secretly enjoys the babying. It gives Afton something to concentrate on too.

She's distracted from her own worries by putting her focus on someone e
lse.

I can think of a thousand moments when we were all in a better mood,
even when the situation was worse.

"Yeah, I guess." Grady can't see if it's a nice night or not. He's staring
down at the planks on the boardwalk, the hair of his mop-top blocking his
peripheral vision so that only the ground is in front of him. He's like a work
animal. Only the burden that he carries is mental.

"Hey, Teddy...is this anything like your homeworld?" I ask, the thought
hitting me out of nowhere. It's fine because I'd rather discuss anything
other than today's debacle.

"Sediment is not prevalent," Original Teddy answers.

"You don't have beaches?"

"That is accurate."

"What a bummer."

"That is also accurate. Teddy has also not inhabited."

I look back at him, my eyebrows squeezing themselves together. A
twinge of regret surfaces somewhere inside my mind. It only confuses me
more because I shouldn't have any regrets about it.

"Wait, you've never been home?"

"That is accurate. Teddy has inhabited vessel solely."

"So, you were born on the ship? How many other Teddys are like you?"

"Crew is similar."

Never in an eon would I have guessed that.

"Were your parents on the same ship?" Grady asks, stopping to turn to
Original Teddy behind him.

"That is not accurate."

"So..." Grady's mouth drops open. "You've never met your parents?"

"Precursor was not available," Original Teddy says, his tentacles droop-
ing. Then I feel it again, a wistful desire to have something that I've never
known.

Whatever it is gets shoved to the back of my brain when Grady's mood
suddenly changes. No longer is he the doomsday guy. His slumped frame
turns upright, and I get a familiar sense of a Grady I haven't seen in a while.
This is "I'm on a mission" Grady. This mode only shows itself when he's in
the middle of a big design job, so I'm wondering why it's rearing its assertive
head now.

"Hey, dude, what's up?" I tug Kayley so we can come around to face
him. She follows with the precision of a drill sergeant and lets me lead. She's

always been more than a little sensitive to what I'm thinking. That's why I can't ever lie to her.

"Guys," Grady starts as we gather around him. "Thanks."

"For what, dude?" Parrish asks.

"For making sure I don't sink, even when I really feel like I want to."

"That's because you're one of us," Kayley says, the leader in her coming out. "And we never let each other down. Right?"

She gets a strong positive confirmation from all of us: clapping, shouts of "Yes!" and a military grunt from Parrish. Grady blushes and smiles but looks away.

"We're here for you, dude," I say, dropping a hand onto his shoulder. The others follow suit, and even Original Teddy gets in on the action, slipping a tentacle between our arms and tapping Grady on the head. That gets a laugh from everyone.

"Teddy, you are definitely on the team too," Parrish says.

"That is not accurate."

"What?" Parrish says. Our faces fall. We've always considered him to be one of us. If he's turning us down, that's totally disappointing.

"You are Teddy. Therefore, you belong to Teddy's team."

"Oh, that's what you meant," he replies. We share another laugh, and Kayley rubs Original Teddy's head right between his ears. He gurgles in what I can only think must be a cheerful sound, but he could also be revolted...nah. No one has ever been repulsed by her touch.

We share a few more laughs, and I wonder if Doc Elizabeth's choice of medication really is doing us some good. It's energized me some, and I'm ready to dive right back into the defense of Grady's parents. The only thing giving me pause is whether Grady has gotten his recharge too. Even if we pick up where we crashed, it's still a risky endeavor.

Well, what the heck. I want to go for it.

"Guys...I don't want to bust down our happy moment, but we've got some stuff to talk about."

"Like what?" Parrish asks as I glance around, connecting my eyes with everyone's. They stay silent and look around at each other. My implied message of duty to Grady is not getting through.

"Wait..." Doc Elizabeth gets a huge grin on her face. "Did you propose? Are the two of you finally getting married?"

I would have liked to have seen Kayley and I execute a synchronous eye roll because I'm sure it happened. There are sighs and groans all around, and I just have to shake my head.

"No way those two are ever getting married," Afton says with a smirk. "They're perma-dating, for sure."

"We are not!" I shoot back. "Or did you forget we're already engaged?"

"Actually, *I* forgot..." Kayley mumbles. I stare at her, my jaw slack.

"So then, tough guy, where's the necklace?"

"If you haven't noticed, Surela, we've been a little busy!"

"Wow," Grady says. "The first Surela in at least two weeks."

"Hey, guys!" I wave my hands in front of everyone's faces. "This is not about Kayley and me. We're supposed to be discussing how we're going to help Grady's parents!"

"Okay, then, go for it," Afton says, folding her arms. I blink. That's not how I expected this to begin. I'm totally not prepared to run a meeting.

"Uh, darling," I turn to Kayley with a hopeful smile. "You want to take it from here?"

"Sure." Kayley smiles back at me, then turns to everyone, her face turning stern. "Okay, we're hunting for evidence...where's the next place we look?"

We pass a few ideas around, none all that good. We've got a suggestion for other Jinse Shaloo execs, another for breaking into Grady's parents' lab, and even one for kidnapping Cecelia Nilsson-Lim. As much as I might like to do that last one, it's the least viable.

"Guys, no." Kayley waves a dismissive hand. "Let's think less blockbuster cine and more realistic and achievable, shall we?"

"Well, like what?" Parrish asks. "All we've ever done is high-stakes missions."

"True, Parry, but we won't find what we need by blowing something to smithereens. We need a bit more sleuthing this time."

"Honestly, I think we should keep doing the blockbuster thing," I say. "We've got the most experience doing that, so we're going to be the best at that."

"Oh?" Kayley turns on me, arms folded. "And what do you suggest we blow up next, *darling*?"

That sweet but spiky tone my girlfriend is using on me right now is a pure asteroid belt of a disaster waiting to happen, should my mouth decide to take a wrong turn and obliterate itself on the massive rock that is Kayley's patience.

"We don't have to blow anything up...in fact, come to think of it, we never intentionally blew anything up. That was always someone else."

Kayley glares at me, her eyes smoldering. I guess that wasn't the point she was trying to make, however true it was. I'm sure we're going to have a little conversation on the side later about it so she can tell me what an unsupportive boyfriend I'm being. That's fine. I've got my own complaint to bring up...I mean, really. How dare she forget about our engagement?

"Let's start at my house," Grady suggests. "Maybe there's still something there."

"Oh, good idea!" Doc Elizabeth says, then frowns. "But, didn't you try that already?"

"Nope." Afton shakes her head. "Government agents took most of their notes and their computers, so there wasn't much of a reason to."

"Ah, I see. But there might still be something there?"

"Maybe," Grady replies. "I could think of a few places the agents wouldn't look."

"Wait a minute..." Parrish says. "We're so focused on what we should do that we haven't even discussed if we should do anything at all."

"What do you mean?"

"Well, think of it this way. What if we find something and it's not helpful to Mr. Moreno? Meaning, what if it actually hurts his defense rather than helps it? Then what do we do? We can't destroy it, or we'll get arrested and prosecuted if anyone finds out."

"But if we do nothing, dude," Grady replies in earnest, "then I will blame myself for sitting around like a dumbass while my parents get torn to shreds in court. They're innocent! I know it!"

"Yeah, I think they are too, and that's why I don't want to be the one to mess their case up."

"You can't let fear rule you, Mr. Beltrami," Doc Elizabeth says, turning on Parrish. "Then we *will* lose."

"Let's vote," I suggest.

"No," Kayley says, observing everyone. "We don't need to. It's obvious what everyone wants to do."

"Damn straight," Afton adds with a grin. It's contagious, and in a moment, we're all smiling.

"Okay," Grady says, "so this is where we're going to look..."

Sixteen

I FEEL SWEAT COVER my forehead as I rush out the university classroom door and trip into the rough grass of the courtyard. Kayley and Parrish are right behind me, gasping for breath in the midnight air. I catch my foot on a clump and take a dive right into the turf. But I'm laughing as I do because I know we're safe. The auto sentinels' wheels aren't big enough for anything bumpier than a building's tiled floor. They can't chase us.

We won this round!

After our little pep talk, we searched all over Grady's house, starting with the places he'd suggested—the secret drawer in his father's study, his mother's old textbooks in the basement. We even tore up a few floorboards because Grady thought he remembered a secret stash there.

As it turned out, our lead was in the most obvious place we never looked—right on top of his mom's desk.

When Grady was about to crash nap on her desk, he found a message to a fellow researcher at Bradbury University. It read:

My dear Professor Burnell,

I once again thank you for the candid conversation regarding our recent accomplishments. It is my utmost hope that you will choose to act as per our discussion. Please communicate with me once you have completed your errand.

In your trust,

Elenora O'Grady-Davies, D.Sc., D.Eng.

This was our best—and only—lead, so like the reckless kids that we are, we went to investigate.

"What makes you think we're going to find anything at this professor's office?" Parrish asks, limping behind Kayley and me.

"We don't really have anything better to go on, dude." I give Parrish a smile and a thumbs-up. As much as I'm happy to have him along, I wish he would have hung back with Grady. If his leg were fine, I would totally choose him over Afton, who's been brooding over that fight with her mom and not exactly on point.

"We could have at least come at a better hour. If anyone sees us, it's going to be completely obvious that we don't belong here."

"This isn't even midterms yet, Parry," Kayley says. "If it was, this place would be crawling with late-night crammers. Not that I think it matters. We're old enough to pass for students here. You'd be the first to get away with it."

Parrish is the oldest of us by a few months. It'll be his birthday soon, and then he'll officially be one year older than the rest of us. Afton is next, then me and Kayley. Grady's the youngest. He's a solid ten months younger than Parrish. One more month, and he'd be a year younger than the rest of us. He's still the smartest, though.

"Dude, I could ace any of those classes," Grady says over Teddy comm. "If you run across someone, I can come up with a good excuse to be there."

We come to the office door of Prof. Burnell. Whether or not it's locked isn't even a concern. We've gotten through high-security military locks before. This one should be a complete—

"What the heck is this?" Parrish leans over to examine the knob, hands on his legs.

"What's up?" I come to stand next to him, looking at what he's looking at. The bulbous doorknob is unusual, for sure, but what is really strange is that there's no keypad or biometric scanner anywhere on it.

"What are you guys seeing?" Grady asks.

"It's a...mechanical door?" I guess.

"So, just break it in, then."

"We can't do that!"

"Why not?"

"Because." Kayley puts her hands on her hips. "We don't just smash things if we don't need to. This isn't some criminal enterprise here. This is a respected professor's office."

I examine the doorknob again, noticing a small jagged slit in the center. I lean down to look closer, and I see there are a few ridges and bumps inside. I've seen devices like this on cine before. The main character needs to break into somewhere, so they use these little picks to get the lock to open.

"Oh! This is an analog key lock!"

"What does that mean?" Kayley asks.

"It means you need an analog key to open it," Grady replies. "Or a set of lockpicks...which we definitely don't have."

"So, how can we get in?"

Parrish stands up and looks around. Then before we can make a comment, he presses against the frosted window in the door and, with a single, hard jolt, breaks the glass. Kayley gasps and gawks at her former boyfriend. I, on the other hand, grin.

"Parry! Why'd you do that?" Kayley is in complete disbelief.

"So we could get in?" He reaches through the broken window and turns the lock on the other side. The door opens with a simple twist of the knob after that.

"Security better not have heard that."

I doubt they did. It wasn't loud at all. Parrish remembered his physics and stopped the window from vibrating and creating a lot of sound. Likely there's no security, anyway. This is Angelcanis. Nobody steals stuff here except for us.

We slip into the office and close the door behind us. There's little reason to do so. Now that the glass is busted, anyone could glance in and see us with ease. I'm not going to worry. We've been through much worse than this. A broken window won't break us.

But Kayley might.

"So now that we've vandalized a Level-1 university, one that *I* might like to go to one day, can we get what whatever we're looking for before we're all permanently banned?"

"KayKay, I think you're the only one who was looking forward to coming here."

"So? I'm allowed to dream. Don't you?"

I do, and my girlfriend knows every one of them as intimately as she knows how I've failed at most of them. That's okay. She'll keep pushing me to achieve them, and I love her for that. But right now, I'm going to keep my head down and avoid any Kayley cannon fire.

I sit down at the desk and power the computer console on. It's a fairly standard machine, and if the security on it is anything like the door, we'll be online in a jiffy.

It takes a little prodding, but with Grady's help, we're in. At this point, I don't know whether I should be counting my blessings or continuously glancing over my shoulder. Parrish is keeping an eye on the hallway, so that's hopefully enough.

"Go to the message folder," Kayley instructs. I make a rude face at her because I know to do that. "Now, do a search for Grady's mom."

"KayKay," I turn around and smile at her. "It's completely unnecessary to state the obvious."

"You want me to do it?"

"No."

"Then get a move on." Kayley smirks and smacks the back of my head. "Darling."

I clack on the keyboard, delving into the messages until a few come up that look like they might be a part of the conversation that Grady's mom was having with the prof. Kayley points to one from the following day, and I open it.

My dear Professor Burnell,

The time has come for action, and I pray you are with us. If you are, please forward all the data to us and triple-delete anything in your possession. We must take advantage of the situation while we can. Remember, this is all for our future profit.

Your colleague in confidence,

Elenora O'Grady-Davies, D.Sc., D.Eng.

"What does that mean?" I frown at the screen and reread the message. Twice. Then three times. I don't want to believe there's more to it than I'm reading, but there seems to be no other conclusion.

"It means my parents were up to something," Grady says, admitting it with some reluctance.

"Yeah, but what?" Kayley taps her teeth together, a bad habit I've tried to warn her about, but she won't listen to me.

"Does it matter?" I rotate in the seat to look at her. "If this is evidence that they are guilty, then forget about searching for something to prove their innocence. We've got to make sure my dad never sees this!"

I spin around and go to delete the message, but Kayley steals the keyboard out from under my fingers before I can even tap a single key. I stare at her, eyes bulging.

"What are you doing?"

"Stopping you."

"But why? This isn't going to help us!"

"It might."

"Explain how!"

"Guys, keep your voices down for a sec. I think I hear something." Parrish puts his hand out to silence us. We freeze and stare at him, waiting for his verdict. He looks at us, anxious.

I slide off the chair and pull Kayley down with me to hide under the desk. The two of us can fit under with a bit of room to spare. Of course, that leaves Parrish out in the open, but he might find somewhere else in the office to hide—a closet, maybe.

"So, how can this help?" I whisper, acutely aware that I've left the computer on without deleting a single thing.

"What if this is Grady's parents trying to protect the technology they created rather than steal it?"

"Where are you getting that from?" Grady responds before I do. "My mom is talking about profit and taking advantage of the moment. If that gets read aloud in court, the jury will only think one way about that...and that's in a bad way. We've got to delete it."

"No!" Kayley shoots back. "We've got to at least show it to Mr. Moreno. He'll know what to do with it."

"The only thing we have to do is get out of here!" Parrish hisses. "Some kind of automated security is coming!"

Kayley and I burst out from under the desk and race to get on the chair. I get there first, but she just drops herself on top of me and pounds away at the keyboard. A few more clicks, and she looks at the printer.

"What did you do?" I glance between the computer and the printer.

"I made a copy."

"Kayley! No! Security is going to hear that!"

Too late. The printer whirrs and buzzes and shoots a hard copy of the message out. Kayley jumps up and grabs it, folding it down so that she can stuff it in her pocket.

"We have to go!" Parrish drops and slowly opens the door. He sticks his head out and peers in both directions.

A whirring alarm goes off, and Parrish jerks his head back in.

"Oops." He looks at us and shrugs.

"Guys, just get out of there. I'll handle security," Grady says. "There won't be any recording of you there."

I punch the power switch on the computer and grab Kayley's hand. Parrish counts down on his fingers and explodes from the room. Kayley and I are not a microsecond behind him.

There's a pair of auto sentinels charging towards us, lights blazing. We spin in the opposite direction and dash down the corridor.

Another robot blocks our escape out the main entrance.

"*Perpetrators must halt and await the arrival of authorities. Halt imme-diately!*"

As if. We're not waiting for anyone. These dumbbots can't stop us—they're not even armed.

"In here!" Parrish bangs a classroom door open and crashes into a series of desks. Kayley and I keep going. There's a door leading out on the opposite end of the room, but somewhere in the middle, I lose my grip on Kayley's hand—she's gone back to help Parrish!

I hit the door and wrestle it open. By then, the sentinels are entering the classroom, speakers blazing their toothless warning. I grin and jump out.

Now all I have to do is talk Kayley into burning that message.

Seventeen

BREAKFAST. MY FAVORITE MEAL of the day. There's just something special about waking up and loading up on a tasty meal. I'm totally spoiled, of course. My mom makes the best breakfast. And lunch. And dinner. The only thing better than having a big bowl of her congee is enjoying the first meal of the day with my buds.

So that's why we found a new place to munch down on all things that pertain to a morning meal. It's no surprise that the owner is the same one from our former spot, Wylde Thyme. Well, honestly, it's just the same place, rebuilt after the military blew it up. Just like my house, the government wanted to sweep as much of the fallout as they could under the doormat. So not only did they rebuild the place...they built it bigger. Twice as big, to be exact. Before, there was only one floor. Now it's got two.

We still wind up sitting in the same place we always have—at the counter.

"Too bad old Mr. Roberts retired," Parrish says. "It would have been good to see him again."

"After *your* place of employment blew up with *you* in it, do you really think you'd want to keep working there?" Afton asks with a straight face, but there's a twinkle in her eyes.

Parrish shrugs. He's just nostalgic, but we all are. Otherwise, we wouldn't have come here, sat in the same spot, and ordered the same thing we always do. Parrish wouldn't be trying to steal my taro fries, and Grady wouldn't have a face covered in pumpkin mash with maple syrup. That's why we get to reminiscing as we eat.

"I really have no idea why we ever came here," Afton grumbles, digging her fork into a strawberry pancake. "The food is bad, the service is worse, and they don't even like having us here."

"That last part is a recent circumstance," I say. "Mostly due to—"

Kayley claps a hand over my mouth and silently motions towards Grady.

"It's okay," Grady says, acting like he's currently impervious to all the problems in his life. I guess Afton's morning cooking isn't all that good. "Let him say it. Most of the staff here is new anyway, and they won't remember us from before."

"At least the owner does," Parrish adds. "We wouldn't have gotten our preferred seats any other way. Even though the place is empty."

"He just wants our money," Afton counters. "He wasn't all that excited to see us."

"Whatever negativity we're encountering is only temporary," Mother Kayley says. "When the trial is over, and everyone sees Mr. and Mrs. Sugiyama are innocent, there won't be any issues with us coming here."

"Not that we've helped that at all."

"What do you mean? We just found a letter from Mrs. Sugiyama—"

"Don't let my mom hear you call her that," Grady mutters between mouthfuls. "She never uses any other name but her own."

There's still a debate going on over what we found at the school last night. Afton and Kayley are on one side, while Parrish, Grady, and I are on the other. It's a real gender battle, and even though we outnumber the ladies, I still think I'm on the losing side.

"Oh, you mean the letter that you had to trash a school to get?" Afton grins. "I'm totally into the fact that you guys did that, by the way."

"Yes," Kayley's cheeks get a little red. "*That* letter."

She may not approve of our means, but now that we've got said letter—printed on paper, even—it was worth whatever academic carnage we created, even if we can't use it. It's a well-funded private school, anyway. They might even use this opportunity to update their dumbbot security system.

"We cannot use that letter," I say. "It's just too risky."

"Well, what do you suggest we use, buddy boy?" Afton points a finger at me. "And no looking to your girlfriend for the answer. You know how to put your pants on by yourself."

"Clearly."

"Face it," she says, "when it comes to investigation, we're so high up on the suck meter at the moment that we can't even break a door down."

"That door was magnesium reinforced carbon-fiber composite woven together in such a way that a nuclear blast at any magnitude wouldn't have broken it." Grady shakes his head, then licks around his mouth to recover any lost syrup. "Though, we could have broken the lock with seven Parrishes."

"Now that'd be a sight," Parrish says.

"With a nuclear blast, there wouldn't have been anything left inside to check out," I say.

Afton is right, though. This entire court case has thrown us off our game. Kayley's kinder, gentler approach—which is all in response to the actions of a certain hand-hunter who shall remain nameless—hasn't helped, either. We need to get back with it so we can really uncover the evidence that we need to clear Grady's parents. Our bud is relying on us to come through for him and his family, and until now, we've done nothing but let him down. The obvious information from Mr. Kesh-Kaeo notwithstanding.

"Guys," Kayley says, spinning on her stool to face the rest of us, "we've got the letter. Why don't we show it to Mr. Moreno and see what he says?"

"Sure, but once he knows about it, he has to submit it as evidence...for good or bad. Or else he could lose his license to practice law." I smile at her, trying to soften the blow of that.

"How do you know that?" Afton challenges.

"Uh...his *dad*?" Parrish says and reaches behind me. I get suspicious instantly.

"Hey! Did you just steal a fry?" I turn to see Parrish smiling and chewing.

"Nope...I stole a few."

"Dude!"

"Yeah, Parrish, you shouldn't do that," Afton says as she reaches onto my plate. "You should do this."

"Come on!"

I spin on her, only to feel Kayley press against my back, her arm stretched out. She retracts it in a microsecond. When I spin back to face her, her cheeks are puffed up like a squirrel's, a reddish tint forming on their edges.

"KayKay, you too?"

Kayley's eyes float up to the ceiling, and she tries to smile. I smirk at her and go to poke her cheeks, but she giggles and grabs my wrists. Before I can break free, she swallows the evidence, and I'll just have to be the victim of a fry-robbery once again. They've stolen my fries so many times now I made up a word for it. I'll have to do a better job of looking out for the frobbers in the future if I don't want to starve.

"So, where were we?" I ask, getting back to the actual crime.

"Letter and failure," Grady says.

"Right, so if the letter is a risk, then we go look elsewhere."

"Where? We've already exhausted Grady's house, and that Jinse Shaloo exec was a waste of time."

"Then we go for something bigger."

"Rance, no," Kayley says. "There's got to be other options…and unlike the rest of you, I'm not ready to give up on the letter."

"I'm not ready to give up on the letter either," Afton says, "but I think we need more than that. A Jinse Shaloo Tech factory sounds like something we can bust up and not feel bad about."

"Let's not bust up anything," Parrish says. "We make one wrong step here, and it's going to reflect badly on Grady's parents."

"So, we don't get caught," I shoot back. "Grady erased the cameras from the school, so they'll never find us."

"Yeah, well…about that…" Grady says, his voice low, but no one but me catches it. Before I can ask him what he means, Kayley pounds a fist on the counter, breaking my focus.

"We are *not* sneaking into a high-security facility, and we are *not* smashing anything up!" Headmistress Kayley narrows her eyes at us and makes sure she's got our attention. "We're already at a disadvantage being connected to this trial. Personally, I think this whole thing is to get back at us because we've uncovered some dirty players in the government. They were well hidden before, but now, thanks to us, others are aware of them. We need to watch our backs."

There's a brief pause before understanding kicks in. Then Afton, Parrish, and I attempt to better explain our positions, all speaking at the same time. We're supporting her theory while trying to convince her of ours. With three of us talking simultaneously, no one is getting their point across.

"Guys," Grady says, loud enough to stop us talking. When we do, he presses his lips into a small smile and continues. "I appreciate all the help, I really do, but I don't want you guys to get hurt for my parents' sake…or mine. That you're here is enough."

Whatever resolve we had to press our agendas forward goes down the drain with the rest of the food particles on our dishes. And our thoughts about busting up some automated stamping machine and discovering the hidden truth of Drs. Sugiyama and O'Grady-Davies' innocence also get washed away.

"Dude, are you sure?" I ask.

"I am. You guys are awesome…I don't ever want to lose you."

"You won't," Kayley says. "But our choices don't have to be so extreme. We can still find ways to help. Interview co-workers…check bank records. Those things don't require any smash and grab."

"But I like smash and grab," Afton murmurs.

"Right there with you, Surela." I smile at Afton, and she lifts her head to smile back, up to the point when she realizes I just used her first name, then the smile turns into a scowl. Definite point, me. "That's for grabbing my fries and encouraging it in others."

Her scowl turns back into an upward curl of the side of her mouth. She knows I dropped one in the net, but this match is far from over.

"Well, I can definitely pop over to the Jinse Shaloo bank data vault and see what I can find out," Grady suggests.

"I'll give Captain Cortell a call," Kayley says. "Maybe some of his people can lend a hand."

"We'll go talk to a few people at the lab." I turn back to Grady. "Maybe even look up that Professor Burnell and see if we can ask her a few questions about that letter."

"Oh, yeah, so, bad idea, dude," Grady says, shaking his head. "The cameras in the school apparently had a backup that I didn't catch. Better not show your faces over there again."

So that's what he was trying to tell me before.

Eighteen

I'm meeting my father in the park, not because I really want to, but because he said it was important. When I spoke with him on Sergo, his voice had an irritated edge to it, like someone who had just found out that they were going to have to take their two years of compulsories over again. I thought it was odd because he never talked to me like that when I was younger.

So when I see him by the fountain of the Three Goddesses with a scowl across his face, my suspicions immediately go up.

"What's up?" I ask. No reason to make small talk. He doesn't look like he'd be interested, and I am more than definitely not.

"Why were you talking to Mr. Kesh-Kaeo?"

Oops. I guess he found out what happened. His laser-focused stare makes that point well. I wonder if I should try to deny it or not. That would likely make him angrier. Not that I care all that much. It's payback for all the agony he put me through. I'm also wondering how he found out.

"Cash-Cow? Funny name, but never heard of the guy."

"He's making an official complaint that you assaulted him." The edge in his voice gets sharper. He folds his arms. "Cecilia is ready to press charges against you. If you're convicted, that's punishable with jail time."

"Cecelia...as in Cecelia Nilsson-Lim? I didn't realize you were on first-name terms with her."

"I'm not!" He gets flustered, but then catches himself before he gets out of control. My father takes a quick glance around, then grabs my arm and pulls me towards the path through the woods. "Let's walk."

I've always liked this forest path, with its towering bamboo and massive greenwood trees. Kayley likes it a lot, too, so when we have time, we take an amorous stroll and gaze up at the sunbeams streaming through the leaves. This, however, is completely unromantic.

"I don't know what you thought you were going to accomplish with that stunt, but I'm very disappointed in you."

"Yeah, well, that makes two of us."

"I know you want to protect your friend's parents, but to attack someone like that? I thought I had taught you better."

"You taught me a lot of things, that's for sure." I don't know why he's talking to me like I'm nine years old, but for him to play father right now is pathetic. His calling me here just to yell at me as if I vandalized the local hardware store is a very poor attempt at being parental. The moment he left was the moment he ceased to be my father.

"Do you understand how this could reflect poorly on me? After all I have worked hard to achieve?" He grabs my shoulder and spins me around. I get surprised by his second violation of my person. That's why it takes a moment for me to realize just how selfish what he said was.

I stare at him, heat coming to my skin as if there's a mass of magma getting ready to erupt straight through it.

"So that's what this is really about, isn't it? How you think whatever I did is going to mess up your rise to the top?"

My father shuts his eyes as if he's the one that just got hurt. But a small shake of his head, and now I'm wondering if he regrets saying what he did. He takes a breath and runs a hand through his hair—dark and thick, just like mine. At least I got one good thing from him.

"Did you do it to get retribution on Ms. Nilsson-Lim because she testified?" His voice is calmer and more focused. I'm glad he let go of me, too, because if he didn't, I was going to pop him one.

"Mr. Moreno discredited her. There was no need to get back at her for that."

"Is that what you think he did?"

That gives me pause, and now, despite my anger at him, I'm doubting how effective Mr. Moreno is. My father could also be playing mind games and trying to psych me out, so I'll give up, accidentally let slip something important, or both. I wouldn't put it past him to take advantage of the fact that I've got a connection to the opposing side.

"Well, at the end of his cross-examination, she was trying to backtrack over her previous testimony. It was clear that she had attempted to make some part of her story up."

"Rance, that's a stretch at best. Mr. Moreno may think all he needs to do is confuse the jury, but the evidence is stacked against his clients."

"What evidence?"

"You'll have to wait for the case to resume before you learn that."

He *is* playing mind games—trying to make me worry about nothing so that I go and tell Mr. Moreno. Then Mr. Moreno will second-guess his strategy or even give up completely. Well, no way am I going to let him use me as a weapon of sabotage.

"But I didn't come here to talk about the case. I came because I am concerned for you."

Then again...

"Funny that you would say something like that now."

"Well, it's not every day that my son assaults a business executive that's connected to Cecelia Nilsson-Lim."

I sigh and turn away. I know how this goes. It's the same tactic he used on me when I was young. He's going to keep bringing that up until I crack and confess. It must be nice to be able to use criminal interrogation techniques on your own son.

"Rance. I'm not asking for anything other than for you to let me know the truth. If whatever you did was well intentioned, if very misguided, we can work with that. Perhaps I can talk to her on your behalf, you know, get this whole thing erased for you."

And there's the next technique...the offer. Give a suspect some hope that everything will be fine, and they'll admit they did whatever you want them to. It's not that easy—it's never that easy with my father. But now that I'm onto him, I've got to be wary of tipping him off. I can't just say we did it and then have that affect Mr. Moreno's defense. Not telling him is equally bad. I may not be afraid of jail time, but I'm not interested in spending any more time in one than I already have.

"Like I said before, I don't need your help. I've gotten this far on my own—"

"Gotten what, exactly? A knack for criminal misconduct? I can see how our time apart has sent you astray. Now how do you expect to fight for the people if you're a wanted outlaw?"

"Ever heard of the man in the green hat?"

"Rance, you can't base your life on a fairy tale!"

"Why not? Someone who steals from the rich and gives to the poor sounds like someone I'd like to know."

My father throws a hand up and shakes all his frustration into it, seething. Good. I'm happy to keep adding to it.

"Alright, listen, you don't have to tell me why, but at least promise me you'll never do it again."

"Yes, I promise that. I can promise that easily...because the next time, we'll be successful."

"Son, what are you trying to do to your life? Destroy it? Because if you do something as dumb as cross Cecelia Nilsson-Lim, prison may not be your biggest concern. I've heard she's not as polite as she pretends to be. She is, after all, an arms manufacturer."

Did my father just let something slip? Did he do it on purpose? Do I have little Mrs. Cecelia pegged correctly? I'm taking a risk hinting that we assaulted Mr. Kesh-Kaeo, but if I get something more important out of it, then it's worth it.

"So, she *is* doing something illegal, isn't she?"

"I never said that."

"Then what are you saying?"

"Only that the Empire is very ruthless about protecting its secrets. You don't want to get on her wrong side, Rance. The security that surrounds her goes very deep."

"You seem to know her really well...why is that, exactly?"

"Because I do my research on the people I put up on the stand. I have to. Especially on a high-profile case like this. I need to do my due diligence, or I could lose the case, and I'm not about to do that. Now, will you promise me you'll stay clear of her, or do I have to have you arrested just so you can learn your lesson?"

He's not joking. I can see it in the sternness of his eyes as he waits for my reply. He may only pretend to care about me, but he's dead serious about Cecelia Nilsson-Lim's inclination for brutal security tactics. That tells me something I didn't know before. Something we need to investigate. But first, let's get the hounds off our trail.

"Fine...I promise."

"Good." He claps my shoulder, and I grit my teeth to tolerate it. "Then I'll see what I can do about there being any repercussions...and please, for your own sake, keep your promise."

I nod.

"I'm glad we had this talk, son."

"Yeah, well, I'm not."

Nineteen

"Cecelia Lim is absolutely up to something!" Afton says after I tell my buds about my run-in with my father. Everyone was concerned, naturally. But when I told them about how I thought he was trying to stop me from checking her out, they jumped right to the same conclusion I did.

"I thought her last name was Nilsson-Lim," Parrish comments.

"It is, but I don't want to say the whole thing," Afton replies.

Our magnificent seven are sitting in Grady's den, keeping an eye on the world around us as he delves into the inner space of the world Infonet. He's searching for any suspicious financial transactions that Jinse Shaloo Tech has had with a government entity. I have no idea how he knows what a suspicious financial transaction looks like, so I ask.

"Simple," Grady replies. "We're going to let the system do it for us. All I have to do is review their normal everyday transactions, and from there, any that don't fit the pattern will pop out."

"Yeah, but that could still be millions of transactions!"

"We don't care about ones that are for a small amount. Only financial transfers in the millions or billions matter. That should filter out a lot."

"How do you know it still won't be too many to look into? Jinse Shaloo is an enormous company. They could have done a thousand transactions just now!"

"So we refine our filter and try it again. No one said we'd find something in the next five minutes."

"As long as it doesn't take the next five years," Afton says and gets comfortable on the sofa by folding her legs under her and dropping her hands into her lap. It's the first non-irritated attitude I've seen from her in a while, which is a good thing.

"How are you going to get access to that bank data in the first place?" Kayley asks. "Do we have to worry about being tracked?"

"Standard hack tool...Teddy-invented, of course." Grady taps a flurry of commands into his lap terminal and pounds on the "execute" button. It's connected to a special Teddy comp they built for Grady. It was only supposed to help him do calculations for his engine design, but they've made some modifications. It still amazes me Teddys can just create stuff that interfaces so cleanly with human tech. I'll chalk it up to the fact that human scientists, in their eagerness to get their mitts on Teddy tech, have provided as much data and understanding as they can to our fuzzy friends.

"You've been busy, Teddy," I say, impressed at their constant ingenuity.

"Teddy is already informed," Original Teddy says from his usual spot on the carpet. "Development has been communicated."

I know Original Teddy has a tendency to speak in a jumble of cryptic nonsense, but this one has got me stumped. It's got everyone stumped. I'd ask him to explain his statement, but I have a feeling that I won't gain anything from it. Besides, he'll elaborate if he wants to.

"So, have you found anything yet?" I ask.

"Getting there...be patient."

"I thought I was being patient."

"Hardly, darling." Kayley brushes a stray lock of hair from my face. I was so focused on what Grady was doing, I didn't even notice it. At least my girlfriend is looking out for me.

It takes another half hour before anything comes up. I take that time to check on what our standard complement of media people are up to. When the trial started, nearly a hundred of them took up permanent residence in the park across the street. Now there are only about twenty-five of the most committed journalists living in tents and broadcast vehicles out there, and even they are looking fairly haggard.

"Okay, here we go," Grady says. That's my cue to turn my focus back inside. I come around to stand over Grady with Parrish and Kayley as he watches his screen. "Twenty-four thousand, five hundred and fifty-six results."

"You're going to pare that down a little, aren't you?" I ask.

"Of course, dude. Working on it already."

This next filter only takes fifteen minutes, so I'm hopeful that he'll have knocked the list down to a few hundred.

"Three thousand, four hundred twenty-two."

Kayley makes the quick calculation. "Twelve and a half percent of what we had before." If I didn't already know she was sharp in math, I would be even more impressed. It's one of the things that I love about her. "That's reasonable," she adds. "Can you find any anomalies in those?"

Grady rifles off a few commands into his terminal and waits for the output. When his face turns sour, I know it's not going to be a positive answer.

"No." Grady taps a bit more, then makes a rude noise by blowing air through his lips. "I'm going to try something different."

This search isn't any better. In fact, it turns out worse. The results are another exponent larger than the last, even when it gets pared down. Parrish drops himself into a chair and sighs while Afton fidgets with the bit of jewelry that her mother had thrown at her.

"I thought you said you didn't want that," I say.

"I don't, but I might sell it. Supposedly it's worth a good sum."

"Can I see it?" Kayley drops into the seat next to Afton, her eyes growing big. Afton hands it to her with a smile and watches as Kayley turns from our courageous leader to a little girl who's just been given a piece of candy.

"This isn't working," Grady groans. "The big transactions show nothing out of the ordinary, and the payments all came from the same Imperial treasury account. They're not for any sort of weird amount."

"What about the small transactions, then?" Parrish suggests. "Could they have broken up the payments so small that no one would take notice? Maybe categorize them as something mundane, like a transaction fee or something like that?"

"Good thought," I say. "I mean, strange-looking transactions would be more obvious if they were large, right?"

"Yeah, but trying to go through millions of small transactions could take days," Grady counters, his brow bending into wrinkles. "We don't have days."

"Can you write a filter or maybe something that might search for the patterns Parrish is talking about?"

"Sure, but that's going to take time, maybe like a few hours, and it's already getting late. I was really hoping to be in court tomorrow."

"Dude, we already discussed this, right? This is the best way for you to help your parents."

"Yeah, I guess." Grady squishes his lips together.

"Tell you what. You get cracking on that, and I'll make you something to eat," Afton suggests.

"No way, let Parrish do it," I counter. Afton flashes me a glare so fast I think a pair of missiles just launched from her eyes.

"Happy to. What do you want?" Parrish's offer silences any objection from her. She makes a grand sweeping motion towards the kitchen, inviting Parrish to go for it.

A few hours more will put us into near dawn, and we're all beat already. If we burn through the night—correction, if Grady burns through the night while we watch—we might get it done, but we'll all be too exhausted to get to court on time. Grady won't forgive himself if he misses it, but he won't help his parents if he's nodding off on a hard wooden court bench.

It's strange that we didn't even find one anomaly yet. Big companies are always doing sketchy things with money. There should be at least some kind of evasive funding thing going on, but it could be we're just not digging deep enough. Cecilia Nilsson-Lim has got to be profiting from this whole fiasco, even if she's pretending not to be.

"Hey, dude, hold up a minute."

Grady frowns and looks up at me. He hasn't asked yet, but I'm sure he's wondering why I'm making such a stupid request. I hope the idea that just popped into my head makes his annoyance worthwhile.

"Could you check Cecelia's personal accounts?"

"What are you thinking?" Kayley sits up. "That she's been directing payments to herself, so if there's dirty money passing around, her company avoids an audit?"

"Exactly."

"Try it." She slides over to the opposite side of Grady, so now both she and Afton are peering over Grady's shoulders.

Grady spends a few minutes rattling away at his terminal while we impatiently try to remain quiet. Kayley's face distorts in all sorts of strange ways as she attempts to make sense of what he's doing. Afton isn't any better, and I bet I'd be the same way if I could see his screen.

"Well?" I ask, running out of patience.

"I can't find accounts under her name." Grady shakes his head in disbelief. We're all a bit confused. Me especially. I thought this was going to be our breakthrough.

"That's impossible. She's got to have accounts."

"She does, but these are all just chump change compared to the company numbers I was just looking at."

"Could she have hidden accounts?"

"Ting Fu," Afton says.

"Well, of course, she's rich." My comment passes my lips before I realize that she's not speaking Common.

"No, dummy, that's her name." Afton's *you really are stupid* gaze says way more than her words. I blink, feeling like an idiot.

"Wait, how do you know that?"

"Because it's on her ID."

"You stole her ID?"

"Wrong again, fungus for brains." Afton rolls her eyes and points to Grady's screen. "It's right there."

We all jump to where she's pointing on the screen, and sure enough, there it is...a secondary name that sneaky Mrs. Cecelia Nilsson-Lim goes by: Ting Fu. It might be an honorary name or a sacred name. Some religions do that. For instance, my middle name—Quigley—was my grandfather's first name on my mom's side.

"Something's coming up," Grady says as he rapid-fires commands into his terminal. I find an edge of the sofa to squeeze myself into, and Kayley leans on me to peer over my shoulder as we wait for a response from the net. I take a breath and hold it, afraid that an exhale will blow away any of the data that we're searching for.

And it works. Up pop a few thousand transactions of varying amounts. There's no rhyme or reason about them, and none are large enough to call suspicious.

"Look at these here," Kayley says and points to a few relatively small ones, "and these too. Could you combine them into one big sum and see how much they total?"

"Why do you think those mean anything?" I ask.

"Because the numbers are too random. Thirty-two seventeen? Four oh three thirteen? Who transfers money to a personal account for amounts like that?"

"Yeah, that does seem weird." I attempt to do the calculations in my head, but Grady's fingers are faster. His brain is faster. He could add up those numbers faster than he types. I'll chalk it up to the fact that he's just tired.

"Whoa...check it out," Grady says, and we all dive into the screen.

"Is that right?" I ask, but I shouldn't because Grady doesn't make mistakes in calculation.

"That is accurate," Original Teddy says. "Ten thousand is precise."

And neither do the Teddys.

"Quick, where are the payments from?"

"A sub-account of Jinse Shaloo, but the account name isn't connected to the company. It comes from a sub-address...on Albion."

"Oh heck no." Afton folds her arms and shakes her head. "We are not breaking into some government office on the Capital Planet just to check on a few odd numbers."

Kayley turns her most resolute gaze on her, and Afton leans back. There's no way she can compete with Kayley when she's set on a decision. Afton won't even try. Besides, she might even enjoy this.

"We're going to do

exactly that."

Twenty

ALBION, THE LITERAL CENTER of the Empire. I never thought I would find myself here, much less sneaking into the home of the CEO of the largest arms manufacturer in the entire commonwealth. From what I can tell, the house and the grounds are massive. Take all our houses, Grady's, Afton's, Kayley's, and mine, and you'd still have room enough for three of Parrish's bungalow—with the veranda.

Security is likely to be tighter here than any Imperial starship, and this being the best and richest planet, the guards will be quick to shoot on sight, leaving very little room for error on our part. Of all the places we've intruded upon, this has got to be—

"The stupidest, the most short-sighted and completely unnecessary mission we've ever done," Afton grumbles, dragging her feet behind Kayley, Original Teddy, BB, and me. "We could easily have just stolen the data right from Grady's living room, and I would have had time for a nap."

"Since when do you nap?" I say.

"Since all the time. Where have you been?"

We're skirting the perimeter, about a block away from the fence that wraps around the entire grounds. The house itself is set back and overlooks a small lake—likely artificial—which means it's the farthest point away from anywhere we decide to enter. So we decide to just walk right through a side gate. Of course, that means borrowing a minor talent from our Teddy friends, but they are only too happy to oblige.

"If you didn't want to come, you could have stayed on the ship with Parrish and Grady," I say, looking over my shoulder at Afton.

"Who'd cover your cute little butts if I wasn't here?"

I throw a side glance at Kayley, whose cheeks are turning a deep shade of pink. She'll jump into this silly little conversation if it goes to odd places, but until then, I'll have to take this abuse from our grumpy guardian.

"The Teddys got us," I reply. "Unless you can shoot antennae out of your head and popsicle someone."

"Unlikely," Original Teddy says.

Afton folds her arms, and I grin. There's a definite point won for me in there. I'm feeling generous, so I'll just put it on hold for now. I've won so many points recently that I must be way ahead. The "cute little butts" comment could be worthy of a point if I were so inclined, but I think she's got a little more work to do in that regard.

"Okay, stay in the shadow," Kayley whispers, "and when we're at the corner of the building across the street, you'll hit them. Got it, Teddy?"

"Copasetic," Original Teddy says.

Once we hit the point, the Teddys pop their antennae and popsicle the three guards in short order. We waste no time and dash across the street, reaching the nearest guard and snatching his security badge. We're through the gate in thirty seconds, experienced as we are.

"We better not have our profiles broadcast all over the Jinse Shaloo vid network, Grady," Afton growls as we slide through and hit the shadows.

"Not a problem, I've got it," Grady responds. "Her security system was surprisingly easy to get into."

Tree-lined avenues and grand flower beds full of a multitude of colors, some local, some exotic, cover the grounds. I can see everything perfectly because of all the light pouring down from the high-powered lamps that illuminate the entire grounds. But I can't stop to enjoy the view because that means we've got very few dark spaces to hide in, so it's amazing that we make it all the way to the main building without being seen.

"Wow...that's tall...for a house." Kayley stares up at the twenty-story glass-and-concrete tower that no one would ever mistake for a house. It's like Cecelia Nilsson-Lim really wanted to live in an apartment but didn't want any neighbors.

"Let's hope Cecelia's office is on a lower floor," I say.

"There's a better chance of me getting married tomorrow," Afton says.

"You have absolutely no interest in getting married."

"I can change my mind if I want."

"Well, for our sakes, don't change it now."

We find the vent access Grady discovered for us and slide through. The Teddys are a supreme help in getting the three humans up and in. A few minutes later, we're climbing up a few levels until we get a reasonable distance away from the main entrance. Most floors are dark, but the one we hop into is darker than the others.

"Good," Kayley says, scanning the space. "We'll make our retreat point here. No one is using this floor today."

As if the building was listening, the elevator chimes, and the car arrives at our level. I drop, snatching Kayley with me. Afton and the Teddys scatter. My heart pounds, and Kayley's breath is fast on my neck. We should learn not to talk in absolutes.

"I'm sorry, Benicio. The lifts are limited to certain levels for security. We can switch to this one here...unless you prefer to walk up."

That sounds like Cecelia Nilsson-Lim! And...Benicio? No...it couldn't be.

"Twenty floors?" It is! My father's voice! I confirm when I peek over the sofa we're hiding behind. My father chuckles and shakes his head. "I'm in good health, but that's too much even for me."

"Lift it is." Cecelia walks over to the panel and taps in a code. A few seconds later, the elevator arrives, and she and my father step in. The door closes, and they're off.

"No way that just happened," Afton says, crawling out from behind a desk.

"Rance...you had no idea, right?" Kayley stares into my eyes as she kneels in front of me. I'm still on my knees myself, in total disbelief over what I just saw.

"That they're on a first-name basis or that her house had elevators?" I blink into the darkness, still seeing the image of my father standing side by side with the target of our mission.

"Hey." Kayley grabs my hand and squeezes it. My eyes slide to look at her and give her the answer she's expecting. Of course I had no idea.

"Guys, I hate to break this to you," Grady says over the comm, "but if the elevator is on a coded signal to her office level, then you're going to have to take the stairs."

"Why?" Afton stands and glares into the air as if Grady can look down on us from the Teddy ship and see her.

"Because, if you put in the code...any code, security will know instantly, and since she's the only one that lives here, they won't be expecting anyone else."

"Is her office really on the top floor?"

"Yup...well, save the penthouse...but yup."

I can think of at least twenty-five exclamations that could come out of my mouth right now, but because it will make no difference to my state of mind, I abstain from saying any of them. Instead I stand, pulling Kayley up with me, and without another word we head for the stairs.

Original Teddy and Blue Buddy are having an absolute ball on the stairs. They bounce from landing to landing, swinging themselves up on the railing while the beings limited to four appendages—that'd be us humans—trudge up every last step on our way to the twentieth floor.

"Why couldn't she be afraid of heights?" Afton, the most fit of us all, leans hard on the railing as she drags herself up the last few steps. Kayley and I are not nearly as worn out. We took a few breaks along the way, so we're a bit more refreshed than Ms. I'm an Athlete So I Don't Need a Break.

"Consider yourselves lucky," Grady says. "My parents know another CEO that has fifty floors in his house."

"Hey, have you guys considered what you're going to do once you get to her office?" Parrish asks over the comm. "I mean...we weren't expecting her to be there, right? You can't just sneak in if she...and Rance's dad are in her office."

Afton turns from the door and wrinkles her nose at Kayley and me. I agree with her, and by the expression on my girlfriend's face, so does she.

"I can tell you what I'd *like* to do," Afton seethes.

I take a deep breath. No need to make a rush decision on this. There's literally a hundred ways that we could screw up here. Failure would mean everything from a certain conviction for Grady's parents to execution for us. We didn't come here for the exercise, however.

"Let's go. If we have to wait until the morning, I'm willing," I say. "We're here for Grady."

"And his parents," Kayley adds.

"Definitely."

"Great," Afton says. "Now, how do you get this door open?"

"You're going to have to go through the ventilation system again," Grady says. "No way to get that door open from the stairs unless you want to blow it open."

"Teddy, can you find a way in through the vent?"

"Roger dodger," Original Teddy says and turns to BB to click and whistle a few words at him. Both Teddys scramble up the wall and surround the grating that will have to be our way in—if we fit. Afton and I might be too wide.

We compromise by having the Teddys go up and open the door for us from the inside. It opens into a bedroom, which is dark, but light spills in from the next room. At first my heart freezes, thinking that we might have slipped in to find Cecelia and my father in a compromised position, but by the grace of the Three Goddesses, I don't have to witness such a revolting scene.

The bedroom is as to be expected. An enormous bed with a white-and-yellow canopy is centered in the room. Gold-trimmed white furniture surrounds it, while a vanity with a gigantic circular mirror occupies an entire wall by itself. This woman has more money than half of my planet, and she's not afraid to show it off. I wonder just how many bedrooms are in this house.

I head towards the door that goes to the next room. As I get closer, I think I hear voices. I pause, but my sense of duty takes over. I need to find out what's going on. My safety be damned. If my father is in cahoots with Ms. Nilsson-Lim for some reason or another, it's on me to find out.

"Yes, of course, Cecelia," my father says. "This is becoming a routine case. The defense can't put our last bit of evidence in any level of doubt. Vid is always the best proof when it comes to a jury."

"Won't that Janek Moreno bring up all sorts of ideas that the vid has been tampered with?" Cecelia asks.

"Sure, he will...but my finishing moment will be when I put Dr. O'Grady-Davies on the stand." My father lets out a haughty laugh. "She will confirm everything that's on the vid, and even if she tries to deny it, my experts will put an end to that."

"So then, it's as good as closed, right? The jury will have to convict the two of them."

"Yes. There's no way anything else will happen."

I grit my teeth, hoping that Grady didn't just hear all that, but, of course, he did. My built-in Teddy comm never turns off. I can ask the Teddys to mute it so I can have some privacy, but to ask them now would make Grady suspicious.

"Ugh, this skirt is so uncomfortable." I hear Cecelia shifting around in her chair. "You don't mind if I go change, do you?"

"Not at all."

Shoot! She's coming! The five of us scramble to find a place to hide before she comes in. Afton dives under the bed. Kayley and I follow, squeezing ourselves under just as the lights come on. I grab the edge of the bed skirt to stop it from moving and hope she's only looking in the closet for her clothes.

"Hey, Cecelia?" My father comes in. "On second thought, I'm going to run. We've got a big day in court tomorrow."

"Oh? Okay then…" Cecelia's voice drops. "Best you get your rest, then."

My father walks out, and Cecelia Nilsson-Lim sighs. Kayley and I share a glance, and Afton pokes me from the other side, so I glance at her too. She raises a hand and shrugs. My reply is just to shake my head.

"That man is so sexy, isn't he, Cecelia?" Cecelia sighs again and flops down on the bed. The entire frame shakes above our heads. Kayley's mouth drops open, and my eyes go wide. I can only imagine what that means—what the current relationship between her and my father is, or what she wants it to be.

Either way, she's got it out for Grady's parents, and we've got to stop her before my father puts them away for good.

But first, we need to find a way out from under this bed.

Twenty-one

I FORGET WHO WAS first to check if Cecelia had fallen asleep, but once she was, we were out of there as fast as we could move. We had to stop Afton from attempting to strangle the woman, though. Then, we made our way out the main door to her office, as we worried that using the door to the stairs might wake her up.

"We should have searched her desk," Afton grumbles as we head down the corridor, looking for another exit.

"And what if she had woken up?" Kayley counters. "How would you explain that to her?"

"Doesn't matter...we're being broadcast all over the cameras right now, so whatever we came here to do is a total loss."

"There are no cameras on this level," Grady says, his voice somewhat subdued from before. "Do you think she wants security to see her in her pajamas?"

"Was she wearing pajamas?" I ask.

"I bet you were hoping to see her in some sexy negligee, weren't you?" Afton smirks back at me.

"Heck no. Do you think I'm trying to make myself sick?"

"I bet you haven't even seen your girlfriend in a negligee."

"I don't *own* a negligee!" Kayley hisses. "Can we knock off the chatter?"

"How about a camisole?"

"No!"

"Baby doll?"

"Afton!"

I'm glad it's dark, or the two of them would see how bright red my face is. As much as I'd like to envision my girlfriend—no, wait! I shouldn't be thinking about stuff like that in the middle of a mission. Still...maybe a little? Keep it together, Rance.

We find an exit to the stairs and begin our descent. I'm a bit down about the fact that 1) we didn't get the evidence we were looking for, and 2) my father is cavorting with one of the case's key witnesses. To what level, I don't really know yet, and as we go down, I wonder if Cecelia is really out to get Grady's parents or if my father's brief visit this evening was nothing more than a social call.

"Hey, there's no more stairs," Afton says, turning back to us from the stairwell she's standing in.

"Did we do twenty levels already?"

"Twenty-four is accurate," Original Teddy says.

"Wait...twenty-four? That'd put us in a sub-basement."

"That is accurate...and unfortunate."

I glance back up the stairwell, but the only thing that's there is Kayley...and lots of steps. She looks back at me with no more answers than I have, which currently number zero. I turn back to Afton and spot a door just ahead of her. It's got a latch on this side, so our downward hike wasn't all for nothing.

"We can get out at this level, at least," I say.

"Okay, but be careful," Kayley warns. It didn't really need saying, but it puts us in the right frame of mind as we gently ease the door open and peek through.

This level is just dark as the rest, but light streams out of the glass-walled rooms and illuminates the hallway ahead of us. My first instinct is to look up and search for cameras. I don't find any, but I'm not ready to jump to conclusions. I should check with Grady, just to make sure.

"There sure are. Motion and sound sensors too."

I freeze the moment it becomes clear just how much trouble we're in. There's no way security didn't notice their alarms going off on this hidden lair of a floor. They're likely now securing all the exits and rushing to intercept us.

"Dammit, Grady, why didn't you warn us?" I ask.

"Because there wasn't any reason to."

The three humans share a squished-eyebrow glance. I'm not sure if Grady has lost his mind or if I just didn't hear him correctly.

"What are you talking about?" Kayley asks.

"Oh, well, I disabled the power to the security office...at least for a little while. They'll be pretty busy trying to figure that out."

"Yeah, but that means they're going to be sending guards to patrol the entire house!"

"True," Grady admits. "So you might want to get a move on."

The three of us groan, and Original Teddy makes a gurgling noise. I'm expecting that he's right there with us when it comes to our sheer level of exasperation. We power down the corridor, searching for the nearest exit.

What we find instead is way more enticing.

Afton is the first to notice the workshop space with a plethora of extra-ordinary-looking devices, most of them quite large. They have one thing in common, which is that I can envision Grady working on every one of them to create his next genius invention.

"Grady, you're not going to believe this."

"I might. Describe it to me."

Afton does her best to explain to him what she found while Kayley and I play lookout. I station myself at the far end of the corridor, away from the workshop. I should have chosen the other side, but Kayley is just as curious about Afton's find.

"What do you think?" I ask.

"Can you get in?" Grady's tone of voice shifts from low and lackadaisical to sounding more like he wishes he was here.

"Sure, but we don't have time to go exploring right now," I say. "Roaming guards, remember?"

"Oh, relax. It's a house, not a starbase. No one's going to be springing traps on you, then taking you in to be interrogated, fed dead animal and tossed in a cell, after which you get rescued by the entire Teddy fleet."

"That's strangely specific, dude."

"That was awesome, wasn't it?" Afton chuckles, and I get the feeling they're having a lighthearted moment at my expense.

"Hey, shush...what was that?" Kayley asks.

I didn't hear anything, but since I'm closest to the stairs, I tiptoe over to the door we just came through and put my ear to it. I hear the rumble of machinery through the cold metal against my face, but no footsteps.

"Alright," Kayley whispers. "Let's find that exit."

Afton's answer to that is to open the workshop door and step in.

"Goddesses, Afton! Saint Sophia is going to smite you good!" Kayley stomps in behind her. I doubt that's the case—if anything, all three of the Goddesses would be putting the smackdown on her. And since I'm going to leave Afton's holy retribution in the heavenly hands of our divine ladies, I guess I'll just go take a peek as well.

"Hey guys, don't keep me hanging! Tell me what you see!" Grady's impatient tone spurs us to stop ogling the pretty tech and start giving him some details.

"Well, let's see." I scan around, trying to think more objectively than I was before. "There are two cylinder things, one box, and a handful of trinkets on a table...oh...and an L-shaped thing that's taller than Afton, with a bunch of buttons, lights, and switches on it. That looks like it could be something."

"Nah...leave that one alone," Grady says.

"Why, what is it?"

"Probably an automated trash bin."

"How about this?" Afton picks up one of the aforementioned trinkets and holds it out to Kayley and me. We get closer to take a better peek at it. As I look at it, I'll agree that she picked the most interesting one of the bunch. It's a shiny metallic box that is vaguely S-shaped. One end is open while the other has a series of circles wrapped around its base. There's also a thumb switch on the top, and if I had to guess, I'd say the back attaches to something larger.

Suddenly the thing blinks. Afton drops it back on the table and steps back. We all step back.

"Okay, enough playing around...let's get out of here," Kayley says. "Teddy, let's go." She pauses. "Teddy?"

My first instinct is to look up because when you can't see them on the ground, that's where they usually are...but not this time. In fact, they're not in the workshop, or the corridor.

"Shoot!" she says. "Of all the times they could choose to go exploring!"

"Teddy," I say, "can you hear me? Come in, Teddy!"

I turn to Kayley, who, at times like this, makes the critical decisions. Her answer is to race out the door and turn the opposite way from where we arrived. Afton gives me a quick look and follows her out. Then I, not putting much thought into it, grab the trinket and follow them out.

The floor isn't that large, so finding another way up and out is easy. We hit the stairs and break out at the next level. With a little snooping and sneaking about we search, but no joy. The next level, which is full of boxes, is the same, so we hit the stairs again, only to realize we're running out of floors to search before we arrive at the main floor—the area where we're most likely to run into guards eager to test out their new and expensive weapons.

I don't remember it being this hot when we were up in Cecelia's office. Heat rises, so theoretically it should be warmest there, not in the lowest levels, but here I am, wiping a sleeve across my forehead. Even the ladies are perspiring a bit. If we don't find the Teddys soon, a little sweat isn't all we'll have to worry about.

"Alright," Kayley says after a deep breath. "Let's get ourselves clear, and then we'll try to contact them again on the comm. Ready?"

Afton nods and looks at me. I nod and look at Kayley. Kayley drops her eyes to my hands and frowns. I squeeze the trinket device.

"Why did you bring that?" she hisses.

"It could be evidence!"

"It could be junk!"

"We don't have anything else to go on."

Kayley sighs. Her nose wrinkles, and she shakes her head. I'll take that as meaning she's got more important things to worry about, like getting us out of here.

I close the door behind me and slip behind Kayley as she tails Afton into the dining room. I'm guessing she chose here because there's a big table we can hide behind or under should we need to.

And we need to!

Footsteps tap the floor in the next room, growing louder as the three of us squeeze under the six-person table. The fact that it's this small is surprising. She must not be very social, or else she must not spend a lot of time at home. Strange that she'd invest so much in a massive space just to not use it.

The footfalls are casual, unhurried. Shuffling, even. That's good—it means whoever it is didn't hear us. As they get closer, I glimpse the feet causing the sound: soft white slippers, beneath the bottom of a yellow robe that the edges of a long white nightgown peek out from under.

This is no guard. It's Cecelia Nilsson-Lim! I thought she was asleep!

She shuffles past us and into the next room. I can see the edge of a tiled floor—that must be the kitchen. So...it's a midnight snack she's after. My father isn't the only thing we have in common.

"Rancid is discovered," Original Teddy says, crawling under the table with Blue Buddy. My jaw drops. I spin on him and slam a finger against my lips. There's no way Cecelia didn't hear that.

"Someone there?" Cecelia mumbles and shuffles to the edge of the tile to stare into the dining room with bleary eyes. She scans around for a moment, then turns back into the kitchen.

"Okay, time to split," Kayley whispers, and a second later, we're sliding out from under the table. Kayley ushers the Teddys in front of her and heads for the nearest exit. Afton goes next, and I'm out last.

As I race to extricate myself from under the table, my foot hits the leg of a chair and sends it tilting into the wall. With a hiss between my teeth, I catch it just before it knocks into the wall. I let out a long sigh and gently put it back into place.

"What are you doing down there?" Cecelia says. My eyes slide up to see her staring down at me. I'm frozen in anticipation as her arm lifts to point a shaky finger at me. "B...Benicio?"

I've never considered the fact that I resemble my father as any kind of blessing, but at this moment, I thank the Goddesses for their extraordinary foresight in molding me that way. Better take advantage of that.

"Yes," I say, getting to my feet. "It's me...I...uh...couldn't stop thinking about you."

"Really?" She bites her lower lip as she brushes a stray lock of her hair behind her ear and tilts her head. "But...you look younger."

She's got me there. What do I say to that? More importantly, why hasn't one of the Teddys popsicled her yet? Are they just going to stand there and enjoy my awkward moment? This is serious! Say something, Rance!

"That's because this is just a dream...you're only dreaming I'm here."

"Really?" Cecelia blinks and moves closer, her face getting closer to mine. She stares into my eyes for what I feel is longer than appropriate, then she grins, her hands reaching up to grab my cheeks. "Well, if this is a dream, I'm sure you won't mind me doing this..."

"Teddy, popsicle!" Kayley shouts, and Cecelia freezes, her lips way too close to mine for comfort I back away, but her frozen body is in the wrong position for standing, and I have to catch her in my arms before she crashes to the floor. Had I not reacted so fast, I might have thought twice about letting her fall.

"Caught you red-handed, you two-timer," Afton says with a pat on my back and a smirk.

"Yeah, funny...what do we do?"

Kayley strolls over, her hand going to her chin. She takes a moment to observe my compromised position and grins.

"Just let her down gently on the floor and get out of there!" Parrish says. Nice of him to finally speak up.

"No way...what if her guards find her?" Kayley counters.

"Put her back in her bed, then. She'll think it was all a dream," Grady suggests.

"Carry her all the way to the top floor? No!" I shake my head and try to get a better hold on the petrified Ms. Nilsson-Lim.

"Any bed, then," Afton says, moving around to grab Cecelia by her ankles. "There's got to be at least a hundred of them in here."

"Okay, fine...but then can we go, please?"

Twenty-two

I GET NOSTALGIC FOR the little cabin that Kayley and I inhabited on the Teddy ship. It was the only place where she and I could be alone when we traveled with our fuzzy buddies. These days, though, sparkle drive works so well we barely use the FTL engine. We can go from Angelcanis to Albion in a split second. That's obviously incredible, but it takes some of the romance out of travel.

Stuffing six humans and two Teddys into that same berth has the same effect. It was my idea to come here, because I thought it would be more comfortable than the canteen. I couldn't have been more wrong.

"So, Cecelia's house..." Afton says, sitting on the bed next to Kayley as the two of them lean their backs against the wall. "You really want to go back?"

"Not especially," I reply, knowing it's not the general consensus. I'm a bit grumpy, mostly because I got kicked off my bed and have to sit cross-legged on the floor next to Grady. "We got the trinket, and we've got her personal bank records. I think that's enough to show Mr. Moreno. Maybe he can come up with a way to use them."

"Dude, this thing may not even be from my parents." Grady shakes the device at me. "I only said that it *looked like* something they'd design. I never said that it definitely was. It's useless to Mr. Moreno."

"Teddy can confirm." Original Teddy chirps to Blue Buddy as they hang from the ceiling—it was the only place they could go—and Blue Buddy drops a tentacle to snatch the tech trinket from Grady's hands.

"Hey! I'm still looking at that!" Grady shoots up to grasp after it, but Blue Buddy keeps it just out of his reach. Parrish has to jump back to avoid Grady's swat, which puts him flat against the entrance. "Give it back!"

"Not a good idea, Mr. Grady," Doc Elizabeth warns, leaning away from him at her spot on the edge of the bed. The rest of us duck and dodge to avoid his open hand across our faces.

Grady jumps up and makes one last desperate attempt to get the thing back. I'm not sure why he wants it so badly. If his parents didn't build or design it, then it's got no value to us. It's got no value to *him*…right?

Blue Buddy squeaks, and the device goes flying from his tentacle as Grady smacks it from the Teddy's grasp. It crunches into the far wall and smashes down onto the floor. There's a stunned silence as Afton leans over the edge of the bed and picks it up.

"Regrettable," Original Teddy says.

"And now it's useless to everybody," she says and tosses it so that it lands on the edge of the bed in front of Grady. He drops his head to stare at it, then huffs and drops back down again.

"Great," I say, pounding a hand on the bed. "Now we're minus points."

"What do you mean?" Kayley asks.

"I mean, for all the energy we've wasted, we've got nothing to show for it. Mr. Moreno is losing this case because we haven't helped one bit. My dad has an army of people working for him. Investigators, legal aides…he's even got a witness in his pocket! Compared to him, we're…we're…"

Less than zero. I don't even want to say the words out loud because then they'll be true. While they're still locked in my head, there's hope that I can make them into something better.

"Rance, we're doing the best we can," Kayley says, reaching out to touch my hand. "We're risking everything to help. No one, not even us, could ask more of us."

"I could," I reply. "I could ask us to actually get something of worth."

Kayley presses her lips together and drops her gaze from me. My heart sinks, knowing I just dismissed her attempt to cheer me up. Great. Now I get to feel bad about making her feel bad.

"Don't get down on yourselves," Doc Elizabeth says. "The trial isn't over. Not by a long shot…and if the fat lady doesn't sing, then the show's not over."

"Fat lady?" Afton asks, leaning towards Elizabeth as her eyebrows scrunch together.

"Never mind." Doc Elizabeth waves a hand. "It's a saying, I can't remember where I heard it…anyway, you get the idea."

Well, that really lifted my spirits...not. I realize it's not up to her to make me feel better, but if we had any sort of direction right now, that would be better than what we had a second ago.

"What do you think would be the biggest help to your parents right now, Grady?" Parrish asks. "I mean, we think we're doing the right things, but maybe we're all wrong about this. Maybe they just need us to do what they asked of us."

"Of us?" Grady shakes his head. "Dude, I get your point, but they didn't ask *you* to do anything...and honestly, who cares if the house is in order if they never get to see it again?"

"Hey, let's not go there," Kayley says.

It's easy to say but far, far more difficult to make happen. We've seen nothing but failure—okay, except that Grady found some bank records—and that just doesn't sit well with the team that took down a minister of Parliament and the head of the Anti-Sedition Ministry, and saved all the colony planets from attack. I know I keep going back to that, but all that we've achieved means something. It means we're capable, even if we're a bit sloppy in our execution.

Court proceedings just aren't our area of expertise. That's why Grady's parents hired Mr. Moreno. He's doing the best job he can. Us, on the other hand...

"I know we're in over our head on this one, but if we could just come up with one small bit of evidence...anything that could help...then, maybe that's all we can do, right?" I glance around at everyone, hoping for confirmation that my idea is valid.

"Yeah, that's what we can do," Kayley echoes, trying her best to be supportive. She'd push for more if she thought we were capable of it.

"Yeah," Parrish seconds. "Anything would help."

I turn to look at Grady, who's still staring at the smashed bit of device lying on the foot of the bed. It's a wreck, crushed on the bottom while the top of it is torn open. Since his sharp retort at Parrish earlier, his eyes haven't moved from that gap. The others must have noticed as well because the room goes silent, and I think I can hear Grady's gears grinding in his head.

"Dude?"

Grady motions me to be quiet, and I obey. He chews on his fingernail, then picks the device up, rotating it around in his hands. I can't understand why he wants to examine it for the fiftieth time. It's not like he hasn't seen everything there is to see on the outside of the device.

But when he flips it over and grabs a broken piece to peel it away from the inside, he gasps.

"Holy hell," Grady says, peering deeper into the gap he just created. "I can't believe it."

"What is it?" If I didn't say it, someone would have. Grady's keeping us all in suspense, and for no good reason. If he found something he should explain it.

"It's a micro transduction array with a charged nanogrid and a photonic beam splitter."

"Once again, Grady, this time in Common," Afton says. "You know...for the rest of us stupid people."

Grady hears his name and lifts his head, his mouth open. He looks around at all the expectant eyes—even the big disk ones hanging from the ceiling—and smiles.

"Grady," Kayley says, softer than Afton, but her voice has some magical weight to it because he turns to her. "What does that mean? Explain it to us."

Grady blinks. "It means the inside of this is my father's design...it's his tech."

"Well done," Original Teddy says and drops from his hangout to plod over to Grady.

My eyes meet with Kayley's, and our minds connect like we're both wired to Teddynet. After knowing someone for so long, you know when they're thinking what you're thinking. She realizes it too, and our mouths widen, the ends turning up into the biggest smiles we've had since we first started dating.

"Hello?" Afton clicks her fingers in front of Kayley's face. "I know you guys are having a moment and all, but how about you share with the rest of us for once?"

"Yes, that would be nice since we're all sitting on needles waiting for you to explain," Doc Elizabeth says.

"Isn't it obvious?" Grady asks Afton's wrinkling nose. "Cecelia Nilsson-Lim is hoarding my parents' tech for her own use."

"Yeah, but how do we prove that?" Parrish asks. "We can't just say, 'Oh, we found this thing in her basement, and we know it's stolen.'"

"We may not need to." Kayley looks at all of us before continuing. "If Mr. Moreno can use this to discredit her as a witness, it might be enough to put some doubt in the jury. If a woman in her standing is dishonest, what does that say about the prosecution's other witnesses? What does that say about their entire case?"

"That was awesome." Afton taps Kayley with her elbow. "You could be a lawyer."

"KayKay could do anything," I correct with a grin, and Kayley beams at me.

"So then, there you are," Doc Elizabeth says. "You've done your part to help. Well done, indeed."

"We're taking this to Mr. Moreno, right?" I ask. All nods meet my gaze as I glance around.

Now that's more like our team.

Twenty-three

"ARE YOU SURE?" KAYLEY asks Grady as we walk towards the prison where his parents are being held. "They actually requested to see you?"

"That's what Mr. Moreno said." Grady's face is a contorted mix of a smile and a wince, caught between happy and confused. His breakneck pace towards the gate says it all, though. Who could blame him?

Other than at court, they've been in self-imposed isolation, refusing to see anyone, including their only child. For someone who's lived all his life under their strict direction and supervision, the sudden withdrawal has been devastating for him. Now that Grady's got the chance to share the results of our hard work with his parents, any second that he's not doing so is a second wasted.

The guards at the gate let us through with little ado. They know our faces well enough at this point that they don't make a big fuss about searching us. We lubricate the process, too, by anticipating their commands and not saying any more than we need to get through. If Grady's parents truly want to see their son, Kayley and I will be rocket boosters, not air brakes.

"Do you remember where to go?" Kayley asks Grady as the three of us head to the visitors' waiting room.

"Yeah," Grady mumbles, not wasting energy on speaking much. I'm sure his poor little heart is pounding so fast that he can't think straight at all. He's so tense that Kayley has to talk to the clerk in the waiting room for him.

"They're waiting for you already," the clerk says, ushering us through the gate. "Table 23b."

"We'll find it." Kayley waves a thank-you to the clerk and ushers Grady down the hall by wrapping her arms about his. "Almost there."

The room where we're meeting with Grady's parents is sizeable, if unimpressive. I count the rows and find twenty-four tables with connected stools filling the floor. They've got enough space to seat six people each, which is one more than we'll need. The ceiling is high enough to allow for a catwalk to sit just above head height, which lines the perimeter of the semi-rectangular space. Five well-armed guards are strategically placed around the room.

Grady halts, his eyes scanning the room. It's not long before he finds them, sitting together side by side at the second-to-last table in the corner. He untangles himself from Kayley's grasp and moves towards them like a comet to a star. His pace picks up until he hits a trot.

"No running!" shouts a guard, and Grady drops his speed. His legs get stiff as he forces them to slow. I touch Kayley on the shoulder to remind her we should follow him. I suspect she wants to give him a little space to say hello before we intrude.

Grady stops before his parents' table and stares. They look back, no tightness in their faces whatsoever. I'd almost think they were getting comfortable in their new surroundings. Grady bows to them, a stiff and formal greeting. With that out of the way, he launches himself towards them but is stopped with a gentle lift of his father's hand.

"Sit, son," Dr. Sugiyama says and motions to Kayley and me to do the same. "Sit, please, all of you."

"Dad...Mom...are you healthy? Are they treating you well?" Grady doesn't wait until he's firmly planted on the stool to fire off questions. His father nods, and his mother smiles in reply, but it's like they're just humoring his son through some formality before he gets to the reason we're here.

"Dad! We found something that could help!" Grady slaps his hands on the table. "Evidence that you're being framed! I've got pictures of it on my Sergo, but they wouldn't let me take it in to show you! It's a—"

"Mutsu," his mother says gently and places a hand over Grady's. "Your father and I need to ask something of you."

"Son," his father says, "we appreciate your efforts, but we request you make no more attempts to search for evidence."

"What?" Grady glances back and forth between the two of them, his gaze blank. But he heard what they said, and so did Kayley and I. We both go rigid against each other, preparing ourselves for some unpleasant explanation.

"Mutsumaji, you are not to investigate the situation any further, do you understand?" His father regards him with a firm gaze. Grady tries to match it, but a second later he just ducks his head. "The most important thing for you to focus on is completing your studies and taking care of the house. I do not want you worrying about us any longer. As you can see, your mother and I are well, and we are prepared for whatever the outcome of the trial may be."

"But...this thing we found could discredit the prosecution's star witness!"

Dr. Sugiyama turns to his wife, who tilts her head and shrugs. It wasn't one of those "Why not listen to what our son has to say?" shrugs. It was more like, "You brought him up to act like this, so you'd better do something about it." He steels his jaw and turns back to Grady.

"No, and that's final."

It's Grady's turn to seek support. He looks to us, a question on his face that he doesn't need to ask. We don't need to open our mouths to give him the answer, either. He knows we're here for him, but this is his battle to fight. For us to intrude would be unwelcome by his parents, and that would be the end of the conversation.

"Why, Dad?"

"I thought I made myself clear enough, Mutsu. We want you focused on your future, not on us. You have much to do in your lifetime, and your mother and I expect you to achieve it all. Now, I wasn't going to bring this up, but we've made arrangements for your engine design to be presented to the top admiral...and you will be the one to present it to him. But before you do, I want you to make sure that you are well prepared to answer the tough questions he's going to ask. You'll work with Dr. Cooper-Wake—"

"That can wait! Mom...Dad...don't you understand you could go to jail for the rest of your lives?" Grady's eyes go wide as his mouth hangs open. "Doesn't that bother you?"

"We're prepared for that inevitability."

"Well, it bothers me!" Grady pounds a fist on the table, and his mother jerks back. "I don't want to have to watch you disintegrate in this place!"

"We are well cared for," his mother insists, but Grady just shakes his head and sighs hard. "There's no need to worry about us."

"Why am I not allowed to want you home?"

Dr. Sugiyama tightens his jaw, and his mother's shoulders fall. His father leans back, his hands on the table clenching. As I look between the two of them, I'm not sure if they're heartbroken or disappointed. Did Grady just break some kind of code between parent and child, or did they, for once, actually understand how he feels?

I turn my head towards Kayley as she slips an arm around mine and presses her shoulder against me. I lean into her as well, seeking the same comfort from the scene before us.

"Mutsu," his mother says softly. "We miss you, too, of course we do, but your father and I have made our peace with our choices. Whatever will happen is what we'll accept. We know this has been hard on you, and should there be a conviction, it will be harder still, but if we didn't think you could handle this, we might have chosen differently."

"W...what do you mean?"

"I mean, we believe in you."

"No." Grady shakes his head rapidly. "No, you said you *chose* to do something...what did you mean? Are you saying that your being here is deliberate? Are you...do..."

Grady stops and watches his parents as they share a knowing look. His jaw drops farther than before, and for a moment, he's frozen, the realization of something pulling him into a suspended state.

My mind is racing when Grady glances about, then leans towards his parents. If he's had some revelation, it hasn't hit Kayley and me yet. Whatever it is, my bud is struggling to comprehend it.

"Mom...Dad...did you...actually do it?" Grady whispers. "Did you steal your own designs?"

His parents once again share a troubled look, and that's when the answer to Grady's question comes to Kayley and me. For whatever reason, Drs. Sugiyama and O'Grady-Davies did exactly what the Empire is accusing them of. The question now is...why?

"Son, you understand why I can't answer a question like that directly. Not here." Grady's dad sits up, lifting his shoulders to a proud height. "But let me explain something to you so you understand the hypothesis behind such an action."

"Go ahead," Grady growls. "I'm waiting."

"I needn't tell you about what a ship that can fold space would be capable of achieving. What you need to understand, my son, is the effects of closing the distances between the planets. There are many benefits, of course, but it would only take one person to utilize the capabilities of our time and space engine to create a first-strike weapon that would put the entire Commonwealth in jeopardy. Once the understanding of that power is out, there is no taking it back, and that's why our Empire is not ready for such technology. We would soon destroy ourselves and any new species we encounter. Your mother and I simply could not accept that our design, meant to bring the Empire closer together, could just as easily tear it apart."

"So..." Grady chokes up but recovers. "You...will sacrifice yourselves for the Empire?"

"Don't think of it that way, Mutsu." His mother's hand slides out to grab Grady's again. "Your father and I had no illusions about our work. We know that what we created could be used for both good and bad, to create peace...or war. We accepted our responsibility before we ever started this project."

"What happens to your designs if you go to jail...permanently?" Kayley asks, interrupting. Now that everything is out in the open, there's no more reason for us to keep quiet. Still, this is not over between Grady and his parents.

"They are secure, just as we planned they would be," his father admits, his face resolute.

"I can't believe this," Grady says. "I can't believe you'd throw everything away, just for an ideal. It's not your responsibility to take the blame, while the ones who would use your tech the wrong way can just continue to do what they want. No...I won't do what you ask of me. You're my mom and dad, and I'm not going to stand by and watch as they turn you into traitors."

"Son." His father reaches out his hand, but it's too late. Grady pulls back and stands, clenching his teeth while his eyes well up.

"No." Grady shakes his head. "No, I don't accept this."

As he walks away, he leaves the four of us staring at each other with jaws slack. Finally, Dr. Sugiyama stands and bows to us.

"Thank you for always looking after my son." He holds out a hand to his wife and helps her to her feet. Dr. O'Grady-Davies makes a reasonable attempt to smile at us, her lips quivering. She nods to us, and then the two of them turn to face the approaching guard.

I turn to Kayley, who is as speechless as I am, but she puts on her leader hat and sets our priorities in place.

"Grady," Kayley says and turns to go after him.

Twenty-four

WE CATCH UP TO Grady just as he's exiting the prison gate. For someone who spends a lot of time in a chair, he can walk really fast when he wants to. At least he stops and waits for us when he hears us calling his name. We break into a jog and are breathing heavily by the time we get to him.

"Dude, you just walked out on your parents," I say, dropping a hand on his shoulder. "I thought you'd want to spend more time with them than that."

"Not when they're acting like idiots, I don't."

I throw a glance at Kayley. We're in uncharted territory here—a mention of Grady's parents and the word "idiots" never find themselves in the same sentence. It's doubly impossible if Grady himself does it.

"Grady." Kayley tries a softer approach. "They're just looking out for you and your future. I think it's amazingly brave of them to risk everything to protect what they cherish."

"And probably some stuff they don't," I add, though I don't know if it's helpful or not. I am trying to be, but I'm nowhere near as eloquent as Kayley. She's had experience public speaking, while I've only managed to piss off every agent of the government I come into contact with.

"I can't be around them right now." Grady throws his hands up, blocking his face from our view, his voice getting tight. "I just want to...do...something. I don't know, or care...just take me somewhere. Anywhere but here."

"Okay, dude." I squeeze his shoulder and try to think of a place to go that won't remind him of his parents—which is a lot more challenging than I expected. The park? No, Grady used to go there with his parents on Sunday afternoons when he was young. Wylde Thyme? Not there either. Grady's mom loves their rice noodle souffle.

"I know where we can go," Kayley says with a smile. She takes Grady's hand and motions me to do the same. We wait for the traffic signal to change, and then we jog across the street together towards the taxi stand.

A big yellow vehicle—not a taxi—skids to a stop in front of us, blocking our way across. It's long and streamlined, like an aircraft. With its chrome tires and trim all around, it shines like our sun. The three of us come to a halt and try to catch our balance before we crash into the side of the lengthy transport.

While I'm choosing some choice words to say to the driver, the passenger door slides open, and out come two hulking men in suits that are way too small and tight for them. One of them steps to the side of the door and holds his hand out. It's taken up by a smaller, slimmer hand that pops out of a trim yellow jacket sleeve. Before I can get my suspicions up, out comes the last person on the planet we want to see, complete in a canary suit and feathered yellow hat to match.

"Oh heck, it's Cecelia Nilsson-Lim," Grady says.

"Let's not be here any longer," Kayley says and tugs Grady and me, heading towards the front to get away from her.

"Not so fast, kids," Cecelia says. Her driver jumps out of the car, blocking our way. "I've got a few questions for you."

As she steps around her vehicle, her two burly men come up behind us to block our retreat. We're staying now, whether we want to or not. Grady squeezes my hand, and I'm sure that was telegraphed from the other side of him where the same thing just happened.

I duck my head down, hoping she won't remember what happened to her two days ago. She wasn't awake...right? Sleepwalking, maybe? There's no way she'll recognize me.

"You, scruffy boy...no, not you." She waves a hand at Grady as he looks up, then points at me. "You...spiky head. Look at me."

Cecelia inhales sharply as I catch her eyes. She takes a step back, her hand covering over her chest. My eyes dart away as she gets closer to examine me. She is so close I can smell her perfume and the mint on her breath. A moment after, her hand comes up to touch my face.

"By Durga, you really do look like him," Cecelia says and strokes her hand down the side of my face as I wince.

"Hey! Hands off!" Kayley shouts. It takes us all by surprise. Even the three massive muscular men, who I'm guessing are her bodyguards, jump.

"Who are you, the girlfriend?" Cecelia teases, her voice mockingly sweet. But then she does a double take. "You...you were there, too, weren't you?"

"Where?" Kayley blinks, playing innocent, but it doesn't fly.

"*My* house...the two of you broke into my house!"

"I have no idea who you are or where your house is," I shoot back. "And why would I want to do that anyway?"

"To help your boyfriend here get his parents out of jail...where they belong, I might add, the traitors." She pokes my chest. "And don't lie, I remember you being there. You pretended to be Prosecutor Cavalcante! I...I almost kissed you! Not that I would have minded, but...but you tricked me!"

"I think you must have been dreaming. I wasn't anywhere near your house, even if I knew where it was, and I certainly wouldn't be kissing you."

"Think you're so smart, don't you? Well, I have you on vid...and I wasn't dreaming. I only sleep in one, maybe two of the bedrooms in my house, and I woke up the next morning in neither of those!"

I glance at Grady, who shoots his eyes up. Once we get out of this, there's going to be some questions about video surveillance and how he was sure that everything had been disabled.

"That's right." Cecelia grins and chuckles. "I've got you, you interlopers!"

"Well, you're a liar!" Kayley fires back. "Pretending to be friends with them and then slandering them all over the networks? What a fake you are."

"Wow, what a little firecracker *you* are. But it doesn't matter. You're coming with me so I can find out what you know. We can't have little kids running around with Imperial secrets in their heads. Boys, put them in the limo."

Kayley swings her leg, and her boot connects with the shin of the nearest big guy. He yelps and grabs his leg. Grady's heel impacts the knee of the bodyguard behind him. He's incapacitated a second after. My turn. But it's Cecelia I'm facing.

No way I'm kicking a lady.

I reach out and grab her. She screams as I throw her into the one free burly man. He's forced to shift to catch her, and that's when we make our break.

Kayley, Grady, and I bolt across the street, dodging the oncoming traffic. Delivery trucks and passenger vehicles swerve to avoid us. Two of them crash, blocking the street and allowing Cecelia's henchmen to chase us.

"Grady, they're not after you!" I push him towards a storefront door. "Call the others! Get help!"

Grady stumbles but manages to slip into the store as he whips his Sergo out. He'll be alright. It's Kayley and me I'm worried about.

I catch up to her as she ducks down an alley, two henchmen on our trail. I hope the third is busy tending to Cecelia's wounded ego rather than finding a way to trap us.

We turn down another alley that takes us into a loading dock. There's an exit on the far side, so we go for that. It's a quick dash, but my lungs are already burning. Kayley must be feeling it too. Her gasps for air are sharp and ragged. We won't keep this up for long.

One of the burly men steps out from the exit and blocks our escape. I grab Kayley's arm and swing her around. I want to turn back, but there's burly men two and three—no going that way. We slide to a stop, searching for another option.

There's a gate in the center of the dock. I motion to Kayley, and we jump on the riser and hit the gate. I pound on it while Kayley looks for a switch.

"Anything?" I pound again, hoping someone will open it. Kayley shakes her head and stares at our pursuers, eyes wide.

The henchdudes are closing in, getting ready to grab us in their meaty hands and carry us like luggage back to the car. One of them is limping, at least. If we can escape this mantrap, we can outrun him.

"Give it up," the driver says, stopping an arm's length from us. "You're not gonna get away."

They might be right. I didn't expect them to be smart enough to trap us like this. I glance between the encroaching human walls. It's not good—I can't see a way to give them the slip. No way to duke it out with them, either. My punch would be like a little kid slapping a bear. That's not something anyone would think wise.

"You're going to answer the boss' questions," says Mr. Limp. "And after that, I'm going to use you to take my frustrations out on."

"What could you possibly be frustrated about?" I ask.

"You'll find out." He grins and reaches for me. I'm away from his muscle-bound grasp in a nanosecond, but I get snatched from behind by the meathead Grady kicked. My leg goes back and pops him right on his knee again. He roars and grimaces but recovers faster than I expect.

"Hold him still. I'm gonna teach this little puke a lesson."

Ah, this is going to hurt...

He winds up, preparing to knock my teeth into next Tuesday. Kayley gives the other one the slip—she's just too quick for his bulky mass—sliding past Mr. Meathammer and jabbing a knuckle into the eye of my re-strainer.

He lets go, his hands flying up to his eye. Just for a little extra, I kick my heel back and get him right between the legs. It's dirty, I know, but nobody's playing on the honor system here.

Kayley and I grab each other and jump off the riser, headed back the way we came. Maybe Grady's already called in the reinforcements. That'd be good.

I'm getting tired of running away.

Twenty-Five

WE BLOW OUT OF the alley and skid right, headed for the store where I sent Grady. It's three steps to get to the door. I let Kayley go first because I want to check something. She's better at spotting people than I am, anyway.

I glance across the street. Cecelia's big yellow limo is still there, but she's nowhere in sight. Did she run? I'm not about to wait to find out. Her goons could be coming around the corner, and I have no interest in starting another stimulating conversation with them. I check once more, then dive into the shop.

"See him?" I whisper in Kayley's ear as she scans the room. I had no idea where I was pushing Grady before, but now I see I shoved him into a tea shop. There are a few small circular tables here, but only a few patrons. A woman behind the counter eyes us warily as she wipes it down. A corridor leads down past the left side of the counter. I think there are a few shelves back there where the public can shop.

"Not yet," Kayley replies. "Better we ask for help."

I nod and, with one final look through the glass door behind us, approach the counter. The woman stops her cleaning and stands up, unsure whether to welcome us or kick us out. She relaxes when Kayley pulls out her all-powerful smile.

"Hi, we were looking for someone who came in here a few minutes before us. He's about this tall," Kayley lifts her hand to the top of her head, "and has kind of a floppy haircut. Do you remember seeing him?"

"Oh." The woman nods and smirks. "Yes, I remember him. He nearly fell through the door."

Kayley glances at me, and I dodge her gaze. Okay...so I might have been a little rough with him when I pushed him through the door, but hey, three big muscle dudes were chasing us.

"Any idea where he might have gone?" Kayley asks.

The woman points down the corridor. "He went back there, but I didn't see him come out...maybe he's using the toilet?"

"Okay, thanks." We both smile and start down the corridor, but the woman stops Kayley by reaching out to her. Kayley turns and blinks at the woman.

"Oh, hey...you're...you're..."

"Yeah," Kayley says, turning the charm back on. "That's me."

"Um...do you mind...a quick photo?"

"Er, maybe later."

"Oh, sure, sure. No problem...you're staying for tea, right?"

Kayley smiles and nods and slides away. I smile too, but the woman is already back to cleaning her counter. If I weren't already used to it, I might be jealous, but we've got more important things to tackle.

The corridor splits off to the left, where there's a long row of shelves stocked full of tea tins. Grady could be hiding back here, but a quick check of both aisles turns up no one.

"Let me check the toilet," I say to Kayley and head back there. I open the door, and as I suspected, no Grady. No anybody. I consider checking the women's toilet, but I doubt Grady would make a decision like that. And besides, Kayley is perfectly capable of checking on her own.

She curls the edge of her mouth down when she sees my discouraged face and folds her arms. I motion towards the back of the shop, and we head that way. There's a small storeroom with a swinging door, and we pass through it until we get to a door heading outside.

The door is ajar, and I raise an eyebrow at Kayley as we share a look. The door might lead back to the alley where we just got trapped, and Grady might have gotten caught in the same predicament if he came out this way.

"Can you get him on the comm?" Kayley asks.

"No, he didn't bring his."

"Neither did I. You're the only one who thought it would be a good idea to get yours implanted into your skull."

"It was a good idea."

"No...no, it wasn't."

"Sure it was."

"Remind me to tell you of my twenty reasons why putting alien tech into your body is a bad idea, Rance."

I give her a half-hearted eye roll and move out the door. We are right back where we just escaped from, but no meatheads to be found. No Grady either. I think he tried to find us and couldn't, so he just headed back home.

"Can you call Parrish or Afton? Maybe they heard from him and told him to get out of here."

"Maybe." Kayley snatches her Sergo from her dress pocket and makes the call. Afton is at Grady's house with Parrish and Doc Elizabeth. He had called them, and they told them to split, but they hadn't heard from him since. I try Grady on my own Sergo, but no luck.

"But are you guys okay? Do you need help?" Parrish asks.

"No, we're fine," Kayley replies, glancing at me to see if I disagree—I don't. We gave those guys the slip, and I doubt they'll be picking up our trail again. They didn't look like skilled trackers of any sort.

"Well, see you guys back here, then. If you need a Teddy pickup..." Afton suggests.

"No thanks, but we may just give the area a quick walk-through in case Grady's still here. He may be scared and hiding," Kayley says. "I don't want to leave him alone. Some...things happened with his parents. We need to tell you guys when we get back."

As Kayley signs off, I search the area for any signs of our bud. I don't expect to find much of anything because he'd have to lose a shoe or rip his clothes for any sort of clue to be left behind. He likely grabbed a taxi and is well on his way home by now. We should be too.

"Is this really worth it?" I ask as I'm checking behind the last trash bin in the alley. Kayley went in the opposite direction to check the other side. It doesn't look like she's had any better luck.

"We're not leaving him," Kayley replies.

"Well, I'm down with that, but maybe *he's* already left *us*."

After a few more minutes of meandering around the back alleyways, Kayley is ready to give up her search. We meet up in the middle of one, eyes meeting and shoulders lowering. She smiles gently at me and moves her head back and forth. We're both beat. Long-distance running is not our forte. Only Afton can burn through the kilometers with any sort of e ase.

"Hey! They're right there!"

We both jerk our heads around and curse. It's two of the muscleheads. They're pounding their way towards us. And we're just standing here like a pair of dolts.

"Move!" I push Kayley in the opposite direction. I dig down to find what reserves of energy I have left. Kayley's right there with me, but she's in no better shape.

At least those bulls on two legs can't run that fast. It helps us save some energy for when we're out in the open. Then we'll really bust loose.

"Right...turn right!" I say.

"No, it's left!" Kayley counters and shoves me towards the turn. I've no choice. We go left and barrel down the alley. It's getting tighter, though, and so is my chest. There's not going to be a lot of escaping if we run out of space, or air.

The alley ends in a tight turn, and we hit it just as Cecelia's two henchmen enter the alley behind us. They're bashing their way through, throwing bins and trash into the air as they barrel down on us. The crashing of metal on metal is enough to wake the dead, and it's definitely enough to drive us harder. We're picking up the pace but not gaining any ground.

A massive arm reaches out as we pass—it's the third guy! Kayley screams as he latches on to her sleeve. I spin and stab down with my Sergo onto his wrist. He shouts as metal meets bone. With a tug from me, she barely escapes his grasp, and we make a dash to the end of the alley.

It's one more turn, and we're home free. I can see the street up just ahead. That's good because we're hitting empty. Any more, and I'm going to fall flat on my face with no energy to get up again.

"Don't stop until we cross!" I shout. It's a risk, but we might make it if we can put some vehicles between them and us.

The exit to the alley is a few paces away. I prepare myself to fly across the street, no matter what. We'll dodge if we have to, but those thickheaded jerks are not going to get us! I glance back. No way they're going to catch up. We're out of here!

"Rance!" Kayley cries, and I swing my head back around. Someone covered in yellow is suddenly blocking our exit—Cecelia! And she's got a gun!

There's no way we can stop. We plow into her and knock her off-balance. She falls with a grunt, landing on her back, and I land right on top of her. I scramble to get up, but she recovers faster than I expect.

"Oh, no! You stay right there!" Cecelia yells, jabbing the barrel of her weapon into my face. I freeze, aware that my weight is still keeping her down. "You too, missy."

Kayley was ready to help me up, but when Cecelia points the weapon at her, she goes still.

I'm staring down at her, uncomfortable for several reasons, one being I'm in a bit of an embarrassing position while my girlfriend sits beside me. She'd totally be kicking me off if there wasn't a gun keeping me where I am.

Cecelia's three henchmen arrive a few seconds later. One of them rips me off his boss and gets me in a headlock, while another grabs Kayley by the wrists and yanks her up. She yelps and glares at the burly man.

"Hey! Don't you dare hurt her!" I shout.

"Of course not," Cecelia replies, dusting herself off. "Not until you've had the chance to answer my questions." She smirks at Kayley and me. "Take them to the lab."

Twenty-six

I was more comfortable in jail.

They've strung the two of us up like bundles of rice, ready to be threshed. But unlike that crop, Kayley and I will not give up anything, not a single grain. We have little to give up, anyway, so keeping secrets should be easy.

It's amusing that she has this bare concrete room in the basement of her office building. It's right out of an action cine, complete with water dripping down the cold gray walls, a single light suspended from the ceiling by its wire, and finally, a solitary table topped with a few random power tools. It's a bit ridiculous, honestly, but it makes me uneasy. I'll be glad when this is over.

What I'm not looking forward to is any attempt by Cecelia's henchmen to make it physical. They won't hurt Kayley—at least they'd better not—but they might want to do a little knuckle dance on my face.

"Hey, KayKay...you okay?" I whisper. They've got my head locked down tight, so I can't see her.

"Yeah." Kayley's voice is shaky. She's not used to this. I'm not either, but I've had a little experience, so I'm not as nervous. "You?"

"Can't complain."

"What do you think they're going to do to us?" Kayley struggles in the metal cords they've got around her wrists. I can't blame her. We've been hanging here for what's got to be a few hours now, and having your hands over your head gets to hurting after only a few minutes. The chain that's wrapped tight around my chest is a bit of a pain, too, the way it digs into my armpits.

"Try to get as much info from us as possible, I would think."

"We don't have any info to give them!"

"No, we don't, but I doubt they're going to believe that."

"They better not try to hurt you!"

"Exactly. I'll go nuts if one of those meatheads touches you."

"I'll be okay," Kayley says after a moment, but I think she's trying to convince herself more than me.

We hear footsteps on the stairs, and Kayley takes a sharp inhale. I strain my eyes to get a look at the door and wait for someone to make an appearance.

It's Cecelia and one of her burly men. I don't think it's the one we capped in the knee—twice—but it's so hard to tell. All three of them are the same shape, and honestly, I wasn't spending a lot of time examining them because we were trying to run away.

Cecelia's got a big smirk on her face as she regards us. She leans back on the table and takes a sip of something in a ceramic mug. It's the kind with the little handle that's too small to do anything other than pinch it with your fingers, yet the mug itself is not some dainty thing that allows for such an easy finger lift. This is bothering me way more than it should and I realize I'm thirsty.

"Any chance you're going to share some of that with us?" I ask.

"Not a stardust's chance on reentry." Cecelia makes a show of enjoying her next sip, smacking her lips and letting out a satisfied breath.

"Well, okay, but if you expect us to talk, a little lubrication in the throat would be helpful."

"Rance!" Kayley's thinking I'm already giving in, but all I'm doing is trying to get us something to drink.

"Oh, you'll talk alright." Cecelia chuckles. "I've got other things that will help."

"You hurt us, and you'll be in trouble!" Kayley shouts. "I'm famous, and I'll let the whole planet know what you did!"

"Yes, famous on a backwater planet...how nice." Cecelia pushes herself off the table and saunters over to Kayley. "People might know you here, ginger girl, but I'm known throughout the Empire. Whose word do you think has more weight?"

"So, what's the reason for this archaic muscle stretch?"

"It's so you know I'm serious." Cecelia turns away from Kayley and comes over to stare up at me. After a moment, she shakes her head. "I still can't believe the resemblance. It's like the two of you are related."

"Who do you mean?"

"Never you mind."

Cecelia's canny. She knows that I could use that little bit of information against her. I would certainly try to do that, especially if things get painful.

I'm not sure she'll believe that I'm her heartthrob's son, but if I'm desperate, I'll have to try.

"Now," Cecelia says and takes another sip, "I have a few things I need to find out from you, and if you cooperate, you'll be free to go. If you decide to be difficult, then I'll be turning you over to the local constabulary with all the vid recordings of you trespassing in my house and assaulting me."

At least now we know what she's after. I suppose I could make something up, but I'm not so sure she's going to believe anything but the truth. If she really has vids like she says she does, then not only will she know we were in her bedroom while my father was there, she'll know we took something from her workshop.

"We didn't assault you."

"You want to see what a jury says about that, bucko? You just try me."

"Goddesses, you're so predictable," Kayley growls.

"Not as much as you are, my dear." Another sip. I wonder just how much liquid is left in that mug. "So, first things first. Why did you break into my house?"

"What makes you think we did that?"

Cecelia drops her mug down on the table, a bit of its remaining liquid splashing out. I can tell now it's tea, and my throat goes drier than ever. She sighs and turns to her henchman. He grins and approaches me as he squeezes his fists. Great. I guess pain time is already on me.

"Yeah..." I try a casual tone, but my voice is already shaky. "That won't help."

"We'll see," Mr. Muscle says and winds up.

"Don't!" Kayley yells.

His fist hits me square on my thigh, and I cry out. It's like all the muscles in my leg just cramped up and exploded at the same time. I fall forward, but my restraints hold me up and dig harder into my sides.

"Do we want to try that answer again?" Cecelia leans back on the table again, crossing her legs at her ankles and tilting her head.

My teeth are still clenched from the nasty impact my leg just took, so I'm not yet ready to give her an answer. At least she doesn't seem to be taking enjoyment from my suffering like some psychotic antagonist from the cine. Still, I think I'd prefer to be elsewhere.

"We were just having fun, honestly," I say. "Your house is so cool, we had to check it out."

"So you were just a bunch of kids messing about. Do you really want me to explain to you why I don't believe that for a nanosecond?" Cecelia shakes her head and nods to her enforcer.

He drives a fist into my gut this time. I retch and cough, doubling over as much as the cords will allow. It's not much, which only aggravates my belly more. Pressure builds up in my throat, and a second later, I spit out whatever I might have had in my stomach. Luckily, it's nothing more than bile.

"Stop!" Kayley cries. "You're hurting him!"

"Yes, that's kind of the point, girl." Cecelia turns her attention to her, allowing me a moment to recover. "But you know, it's totally in your power to stop it. All you have to do is give me a truthful answer. If I get what I want, then we can end this. Believe me when I say I've got much better things to be doing."

"Like making the moves on Prosecutor Cavalcante?" I ask, rubbing my lower lip across my teeth. The taste of stomach acid and bile is sour in my mouth, and it burns my throat. Still, it's minimal discomfort compared to the demolition machine that just struck me twice.

"What's that?" Cecelia gets close to me so she can gaze up into my face as it hangs. "So you've figured out who you're a clone for, is it? Smart boy, you are...but you know, I'm also pretty sharp. I think I'm beginning to put the clues together."

Cecelia paces between Kayley and me, rubbing a finger on the side of her mouth. She stays quiet as she thinks through whatever she thinks she knows. That could be a lot at this point.

"Let's see, I caught you with Sugiyama's son, which means you know about the case."

"Everyone knows about the case," Kayley counters.

"True, but I'll bet the two you have some real info on what's going on, including anything the defense might be holding back. And I'll also bet you broke into my house looking for evidence of wrongdoing...which means the defense thinks I'm trying to frame the accused."

"Are you?"

"Shush, girl, I'm thinking."

"*I* bet you planned to get Dr. Sugiyama and Dr. O'Grady-Davies arrested and charged with treason so you could steal their designs."

"Enough yapping from you, already. Don't you know when to be quiet?"

"I will not be quiet!"

Cecelia rushes up to Kayley and strikes her across the face. Kayley whimpers and goes silent. I can already feel the hair on the back of my neck rising. No one hurts my Kayley...this witch is going to get it. I'll make sure of that.

"Where was I?" Ms. I'm Asking to Be Punched in the Face turns from Kayley as if she had done nothing but talk to her. "Right. My house, your trespass, and the stealing of my device. Where is it?"

She grabs my face and squeezes, lifting my head so she can look me in the eye.

"Where's my device?" She glares. "Not going to answer? Fine, but you're not going to stay silent for long. So, tell me now, or you can enjoy getting pummeled for a bit."

If those two hits were a hint of what might be coming, I'm already freaking out. Yes, I could tell her that it's safely at Grady's house, but that puts Grady at risk, and I just can't let my bud be put into a situation like this. He'd never last. I don't think I will, either, but he's already been through enough. That said, I'm not prepared to take a beating.

"We don't have it," I try, but she sees through the weak dodge easily.

"This is getting really tiring." A nod and Burly Man goes to work on me. His pounding is brutal. With every strike, I feel my eyes roll back into my head. My body goes limp and numb after a minute. All I can see through my darkening vision is the floor beneath my feet.

"We don't have it!" Kayley shouts, her voice breaking into a sob. "Please, stop!"

"Then give me something I can use, or I'm delivering you two to the authorities in an ambulance."

I can only imagine what's racing through Kayley's brain, and as my consciousness drifts away, I try to hold on to that thought. I know she's trying as best as she can to protect our secrets, but I'm not so sure how long she'll be able to hold out.

"Okay...okay..." Kayley sobs again. "I'll tell you...I'll tell you...please, just stop hurting him!"

"Fine, I'm listening, but I don't need you to tell me what you were doing in my house. I've already got that figured out. No, if you want..." Cecelia goes quiet for a moment. Your boyfriend..." Shoot, she figured that out. "To not have to use a wheelchair for the rest of his life, you're going to have to give up whatever secrets Mr. Moreno might be keeping from the prosecution."

"Don't tell her." I don't know how I croaked that out, but I had to try to stop this.

"Quiet you." Burly Man smacks me across the side of my head. I jerk from the strike and fade out.

I'm not sure if I lost consciousness or not, but the next thing I know, I'm lying on the ground, my head in Kayley's lap. She's looking down at me with wet eyes, but at least she's not crying. Still, her jaw is set tight, and her lips are pressed together.

"My secretary will show you out the back door," Cecelia says. "Remember, you've never met me, or you know what will happen. Nice doing business with you."

As Cecelia walks away, I stare up at Kayley.

"What did you tell her?" My voice is weak and broken and that's exactly not what I wanted because it's making Kayley freak out.

"Don't worry," Kayley replies and strokes my head. She's trying to be calm for me, but I can feel her hand shaking. "The Teddys are coming to take us up to see Elizabeth. You'll be okay...you'll be okay."

Twenty-seven

AH, DOC ELIZABETH'S EXAM chair. It's the most comfortable, most supporting deathbed anyone would ever want to lie in. I'm not ready for reincarnation just yet, so I push my eyes open and make a solid effort to move my arms and legs. There's a definite soreness throughout, so I stop moving once it gets to be too much. It's enough to catch Doc Elizabeth's attention, however.

"Ah, there we are," she says as she turns back around and looks down at me. My eyes instantly catch the hypodermic pistol in her hand with the rather large needle projecting from it. "I suppose I won't be needing this after all...shame, that."

"What. Is. That?" I can feel the edges of my eyes growing bigger.

"Oh, this?" Doc Elizabeth glances at it. "Just something that I was developing with the Teddys...I'm not sure it's ready, but—"

"You were going to put some chemical in me, and you don't know if it's ready or not?"

"No, of course not, I'd never do that!"

I let out a sigh of relief. The last thing my aching body needs right now is another shot of physical misery. A nerve blocker would be more welcome than a gigantic needle.

"No," Doc Elizabeth says again, "this is a nanobot injection, not chemicals."

"And that's supposed to be better?" As much as I trust the Teddys, I'm not interested in becoming a walking medical experiment. I press my hands down on the chair to push myself up, but it's tough going. Doc Elizabeth is faster, and she puts a stop to my slow-motion escape.

"You realize you already have nanobots in you, don't you?" She keeps her hand on my shoulder and catches my confused look. "What did you think Teddy comm was, exactly?"

I blink—I had never considered that. I'd always thought the Teddy comm implant was a big block of tech stuck in the back of my neck. That I had never felt it there hadn't occurred to me. I don't know whether I should be amazed or annoyed.

"And there you have it, my little hummingbird. These nanos would help your body recover faster, but since you're so averse to them, I think I'll have to try them on someone else. Your leg is just going to have to recover by itself."

"What's going to have to recover?" Kayley asks, stepping through the portal. She's oddly got her hair pulled back into a ponytail, but once I catch the hand-shaped bruise on the side of her face, I understand.

"She...did that to you?" I ask, my teeth biting down into a snarl.

"She did worse to you, darling," Kayley replies, leaning over me to plant a kiss on my forehead. "How do you feel?"

"Not so bad anymore." I give her a cheeky grin, and she grins back, catching my meaning.

"If only it were that easy," Doc Elizabeth comments, headed towards the portal. "Two weeks at least before I clear you for fieldwork again...of course, if you change your mind, there are always the nanos. Anyway, I'm hungry, so you two keep each other company for a bit, yeah?"

Kayley looks down at me with a pout. I return her gaze with a quizzical look of my own. I guess she might feel sorry for me, but I also suspect she's happy to not have me move around all that much. Still...two weeks is right out. I have to be there for Grady when they read the verdict. Whatever it turns out to be, it will be a very emotional moment for him, and lately, he's been totally overloaded with emotions that he doesn't know how to handle. I won't let him down because I've got a few sore muscles.

"KayKay. What did you say to Cecelia to make her let us go?"

Kayley averts her eyes, and that's a sure sign that I'll have to do some prodding if I want an answer.

"KayKay," I say again, taking her hand. "Come on. It can't be that bad. Right? I mean, you made something up...right?"

Kayley turns, but I do my best to hold on to her hand so she doesn't walk away. She's still holding my hand, too, so that's a good sign. But she's not replying, which isn't good. Eventually she sighs and drops down on the edge of the exam chair."Not exactly," she replies, her voice just above a mumble.

I push myself to sit up, as much as it hurts to do so. There's an itch running down my back that's more insistent than any ache I've got.

"What are you saying?"

She swivels and smiles down at me, her mood flipped right side up. But whatever she's trying to avoid telling me, she's going with playing the cheerful girlfriend instead for the moment.

"I'm saying that it's better if you forget it and get some rest, okay? Your recovery is what's important."

"I'm not worried about my recovery...I'm worried about what you told that devil woman!"

"Just forget it, Rance." Kayley sighs. "It won't change anything, anyway."

"What are you talking about? Do you think Cecelia's already won? Well, she hasn't!"

"No, that's not it."

It's my turn to sigh and look away. It's so unlike her to be purposely cryptic. Why is she avoiding telling me? I don't exactly have all my brain cells firing in sync, so figuring it out is going to be next to impossible right now. Maybe it's best to try another angle.

"KayKay, if you're worried about how I'm going to react, I promise I'll be cool, okay?"

"I know you will."

"So?"

"I...it's not you." Kayley puts a hand on my face, her thumb stroking my cheekbone. Our eyes connect again, and I see the torture there. My whole body slumps. What am I putting her through? Is she struggling that much?

"Talk to me."

"You passed out, Rance...and I was alone. I had to decide."

"No, KayKay." I shake my head—now I see where she went wrong. "You totally misjudged the situation! I told you not to tell her anything!"

Kayley's eyes widen, and she backs off, swallowing hard.

"I know, I'm not proud of myself...but, understand how scared I was! You were...well, the moment I got you back, I prayed to the Goddesses that they wouldn't take you. That's how bad you looked. And honestly, your face is still..."

Shoot, I'm an idiot. I was just trying to give her a clear understanding of the situation so she could stop blaming herself. I should have just shut my mouth and listened. Instead, I made her feel worse.

"Hey, I'm sorry." I reach up and touch her face, careful of the wound she received trying to protect me. She leans into my hand and closes her eyes. "That must have been terrifying for you."

I slip my arm around her and pull her close, and Kayley slides into my arms and puts her head on my shoulder. I smile a little because I'm glad I can comfort her for once. It always seems like Ms. Perfect does all the heavy lifting in our relationship, and that's something I know I have to work on.

"Wasn't it for you?"

"Sure it was. I didn't want to get hit by that guy. Not even once. I hate to say it, but I've been in front of people like that before. Cecelia is just another minister or deputy that thinks they're more important than they are. And people like that, I'm not afraid of."

"Don't act so tough. You don't have to face them all by yourself."

"Neither do you, KayKay."

Kayley sniffles and pushes back to look me in the eyes again. She's searching for an answer to something.

"What is it?"

"Rance...I told Cecelia the truth. I didn't know what else to do. Now she knows Mr. Moreno's plans, and it's my fault."

The thing is, I'm not surprised. I get why she'd want to keep that a secret, and it's not because she was afraid of how I'd react. Speaking it out loud means she's admitting what she did to herself, and for Kayley to think of herself as fallible is pure self-persecution.

"And now she's going to go tell my father, right?"

Kayley nods reluctantly.

"Well, we're going to just have to put a stop to that."

"How?" She asks, turning a suspicious eye on me.

"I've got a plan."

Twenty-eight

WE JOIN DOC ELIZABETH and the others at the human table in the ship's canteen. It's literally our table now, as the Teddys modified it to only grow human-safe veggies, and they moved the small furry things elsewhere. This means that no Teddy who has any true level of hunger can eat here. It's turned more into a snack bar for them, and not even a good one, at that. So while we humans don't own it—no one owns anything in Teddy culture—it's been graciously surrendered to us. I hate to say it, but I think we're rubbing off on them just as much as they are us.

Save three blue buddies who came to keep us company, it's just us in here at the moment. We're still on Angelcanis time, which is the late shift here on the ship. All the Teddys on this schedule already ate, and the others coming online aren't due in here for a few hours.

"So they don't speak Common?" Afton asks, staring at the blue guys. They don't seem to mind as they chirp and gurgle amongst themselves. It's not just on our homeworld where we're celebrities. I'm guessing these three must be new recruits. If autographs had any value—or meaning—for Teddys, we'd be scrawling up a storm.

"Not a lick," Doc Elizabeth replies.

"Guys," Parrish says. He snatches bits of black celery and orange cabbage and molds them together. "Try these two together...it tastes just like deep-fried fermented bean curd."

"I thought Elizabeth told us to stay away from the orange cabbage," I say.

"I tried it...it's disgusting," Afton adds.

"Not like this, it's not! Try it!"

But no one does.

Parrish has been on a roll with his cooking, and I totally support that, but some ingredients you just should not mess with. My mom would chop my hands off if she caught me putting chilies in my broccoli.

"Hey, everyone," Kayley calls. "Let's get this meeting started. We've only two days before the end of the trial. If we're going to come up with some way to do something for Grady's parents, we need to figure it out now."

"Why bother?" Grady grumbles. "We did our best, didn't we? But it wasn't good enough. I don't blame any of you for that. I appreciate all you've done for me. Whatever happens, happens at this point."

Everyone knows by now that Grady's parents admitted to breaking the law. I think that we all understand their reasoning, too, and no one—Grady especially—wants to see them go to jail for life.

"It's not over yet, dude," I say, limping over to stand before him. "We still have time...and the smallest thing could make the difference."

"Thanks, dude, but no way can I just waste myself banging up against that wall. It's over...they're guilty, so that's it."

"What they did wasn't for some selfish reason," Kayley says, coming to my side. "They were trying to save the Empire. Even if the jury never gets to learn that, we owe it to them to keep trying. It's up to us to get the truth out there."

"And who would believe it?" Grady hangs his head. "They admitted they did it. If that comes out when either of them takes the stand, it's all over."

"Yeah, they broke the law, sure," I say. "But it was for all the right reasons...haven't we done that a few times?"

"True."

"Then," Kayley says, picking up my thought and continuing it, "don't they deserve us to keep trying, all the way to the end...and after?"

"I..." Grady slumps and sighs. "I don't know if I've got the energy for that, dude."

"Don't worry." I smile down at my forlorn bud. "I have an idea that won't require much effort at all."

Grady wrinkles his nose and turns his head away. But he makes the mistake of glancing at Afton, who's swinging a finger in my direction. I'm thinking positively and going to say that she's backing me up...for a change.

"Rance was hoping to share it with you, Grady," Kayley says. "Could you at least listen?"

"Fine."

"Okay." I drop onto the stool next to him. "So, Cecelia Nilsson-Lim thinks she's got the advantage on us because she's got a direct connection to my dad and can share with him anything she learns about the defense."

Parrish and Doc Elizabeth get closer as I begin my pitch. I'm hoping that Grady sees the logic of my idea, especially since it doesn't directly involve him. I know he wants to help his parents, but he's still stunned by what they dropped on him two days ago.

"That doesn't help us, dude," Grady comments, but I hold up a hand and continue. He'll understand soon enough.

"The thing is, she doesn't know that I'm related to him. All she thinks is that I look like him, but she has no clue that I'm his son."

"You try pretty hard not to be," Afton comments, playing with some shiny trinket in her hands. It's true—I have absolutely no interest in any association with him. I think. I still have so many wonderful memories of my childhood with him, but they're tainted by what he's become, and worse—what he's doing now to my best bud's family. I want to forgive him and move on, but he's making that near impossible for me to do.

Well, either way, I'm still going to use him to help my bud.

"Alright, get this." I hold up my hands to frame the idea for him. I'm not sure why, but I saw Kayley do it once, and everyone loved her speech. "I'll go talk to my dad and ask him to drop the case. I'll tell him everything that's happened—"

"Besides the confession," Kayley adds, smiling at me, "an admission of guilt's not likely to help at this point."

"Yeah, so not that...but I'll tell him how we think—I mean, *know* that Ms. Nilsson-Lim is dirty. I'll tell him everything about how her goons beat me up and threatened to do worse...I'll show him the bruises and everything. He'll totally fall for it!"

I watch Grady for his reaction. At first he stares at me blankly, and I'm wondering if I didn't explain it well. I glance at Kayley, she nods. Then his forehead crinkles, and his eyes get narrow.

"Dude, no," Grady says. "No offense to you, but your dad is our adversary. You can't trust him with anything. He could use it against us."

"But I don't think he will. I've seen the good in him, and I really think he doesn't want to convict your parents, dude."

"Maybe he doesn't, but he's about to."

I turn to Kayley for some backup, but she's got nothing. She might come up with something still, but right now, I'm on my own.

"He could still change his mind," Doc Elizabeth says. "It just depends upon how convincing Rance can be, and some of those bruises he's got will do most of the convincing for him."

"It's still risky," Parrish counters. "You know your dad best, Rance, but you should be really careful with what secrets you give to him."

"Definitely," Afton seconds. She stretches out the shiny thing in her hands, which I realize now is the Matha-something that her mother threw at her. "Blood relations are not a guarantee someone's going to be on your side."

This isn't going the way I had expected it would. I thought I'd just break my idea to Grady, and he'd be all into it. Now Parrish and Afton are taking sides with Grady against Kayley and me. If this devolves into a shouting match, then all is lost. I think I could still convince them, but I'm going to have to work for it.

"Doing nothing is also risky." To my relief, Kayley gets in with a valid point. Grady shifts on his stool in response—that's a good sign. It means he wants to try *something*.

"What's given you any sort of idea that Rance's dad would do the right thing with this information?" Parrish looks at me. "What if he arrests *you* for robbery? Then what? I'd rather not have to go to another trial."

"He's trying to reach out to Rance," Kayley says. "We wouldn't be thinking this way if he wasn't making that effort."

"Maybe he's just using you to get information," Afton says.

"Guys, listen." I try to take the opportunity to close the deal. "I'll be the first to tell you that my father is not to be trusted. He walked out on my mom and me just when I thought everything was going great. But I think he realizes he messed up...and I have to take advantage of that."

We all turn to Grady because only with his blessing do we get to do this the right way, but he's not giving any hint about which way he plans to go. I could really use his support on this.

"I'm sorry," Grady says suddenly. "I'm sorry, Rance. Maybe he is trying to make up with you, but that's separate from my parents. He has a direct commission from the Emperor to prosecute this case, and you can't say no to the Emperor. Not if you want to stay the top prosecutor in the Commonwealth."

"I understand, dude," I begin, thinking of what to say next. "But—"

"Promise me, dude." Grady looks straight at me.

"Promise you what?"

"Promise me you won't go talk to him."

Wow. It was one thing to tell me he doesn't approve, but to ask me to promise him not to do it? He just thickened the air around all of us to the point where none of us seem to want to breathe in too deeply. No one wants to fight over this, but that hasn't helped ease the tension in the room.

One look at his adamant face, and I know more words won't convince him to change his mind. Kayley must realize it, too, because she's keeping her mouth shut and sliding closer to me. I'll take that as a silent message that she's still on my side about this.

"Okay." I sigh and nod in agreement. "I won't talk to him."

Grady lets out the breath he was holding and smiles.

"Thanks, dude. I knew I could count on you," he says, standing. "Now, if you guys don't mind, I'm beat. It's been a long couple of days."

He shuffles off, with Afton and Parrish waving their goodnights to us as well. While I think that's a little odd, I'm relieved. Having them hang around after that tense moment would just be awkward. We all need a moment to cool off before we can return to our normal selves.

Doc Elizabeth is still here, though. I think she was silently on our side, and when she walks over to us, that idea is confirmed.

"If the two of you still think that talking to Rance's father is the right thing. I'm behind you," she says. "It might have occurred to you that breaking your promise would be best."

I glance at Kayley, and her smile is enough to let me know where her thoughts are. I feel a small surge of energy run through me as I choose a path that could cost me a friendship...but it could be the only way to clear Grady's parents. I grin up at the doc.

"Yes. It did occur to me."

Twenty-nine

"Arrival is imminent," Original Teddy says, hopping out of the shuttle's front cabin and into the main one where Kayley and I are sitting.

"Thanks, Teddy," Kayley says, reaching over and patting him on his head. Original Teddy bounces in happiness and makes circles with his pupils.

It's becoming apparent to me how absolutely valuable being a Teddy can be. While neither Kayley nor I will grow copious amounts of fuzz anytime soon, the fact that the Teddys see us as their own has made it so easy to get their help whenever we need it. I wonder if the nanobots that I got from Doc Elizabeth for my leg are any sort of help in that regard. I certainly haven't had much trouble talking to Captain Teddy about our needs for this most recent escapade.

So Kayley and I ride the shuttle down to the surface in near luxury with Original Teddy, Original Blue Buddy—I'm going to call him BB One from now on—and the three other blue buds who have joined us. They'll just have to be BB Two, BB Three, and BB Four. It'll be tough to tell them apart, so I'll need to observe them for differences.

"Preparation for departure is recommended. Heave to."

"We stand once the ride stops, Teddy," I say with a smirk. He gets it—Original Teddy has been around us long enough to figure out our colloquial nonsense. In fact, he's obsessed with Empire Common idioms. I have no idea why, but I know I need to keep my patience when I'm around him. He's still learning how to use them.

As promised, the shuttle touches down at the local port. Kayley, Original Teddy, and I grab the nearest taxi and take the short ride to my father's office. We're going to position ourselves in an obscure spot across the street so when he comes out we'll be able to tail him until we find the best spot to have a conversation.

"Do you know what you want to say?" Kayley asks as we duck into a recessed doorway.

"Yeah, I think so," I reply.

"Rehearse it. You may only get one shot at this, and if you stumble over your words..."

"When have I ever done that?"

"Do I need to actually respond to that question?"

"Okay, fine." I try to put the words right in my head, but I keep losing my train of thought as I watch for my father to come out. Then when I try to pull my focus back, my mind floats away again with other concerns. How will my father respond? Can I trust him? Or...was bringing Original Teddy with us a complete contradiction in remaining inconspicuous?

"Predecessor is observed," Original Teddy says. "Kick out the jams."

"Teddy, you see him?" I forget about everything I was just attempting to accomplish and focus my gaze across the street.

"There he is!" Kayley points with her arm fully extended, further lowering the possibility of staying out of sight. At least we spotted him when he came out.

"Okay, he's going to cross the street," I say, creeping out of the doorway. "I bet he's going to get a taxi. Maybe we can grab him while he's waiting at the stand."

Like a marching band dragging a parade float behind it, we power across the street, not waiting to get the walk signal. A truck that's going a little too fast blasts a warning at us when he nearly runs us over. So much for low-key.

I call it right—my father is walking to the taxi stand just around the corner of the street he's on. We're just behind, keeping to the edges of the buildings along the block. He won't see us, but we're not exactly experts in stealth.

"What are you doing?" an elderly woman asks, her eyes narrowing at me.

"Uh...playing a game?" I shrug, and she continues on her way but stops to glare back at me before heading off.

"Maybe it'd be better if we didn't try to hide?" Kayley suggests. I throw my hands up and continue on after my father.

As expected, he gets in line at the taxi stand, and we do the same, careful to keep a few people between him and us. He's lost in thought, so I doubt he'd notice us anyway, even though everyone else does. They're mostly glancing at Original Teddy, but—a side benefit—they're keeping a respectful distance from him. Even the woman in line behind us is a few strides away.

My father's Sergo chimes and he picks it up. I step out of line and walk up just behind him to see if I can eavesdrop on his call. Who knows? I could overhear something that might be useful.

"Cecelia," my father says, and I grit my teeth. Why did it have to be her? "Yes...yes...right. The Tongjian Hotel? Yes, I know where it is. Sure...yes, I'm on my way. See you soon."

Shoot. That's even worse. There's no way we can talk to my father about Cecelia when Cecelia is standing right there! I slide back to Kayley and tell her the bad news.

"Shoot," Kayley says, scrunching up her mouth. "We have to grab him before he gets there."

"Then let's get him now!"

I turn to do just that, only to see my father hop into the taxi. He adjusts his coat and glances out the window as the taxi pulls away.

"Look away!" Kayley hisses and spins. I grab Original Teddy and pull him out of the line. Hopefully his pink fur will be hidden from view by everyone's legs.

"Do you think he saw us?" I ask my fuzzy buddy.

"Unlikely," Original Teddy says. "Well done."

"Now what?" says Kayley.

"We know where he's going, right?"

She nods.

"Do you know where it is?"

"Sort of. I've never been there before." She reaches into her pocket to pull out her Sergo.

Original Teddy suddenly rattles off a bunch of numbers, then repeats them again in the same sequence. Kayley frowns at me, but as he does it again, I get the sense that they mean something familiar. Kayley catches on, too, and a second later we both figure it out.

"Coordinates!" we shout together, disturbing the line of taxi-goers. She flicks open her Sergo and plots in the numbers. I peer over her shoulder as the map comes up.

"About ten minutes by taxi...that means it'll take us like twice that by foot." I glance at the growing line of taxi-takers and calculate our wait—not good. It's rush hour, and available vehicles are growing more scarce by the second.

"Look at the traffic," Kayley says. "It's going to take him more than ten minutes. Maybe we can beat him there if we run."

"Us? Run?" I shake my head. "Not that far or for that long...we'd collapse less than halfway there!"

"You and Grady made it to my place running from his house, remember?"

"Yeah, that's because the world was exploding around us! And Afton carried me some of the way."

We're wasting time standing around debating this. My father could grow impatient and request the system choose another route, erasing any gain we just made because of the vehicle congestion downtown.

"Alternative is recommended," Original Teddy says.

"Yeah, got you on that, Teddy, but what alternative? It's not like we can fly."

"That is not accurate."

"What does that mean, Teddy?" Kayley peers at him, her forehead wrinkling.

"Giddy-up!" Original Teddy takes off down the block and darts into a building. It's a few seconds before Kayley and I can react and follow. Once we enter the building, already breathless, we spot him at the door for the elevator. He spots us and taps the call button with a tentacle.

"Teddy, where are you going? We don't have time for this!"

"That is not accurate. Acceleration of time is imminent."

I sigh and follow him into the elevator. He taps the button for the top floor, and Kayley and I spend the next minute pacing around the elevator car. The moment the doors open, he bursts out and hits the stairs that go to the roof.

"What is he doing?" Kayley growls.

We break out onto the roof and look around. It's familiar, but there's nothing really special about it. Antennas crowd around the center mast while various pipes and conduits make their way to and from the massive cooling unit on the far side. Teddy bounces around the corner of the stairwell house, and we follow.

Then I see it, even though I don't believe it. It's the glider from when my father and I saved that man. I remember just how precarious that situation was, and I can't believe I'm considering strapping myself into that thing just so I can beat my dad through traffic.

"Teddy, how did you know this was here?" Kayley asks, even though she knows the answer already. So do I. One of our fuzzy buddies must have spotted it when the shuttle was landing and loaded it up to Teddynet for future reference. As it turns out, it was a good call.

"Hang twelve," Original Teddy says and lifts the entire contraption up by the control bar on the bottom.

"Oh, absolutely not!" Kayley says. "Teddy, do you even have any idea how to control that thing?"

"It'll be okay," I say, taking her hand and walking her over to it. "He can do it."

I don't know why I say that, but it's a feeling I get. Original Teddy's got the ability to make the glider soar, and it's not the first time he's been on one. I wonder briefly if the Teddys have them on their home planet, but Original Teddy has never been to his home planet...are we making a terrible decision here? Are the three of us about to become pancakes on the sidewalk eighty floors down?

"Rance, you can't be okay with this!" Kayley's protesting, but she's not stopping me from strapping her in. I'm amazed that I even know how to do it. She blinks at me, watching me bind us to this soaring frame of death.

"We've got no choice," I say, taking hold of the bar and walking to the side of the building. Original Teddy squats on the ledge, the claws on his feet digging in. I follow suit as best I can and prepare to push us off. Before it happens, I get a glimpse of the ground far below, and I have to catch my breath. It's a really long way to drop if this thing doesn't fly.

"Yes, we totally do!" Kayley shouts and peers over the edge, eyes wide. "We can absolutely choose not to do this!"

And then we're airborne. The raucous sounds of the city fade away, and all I can hear—other than Kayley screaming—is the rush of air past my ears. I feel the wind in my hair, and for a moment, life is suspended around us. Any sense of fear I had disappears, and I begin to enjoy soaring through the canyon of buildings.

Kayley realizes that we're not plummeting and her panic subsides. I glance over at her and see a hesitant smile appear on her face. Then Original Teddy banks hard, and she yelps, but then grins and laughs at herself. We lock eyes and share a moment of pure exhilaration.

But it doesn't last.

"Preparations for abandonment," Original Teddy suddenly says.

"What? Don't you mean land?"

"That is not accurate...unfortunately."

"Rance!" Kayley shouts. "We're going to crash into those bushes!"

We make our best effort to slow our descent, flaring the tip of the glider at the last possible moment, but our feet catch the top of the hedge, and the front of the glider swings back down faster than we were prepared for. It's a good thing the harness is as tough as it is. Otherwise we'd be grated carrots.

As I try to free myself from the now-collapsed frame, there's a commotion forming around us. The voices are full of confusion and worry, and I think there's some debate about whether someone should come in to save us. It's disappointing if you ask me. My buds and I would have dived right in and pulled out anyone who needed help.

The edge of the sail lifts up, and a pair of men duck under, looking for someone to rescue—finally. It doesn't strike me as odd at all that one of those men is my father. Original Teddy got us to the right place, and just in time, too.

"Rance?" My father blinks.

"Hey, Dad, uh...I need to talk to you."

Thirty

"Rance, I've had many people petition me for a conversation, but that was the most bizarre out of any of them." My father helps Kayley detach herself from the bushes and gets her to sit down on the grass next to our crash site. "Why didn't you just call me?"

"Because it's kind of confidential."

"Rance." My father gestures to the collapsed glider. "This...method of reaching me is hardly confidential." He takes a closer look at what's left of our flying transport, his forehead wrinkling. "Is this...did you..."

"No...it's not it. It's a totally different one," I reply, hoping he doesn't clue into the fact that it actually *is* the very same glider.

The small crowd that surrounded us disperses now that they've realized there's no carnage to get some vid of. I'm sure they're all disappointed they won't be on Angel-1 tonight with their award-winning coverage of what was essentially a large paper airplane coming down to do some hedge trimming.

"Well," I say, "we were trying to get to you before you met with Cecelia because it concerns her."

"You mean, Ms. Nilsson-Lim?"

"You called her by her first name before," Kayley comments. My father's face gets a little red, but he dismisses this with a jerky wave of his hand. I'm glad he's too embarrassed to make the connection between his phone call earlier and Kayley's comment.

"Yes, well...what was your rush?" He opens his hands and shrugs. "She won't be here for another twenty minutes. I was going to wait for her in the bar."

My eyes slide over to Kayley to catch her expected angry stare focused right at me. She flips a few strands of hair out of her face and folds her arms.

I can't blame her for being annoyed, but hey, how was I supposed to know that little detail?

"Alright, so...does that mean you have a few minutes?"

"It does." He looks around and points out a bench in a secluded grotto. "Since you were hoping to keep it confidential, let's have a seat over there, and then you can come back and clean up your...transportation. Hopefully the hotel won't want to make you pay for the damage to the hedge."

The hotel will be lucky if I don't make *them* pay for the damage to my face. I hope Kayley's not hurt. It didn't look like it, and I think Original Teddy—

Wait a minute, where did he go? Is he alright? I turn to Kayley and mouth his name, and she nods and goes to find him. I think she would prefer to do that anyway, but that means I'm one-on-one with my father, and that's going to make my job all that much harder.

"So you're alright, then?" My father glances at me as he sits at one end of the bench. I wouldn't say it's a concerned look, but it's not completely unconcerned, either.

"Fine. We've done that kind of thing before." That's not an outright lie, but it is bending the truth a bit.

"You have?"

"Sure."

My father gives a quick shake of his head and rubs his jaw. I'd like to tell him just how much he doesn't know about his son, but I'll have to save that for another time. If there is another time.

"So what's this about Ms. Nilsson-Lim?" My father asks.

"She's crooked, Dad. I think she's trying to frame Grady's...I mean my friend Mutsumaji's parents, so that she can steal their technology."

"That's quite the accusation, Rance. I doubt this is just speculation, coming from you. What proof do you have?"

"First, we decide motive, don't we?"

"Very good." My father nods a few times. "I'm glad you haven't forgotten what I've taught you."

Oh, Dad. When it comes to you, there is very little I've forgotten and a space freighter's worth of stuff I'm dying to forget. But I'll ignore this for the moment if it gets my father to pay attention and listen to me. And if he then decides to arrest Cecelia, all the hard memories will be worth it.

"Jinse Shaloo may be a subcontractor for the Empire, but I think what she really wants is to be the principal supplier. Consider this—her company is one of only two capable of building the designs that the Sugiyamas create.

The other is already owned by the Emperor, so they'll only do what he commands. Then, consider her testimony, and then her total trashing of my friend's parents on every broadcast she could get herself on."

"Wait a moment, Rance. Cecelia's testimony was rehearsed. That is a completely normal procedure in court."

"What about her interviews on Angel-1, 3, 4, *and* 7?"

"She didn't discuss the case, so there's nothing wrong with that."

"She's trying to turn public opinion against them!"

"Now *that* is just speculation, son."

"Well, there's more...and it's not speculation."

I stand up and face him. My father glances up, but his face remains passive. I have to give him credit for picking up some serious skills on his way up to the top. This could turn out to be more difficult than I expected, but I'm still going to play the wounded-son-in-need-of-his-father card. It could work...actually, it has to.

My father's forehead wrinkles as I open the buttons on my shirt. When his eyes go wide when he sees all of the cuts and bruises across my torso, I know my little stunt has served its purpose. He takes a slow inhale and leans back on the bench.

"What happened?"

"Cecilia Nilsson-Lim's bodyguards happened...on order from her! They strung us up, Dad...Kayley and me both! She even slapped Kayley across the face!"

I'll leave out the part where we snuck into her house looking for evidence and also neglect to mention that she was after us because we had stolen something from her. He may yet find that out if he questions her, but if I can at least put doubt in his mind that she's not the puritan he may think she is, then breaking Grady's promise will be well worth it.

"Rance...that is a very serious allegation, and it makes your little stunt back there with the..."

"Glider."

"Glider all that more curious, but how do you intend to prove any of this?"

"Well, I'm hoping that you'll just believe your own son."

My father tightens his jaw and narrows his eyes. I didn't mean for my words to come out like that, but they just kinda did. His question struck me as a bit insulting, and once my blood got fired up, I wasn't going to just stand there and take it.

For a long moment, we just stare at each other. It's a face-off unlike I've ever had. My father wasn't around for my rebellious teenage years, and my mom didn't put up with my nonsense, so I never experienced this. To be honest, it's not what I had expected. Going by the cines I've seen where something like this happens, he should just sympathize with me and that should be that.

"Rance, I have no idea who did that to you, and if indeed it was someone else, then I'm sorry for that, but I've also taught you better. You can't simply make an accusation without proof, son! And the fact that the woman you're accusing is a key witness in a very serious trial doesn't work in your favor. You want to talk about motive? I see a very obvious one. You could want to blame her for something you could have done to yourself."

I take a step back, closing my shirt, suddenly feeling ashamed for having tried. A knot forms in my stomach, and I wonder just why I ever thought he would take my side. I might be his offspring, but once he was out the door, I ceased to be his son. But I try one more time.

"Are you really going to take that line? I come to you in confidence, and you don't even consider for a minute that I could be telling the truth?"

"Son." He puts out a heavy sigh and opens a hand to me. "That's not what I think at all. You have to understand—"

"Oh, I understand, alright. I understand that you'd rather protect your own self-interests than consider that your star witness might not be as reliable as you think she is."

"Now, just wait a second, Rance!" My father's hands tighten into fists, and he leans forward, a scowl on his face. "I don't at all appreciate your assumptions here! I am taking time out of my busy schedule to listen to you, and all you can do is try to blame me for playing sides? I really don't need to sit here and take this from you."

I should have expected this. He always chose himself over his family. If believing me means he might have to withdraw the charges and lose face, then he will never choose that. I should have realized it, and instead I get a laser beam through my heart.

"If you were really my father, you would!"

"Rance, I am your father." His aggressive stance collapses, and he leans back on the bench again, my point scored. I don't regret it, but I'm not celebrating, either. "I have always been your father."

"Well then," I say, ready to go in for the winning point. I won't hold back anymore. I need to know if he's going to choose me over her...or not. "If that's really true, you'll say, right here and now, that you believe me, no matter what...that you're on my side, and that you'll believe what your own son is telling you over some greedy executive!"

When his mouth closes, and his lips press together, I know his answer, and it's not the one I want. But it's my fault. I pushed him into this position. Again, my desire to get something from him has gone astray. Now I know. I should never expect anything from him, ever again.

"You know I can't do that, and I'm disappointed that you used an ultimatum to force my decision." He stands and adjusts his jacket. "I really expected more out of you, Rance, but I see your mother didn't maintain the proper level of discipline with you as she should have."

"You leave her out of this! Don't you know how much she suffered because of you?"

"Unfortunately, I do, son." He walks from the grotto but pauses and turns back. "As you requested, I'll keep this conversation between us, but don't come to me with anything else like this."

Kayley enters just as my father leaves. The moment she spots me she runs over.

"What happened?" she asks, her voice full of anxiety. I must look completely miserable.

"I shouldn't have bothered. I shouldn't have gotten my hopes up."

"But we didn't know—"

"I don't mean just today, KayKay," I say, my voice falling. "I shouldn't have hoped he'd be different...he's not. My father is the same selfish bastard that he's always been."

Thirty-one

My mom was so amazingly generous to cook breakfast for Grady this morning. Like always, she made his favorite: rice porridge with chives, goji berries, and—for a change—mushrooms. He not only dug in before anyone else, he asked for a second helping without batting an eye. My mom grinned and slid back into the kitchen faster than I've seen her move in five years.

Mom would have cooked for everyone and enjoyed it, now that she's got Parrish as her sous chef, but everyone, save Grady, spent the night in their own homes. Afton's dad came back, so she went, unable to resist that pull. And Parrish apologized, saying his mom needed his help with something.

I think Kayley expressed it best when she told me she just wanted to give her parents a big hug because she missed them. That wouldn't be such a hard thing to do if they weren't out of the house as much as they are. I guess she had to take advantage of the moment.

As I help her clean up, I give my mom a hug, too. She seems surprised. Hugging is not all that common between us. There's a definite time for it, and I'd have to say this is one of those times.

"Come on now, Rance," my mom says, "breakfast wasn't that good."

"Grady seems to think otherwise."

She throws a quick glance over to Grady at the table. He's scraping the last bits of porridge from his bowl and paying no attention to us whatsoever. That's fine. I'm glad he can distract himself with something other than his parents' trial. It ends today, and that's got to a be tough way to start the morning.

"Uh, thanks as always, Mrs. He'. It was amazing as ever." Grady bows until his head is parallel with the floor. My mother brushes it off with a "pish" and pulls him back up.

"Go, clean yourself up." My mother pushes him gently towards the guest bedroom. Since no one else stayed last night, he had the best bed in the house all to himself. I doubt he got much use out of it.

Grady bows again but only gets down to a minimal angle before my mom threatens to swat him with her stir-fry spoon. I chuckle as I watch their interaction. Grady is the closest thing I've ever had to a brother, and my mom wouldn't argue one bit if he asked her to adopt him. I wouldn't mind that, either.

"Mom." I wait for Grady to be out of earshot before I continue. "I saw my father last night."

"Oh?" She pretends not to be interested and keeps wiping down the table.

"Yeah...I needed to tell him something."

If I expected my confession to break her away from her task with some level of shock spreading across her face, then I should be severely disappointed. Maybe she has no level of interest in knowing anything new about him, but I'm going to keep sharing because I think it's the right thing to do.

"I was trying to help Grady's parents out by telling him his star witness was a gangster."

"And how did that turn out?"

"Not well...he blamed you for not disciplining me properly."

That gets a reaction. She tosses the rag back on the sink and turns to me, leaning on the edge of the counter. Now I know she's ready to listen.

"That was only after I gave him a piece of my mind for being a jerk...not that you don't know that already. But I really thought he'd see reason when I presented him with my story."

"Did you have any evidence to show him?"

"Of course!" I pause. My mom hasn't seen the bruises on my body, and I only started walking without a limp this morning. She was already asleep when we came in last night, so she wouldn't have noticed then, either. I don't want her to worry, so I think I'll just not mention it.

"And?"

"And he didn't believe me!"

"Well, did you really expect him to?"

"Yes! He—"

I stare at my mom for a moment as she waits for me to finish my sentence. When I don't, she just goes back to arranging the cookware back on their hangers. I don't get it— her nonchalance about my story is making me feel awkward. My mom hasn't forgiven him for what happened. Not in the slightest. And now, as I tell her about his poor reception of my petition for help, she doesn't seem to care.

My father even called into question her parenting skills, and she said nothing! My mom is rightly proud that she raised me by herself for the last seven years. For anyone, especially my father, to accuse her of being a negligent parent should get them chased from here to the next continent, with her heavy cleaver—the one she uses to chop branches off trees—in her hand.

"Mom...why are you taking this so calmly?"

"Because you're not a child anymore, Rance. You can take care of yourself."

"Is that why you weren't shocked when you heard he wanted to talk to me the first time?"

"That's right." She nods. "You have a right to talk to him. He *is* still your father."

"But, Mom, you were so upset when he left! I remember you cursing him...several times."

My mom shrugs, and I'm more confused than before. She really doesn't seem to care, and I just can't believe that. If I can't even look at my father right now, she's got to be building up one heck of an explosion inside her. How she's holding it in is beyond my understanding of the universe.

"Was there more you wanted to tell me about meeting your father?"

"No, not really." I shake my head. "It ended just how you might expect."

"I see." She turns her focus back to her cleaning.

I'm at a loss as to how I can continue this conversation, but then I notice something odd. She's cleaning the same thing she just cleaned five seconds ago. My mom likes her kitchen clean, but that's beyond scope, even for her.

"Okay, Mom, what's up?"

She turns to me, a failed attempt at innocence betraying whatever she's trying to hide from me. We face off, her insistence of nothing to mention faltering. Perspiration forms on my forehead, and my chest gets heavy. I'm not really sure I want to hear what's she hiding anymore.

"Fine," she says, standing straight and folding her arms in front of her. "But you need to understand something first. What I did, I did for you and your future."

"What did you do, Mom?"

"It's not what I did. It's what I've been doing."

"Which is?"

"Rance." She sighs, and for a second, she reminds me of myself. "You father contacted me not long after he left. He realized he had left us with no source of income and wanted to help by sending us money when he could."

"And you accepted?"

"Yes, Rance. I hid away my pride so you could have a place to sleep and food to eat. He still sends money, even though I told him to stop. I guess he thinks sending money means he's still taking care of us. I knew about the case before it happened, too. He felt he needed to tell me."

Words fail me. My mom sacrificing her dignity so that we could survive? My dad still trying to be a part of our family even after walking away from us? I have no idea how to feel about any of it. I can't blame my mom, and I can't forgive my father. It's like I'm stuck inside some extra dimension where time doesn't exist, but reality is still there, smacking me in the face.

"Have you talked to him since the trial started?"

"No."

I guess I couldn't be angry at her if she did. She only ever wanted the best for me. I give her an apologetic smile, and for a record-breaking second time today, I open my arms and wrap them around her.

"What's this for?" she asks, hugging me back.

"It's for...everything, Mom. Just...thank you."

Thirty-two

"WE'LL SEE YOU THERE in a few," I say to Kayley and then disconnect, pocketing my Sergo in my jacket.

We're meeting everyone else outside the courthouse and then going in together. We're a team and we're going to support each other as much as we can. None of us knows what the outcome of the trial will be, but we are going to handle it together.

"They're on their way?" Grady asks, adjusting his shirt collar. He's decided that today will be the day that he dresses up. I guess he's trying to show his parents that he's okay so that they won't worry. Maybe it's kind of an apology to them, too, for walking out on them the other day.

I give him a thumbs-up and a nod. He curls the side of his mouth up and raises his eyebrows. I know that he's a full-on earthquake inside, but he's doing his best to make himself look like a placid lake. It's working...mostly.

We head across the street from my house to get to the taxi stand. There's a vehicle coming, but in the middle of the morning rush, it's going to take a few minutes before we can get one. Not much of an issue, really. We were up way early just for this reason.

"How are you feeling?" I ask. I already know, of course, but I'm just trying to pass the time.

"Horrible." Grady stares out into nowhere.

Yeah, I should have chosen a different question. In fact, I think I'll do that now. I turn to him, putting a smile on my face. It's as fake as you can get, trying to stay positive for your bud and not feeling that way yourself. He's not even looking at me, so I'm not sure why I'm doing it.

"Oh, I meant to ask you, dude...how's your engine design coming along?"

"You know it's finished. I told you that already."

Shoot...two for two.

"Yeah, you did…that must have gotten knocked out of my head when that branch hit it last night."

Grady swivels towards me, an eyebrow raised. I realize he's going to ask what happened, and then I'll have to make something up. I can't exactly tell him it happened when I met my dad because I promised him I wouldn't do that.

"What happened?"

And there it is.

"Oh, well, Kayley and I went for a walk last night, and she was just, you know, looking amazing as always. So I stared for a little too long and wound up walking into a tree."

"You did not." Grady snickers and grins, then shakes his head a little. I feign embarrassment as best I can, but I can't just force the red to come to my cheeks. "You are so hopeless around her, dude."

"I totally did!" I play it up by miming a reenactment of the scene that never actually happened.

"Wait a minute…" A frown comes to his face. "Kayley was home last night! And I came back to your house with you!"

"Well, this was before that." My heart beats faster, and I think Grady knows it, too. He must see the pulse of it because right now, it's in my throat. He leans in towards me, narrowing his eyes and examining my face for signs of something. Like how my story is completely fabricated.

"Where did you go?"

"Just to the park."

"Which park?"

"*Our* park."

"How'd you get there?"

"We took a taxi."

"How much did it cost?"

I've never taken a taxi to our town's park. There's no need. It's only about a twenty-minute walk, and all of us have done it a thousand times. But I said it, and now I'm trapped. The only thing I can do is come up with another lie, and that's really asking for trouble. In the meantime, I still have to come up with a price for the taxi ride or backtrack, and neither is a good option.

"Wait, sorry, dude…we didn't take a taxi. I was thinking about another time."

Our taxi arrives just before Grady opens his mouth to admonish me for lying to him. Instead, he turns and hops in, taking the far corner. I take the near one and stare out the window, hoping he'll do the same. If he can get distracted by the scenery as we commute, then he might forget the whole thing, and I can throw my life savings at the nearest temple the moment I can get to one.

Besides, I've well proven today that my mouth is going to get me into trouble anytime I open it.

As we make our way, my plan takes effect. Grady presses his head against the window, staring out at the buildings and houses along our route. They're all nondescript enough to numb the brain into a perfect daydream where the dull browns and grays meld into a lush bath of nothingness. I think that's just what Grady needs now. I'm going to stay silent and hope hi s pseudo-meditation gives him a bit of relief. It might also save me from telling him the truth.

"What route did you take?" Grady asks, catching me by surprise.

"The usual…just up the avenue until you get to that stupid municipal call box, then the left, and the right just after that."

Grady's lack of follow-up is a positive sign that I'm free and clear of having to beg his forgiveness. When he turns back to gaze out the window again, my optimism goes up even higher.

I will tell him the truth, but not now. After the trial is over, and he's got that load of dark matter off his shoulders. Trying to explain it now, when it's doubtful he's thinking clearly, is a sure recipe for a major crisis.

We turn the final corner and get in the queue for drop-off at the courthouse. It's quite a line we've got to wait in, but if I were Grady, I wouldn't be in such a hurry to get there. The chances of the case ending well for his parents is at an all-time low, and my failure to come up with any sort of evidence that proves their innocence is just the final lock on their box of hope.

"Why did you go that way?" Grady asks, still staring out the window. "Kayley doesn't like to go that way. The street is all bumpy at the box, and she always trips. Don't you remember?"

Shoot. I absolutely do remember. I would never go that way with her unless I was carrying her on my back, and there's little chance of Kayley ever allowing me to carry her all the way like that. Ten years ago, maybe, but even back then she would have insisted on walking by herself.

So, now how do I answer? Every time I try to explain, I just bury myself in another layer of dirt. I could try to change the subject, but Grady knows me too well, and he'll catch on the moment the first word comes out of my mouth. It would be great if the taxi would just drop us off now, without my having to request it. Grady would also take that as a sign.

"Not sure, really." I shrug. "I think we were just so into our conversation that we forgot."

Grady swivels away from the window and eyes me. I try to maintain eye contact with him, but I get a little twitch in my shoulders every time I do, and I have to look away. Grady doesn't flinch at all. He's onto something, and when he gets it, I'm going to hate myself.

"What were you talking about?" he asks, his voice even, like a lawyer cross-examining a witness. I hope to get off the witness stand very, very soon.

"The trial. Mostly. We were just hoping that everything turns out okay so you don't have to worry anymore."

"Thanks, but that wasn't it at all, was it? You and Kayley weren't talking about the case at all."

"We were!" That much isn't a lie. It's just who we were talking with that he's going to object to. I glance out the window. We're just a few spaces away from the drop-off. If I can hold out that long, the others will become the diversion that I need.

Grady crunches some possibilities in his head as he stares at me. I can see the electrons firing off between the neurons of that supercharged computer in his head. It's going to spit out an answer soon, and he's not going to like it.

"Rance." Grady narrows his eyes. "You didn't go to the park with Kayley last night, did you?"

My mouth opens to let out words I don't have. I'm stuck trying to figure out how to answer. So far every reply I've made has failed. Maybe it's time for some truth.

"No," I answer in a sullen tone. "We didn't go to the park."

"Then what is it that you don't want to tell me?"

I take a deep breath. How to break it to him? How to tell him I broke a promise because I thought it was the best thing to do for my friend? I don't know if he'll believe that, but I'm out of chances.

The taxi stops and the door slides open. Grady stays put, never moving his gaze from my face. This time I keep my eyes locked on his. No use becoming evasive at this point.

"Alright. I'll tell you, but please remember dude, Kayley and I only want to help you. That's all we ever want."

At first his face softens. I let the side of my mouth curve up to show that I'm sincere, and I am.

A microsecond later, his eyes get hard, and I freeze.

"You went to see your dad!" Grady's fist comes down on the plastic fabric of the bench. The sound is explosive like a firecracker. I jump back, my eyes widening. "You promised me you wouldn't! Why?"

"It's like I said. We were just trying to help. I thought I could—"

"But he turned you down, didn't he? Or you would have told me that already."

I'm suspended between being speechless and wanting to assure him we did our best.

"Grady, all I was thinking about was you and your parents. I know how much they mean to you, and I know you mean everything to them. My dad, on the other hand, might as well disappear from this universe. He's never going to come back and live with my mom and me. But, if I could have used him, just once, so that you could live as a family again, then I had to try. Please try to understand."

Grady swallows as his eyes get watery. I know he's thinking of what I just said and struggling to believe my words. As I watch him, the others appear outside the taxi. They spotted us because we're holding up the line, and they came over to see what was going on. Kayley smiles at me, only to lose her cheerfulness when she sees the look I give her.

"Why? Why, after you promised me!" He shakes his head. "What if you had given him something he could use against them?"

"I didn't. I promise! Please believe me. I would do anything to save your parents!"

"Yeah, but why that, dude? What that? He's the enemy! You could have done anything else."

"This was the best thing! I could have gotten your parents free!" I plead, but Grady doesn't listen.

"It doesn't matter, does it? You broke your promise to me and risked my parents so you could feel good about yourself." He steps out of the cab, glaring at me.

"Come on, it's not like that."

"Yes, it's *exactly* like that."

"Grady, please, let me explain." I move to slide out of the taxi. Grady steps up and blocks my way.

"No! Don't follow me in. In fact, don't come in at all!" And with that, he stomps away. I'm left staring at my confused buds. All except for Kayley, who knows exactly what that was about. Her shoulders drop. She tries to give me an empathetic smile, but the distress in her face forces any upturn of her lips straight down.

I hope I didn't just lose my friend. My best friend.

Thirty-three

THERE'S NO WAY I'M going to stay outside and wait for the trial to be over to find out what happened. Grady may not want me in, but he never said Kayley, Parrish, or Afton couldn't enter. So they—great buds that they are—gave me a screen while I snuck in, squeezing myself into the last bench in the gallery. I can't see much from here, and that's fine. I'd rather not let anyone see me turn into a total mess if this trial ends the wrong way.

"Mr. Moreno," Judge Hamlin says. "You may proceed with your closing statement when you are ready."

"Don't let him speak!" a man shouts from a few rows ahead of me. This sets off a glut of Emperor supporters around him, and Judge Hamlin has to shut them up by threatening to remove them.

"Go ahead, Mr. Moreno."

"Thank you, Your Honor. It will be just a moment." Mr. Moreno picks up his tablet and scrolls through it while he walks to the center of the courtroom. I shift myself up just a little, so I can see a bit better.

"Your Honor," my father says, his voice full of mock annoyance. "Defense continues to delay the people's business. Could we get on with this already?"

"You had your chance to speak already, Mr. Cavalcante. We do things here by the book, so the defense will have their chance to close, even if it takes him another minute to prepare."

Mr. Moreno strolls over to the jury, a pleasant smile opening up his face. Only one woman in the jury box returns it. He pulls out his box of chocolate-covered pretzels and offers the woman one, but she declines. He's unfazed. I'm sure he's not as calm as he looks, but I'm also sure he's got a plan. What I've seen from him so far makes me think that he's been holding back on purpose.

"Ladies and gentlemen of the jury. My fellow citizens of the Empire. We've seen a lot of speculation by the prosecution in this case. However—"

"Objection!"

"Overruled, Mr. Cavalcante! Give the man a chance to speak before you go complaining about his choice of words."

"Thank you, Your Honor." Mr. Moreno adds an extra flourish to his bow, which gets a chuckle from the woman juror. "Now, I personally believe that the prosecution has done their due diligence in providing witness testimony, facts and figures, dates, and all the other assorted nonsense that they need to paint a horrendous image of my clients. However, the one thing they have failed to deliver on is the one thing they actually need to prove their case, and that, my fellow citizens, is real hard evidence."

Mr. Moreno smirks over at the prosecution's table and holds someone's gaze over there for a moment. I'm guessing it's my father but I can't tell, as some tall man in a black suit is blocking my view. When Mr. Moreno is satisfied that he's agitated the appropriate person or persons there, he turns back to the jury, that pleasant smile floating back onto his face.

"So! Let's review the prosecution's points, and I will show you where they need...and lack...the necessary evidence to convict Tadao Sugiyama and Elenora O'Grady-Davies. Shall we begin?"

A few heads in the jury box nod in confirmation. I'm hopeful that means they're coming around to his side. There may be a chance yet.

"Point one—that my fine clients are traitors because they knowingly and willfully stole *their own* designs so that they would not belong to the Emperor." Mr. Moreno opens his arms and shrugs. "Where are these alleged designs? For the entire trial, the prosecution has procured no data related to said designs and has failed to produce the originals or even a copy of them."

"Your Honor! Please!" My father stands. "That's an outright lie! We had a special closed session just to review the data on that memory chip!"

"Mr. Moreno, explain your claim, or you'll have to retract it."

"Of course, Your Honor. Yes, I agree we had a closed session, and I will agree that there was data on that memory chip, but I will also state that no one could confirm the contents of that data. No expert witness, no colleague, and no member of the military with proper security clearance could verify what we all—I'll say that again, *all of us*—could not understand nor agree on what we were seeing, and *that* is in the court record! Therefore, as I correctly stated before, the prosecution does not have evidence to support their claim of treason."

"Objection!"

Shouts burst out from the gallery. Mr. Moreno's name and family get cursed not a few times, and general pandemonium breaks out to the point that they call another pair of court officers in to calm the situation down.

I smile because this is going even better than I would have expected. Grady must be ecstatic. I stretch my neck out to see him, but he's hidden somewhere behind several rows of large men. Only a flash of Kayley's scarlet hair peeks through the rows of dark clothes and gray heads. I wish she'd turn around to look at me, but that'd be a bad idea. Giving any hint that I'm here would risk freaking Grady out, and I don't want that to happen.

"Point two—that Tadao and Elenora attempted to sell off these alleged designs for profit. Yes, so we've heard from a few witnesses. The most important of those, a Cecelia Nilsson-Lim, chairperson of Jinse Shaloo Technology, may have hinted at some kind of financial transaction, but again, where's the evidence? She transferred no funds. They made no unusual purchases. And, where this would certainly be standard in any large exchange of monies, no contract. So then, how could anyone expect to believe this is the case?"

"You're a heretic, Moreno! I hope you meet your end soon!" It's not the same man as before, and the heated remark came from the other side of the aisle. Whoever it was had some genuine outrage in their tone. The court officers scan for the owner of the offending voice but come up empty. One of them slides his hand to his holster, his fingers touching on the release.

"Anyway, shall we continue?" Mr. Moreno does his own quick sweep of the gallery, then spins back to the jury box. "Point three—this point of transgression against the Emperor. Come now, are we really to believe this? After all, my esteemed colleagues in the prosecution spent very little time on this point, mostly, I would say, because there was no way to prove it. Interestingly, the one solid piece of evidence that Mr. Cavalcante and his team actually had—the decree by His Majesty, the Emperor Joris Regis the Fourteenth—they did not even use. Why did they not use it? Because there was nothing my clients did that went against it."

"Are you calling *me* a liar now?" my father spits. "Or are you claiming that His Majesty himself is in the wrong?"

Half the gallery launches to its feet. The roar is so loud that two of the court officers can't even communicate through their headsets. One of them rushes out of the courtroom—maybe going to get backup.

As I jump up on the bench to get a better view, all I see is a mass of raised arms and shaking fists aimed at Mr. Moreno. He's watching the whole thing with a look of amusement that I suspect hides a lot of fear.

"I will have order! Order, I say!" Judge Hamlin isn't even pounding his gavel. He's pounding his fist. There's little response to his command, so he stands and grabs his microphone. "Officers of the court, remove everyone from the gallery at once!"

"Death to Moreno!" a man shouts as he hurdles the railing and charges him, fists raised. There's no one to stop him—the court officers are all in the wrong place. Mr. Moreno throws his hands up to protect himself as the man slams into him, knocking him against the jury box. Both men go down. The attacker stays on top, pummeling the lawyer.

I look for a way to get up there. Impossible. I'm about to get shoved out the door. Two young men from the prosecution bolt towards the attacker. Parrish does too. A few seconds later, they subdue the man, and it's over.

But the damage is done. The last thing I can see before I'm ejected is Parrish and Grady attempting to stop blood from gushing from Mr. Moreno's head.

A few minutes later, Kayley and Afton find me outside, grim looks on their faces. As they approach I give Kayley a questioning glance, and she just shakes her head.

"It's that bad? Mr. Moreno was hurt that badly?"

"Badly enough that they're taking him to the hospital," Afton replies. "He's not going to be able to finish his closing statement."

"Well, sure, he can't finish it today, but the judge will just suspend the proceedings until he can come back, right?"

They just stare back at me. It seems like they're already trying to prepare for a bad outcome to the situation. I was hoping for one of them to agree with me and tell me that this will all turn out to be okay.

"Let me see what I can find out," Afton finally says. I know she's itching to hear some good news, too. She jogs up to the guard at the gate and chats him up. The guard shrugs and points, and the conversation continues from there. I can't believe there's even a possibility that the judge won't postpone this trial.

"So if the judge doesn't stop the proceedings, does that mean Grady's parents don't get the chance to have Mr. Moreno finish his closing statement? Is that even legal? Or fair?" I stare at Kayley and she replies by taking my hand in both of hers, a wistful smile touching her lips.

"Did you really think any part of this trial would truly be fair?"

Thirty-Four

"The judge isn't stopping the trial," Afton says, trying to keep the emotion out of her tone. "He's ruled the defense's closing statement sufficient and 'in the name of public safety' has ordered the jury to immediately begin deliberation. They'll begin the moment it's safe for them to transfer to their room."

"What? That can't be right!" My jaw goes slack, and I wait for her to say it's all a joke, but that never comes. It'd be a poor joke, and too low even for Afton. She's not in much of a humorous mood, anyway. Who would be?

"I checked with those prosecution guys. They confirmed it, too." Afton glances back at them. "If it's any comfort, they didn't like the judge's decision, either."

"Just make sure you guys look after Grady when you get to go back in." I feel the acid in my stomach trying to force its way up as I think of my bud having to endure this. "Actually, where is Grady?" I look around, suddenly getting self-conscious.

"Parrish is with him, trying to get him to eat something." Afton snorts. "That's going to be a challenge. Those two have no taste buds in common at all."

"You guys should go help. That's important. Grady needs to eat. I can wait here."

"No way." Kayley grabs my arm and slides hers around it, locking me to her. "Grady might be mad, but he's going to need all of us if this turns out badly."

"Don't worry. If you stick with us, we'll get you back in. We've got special family passes," Afton says, "Just keep an eye out for the guards when they call the prosecution team back in."

I watch two young men and an older woman chatting in a corner by the security gate—the prosecution team Afton just talked to. They shake their heads and fold their arms in general discomfort with the entire situation. I'm glad to see that even though they work for my father, they're not monsters.

"Who's going to act as their lawyer?" I ask Kayley. I'm looking at her, but my eyes are only seeing a vision of Grady's poor parents pining over Mr. Moreno. He was really killing it with that closing statement.

"You'd know better than me," Kayley replies with a sad shrug. "I guess the court will appoint one for the end of the trial. At least they won't have to do much."

That's the only redeeming fact in this entire disaster. A lawyer who only has to go through the routine procedure to close a trial has no way to damage the defense's case. The court could assign the most junior of public defendants, and the worst they could do is spill their coffee all over their document reader.

Of course, thinking on the positive side of things, if the jury clears them of all the charges, they can just walk free. And for that, all they need is their son to take them home.

"Oh hey, here we go." Afton points at the guard walking over to the prosecution team.

"Wait," I say as Kayley puts a hand on my back and moves me forward, "does that mean the jury completed their deliberation? Wasn't that too quick?"

"Maybe it's something else," Kayley replies, keeping the pressure on my back. "Either way, we should go."

If there's another reason to call us back, I'm all for it. Or if the jury is coming back now, maybe the judge will send them back and tell them to think it over more. That's just hopeful dreaming on my part. I know that Grady's parents admitted they were guilty, as the law sees it. I only wish that the jury knew to take that into account. Wanting to protect humanity from destroying itself must have some meaning. If it doesn't, we're all doomed.

I'm able to get through security with them, but only because the guard remembers me from the times before when I came in with Grady. I have to lie and say I left my family pass in the courtroom when I ran out.

"Go in and see if Grady's in there." I give Kayley a gentle push towards the door. "If he is, you guys go in, and I'll come in after so that he doesn't see me."

"Will you stop being such a wimp?" Afton says, turning on me. "No way he's going to even think about you being there as a bad thing. He's going to have too much on his mind."

"Yeah, but Grady's got a lot of mind to think about things."

Afton considers that for a moment.

"True, but just don't worry about it, okay? You're with us." She grins. "You're a Teddy, too."

Grady and Parrish are there on the bench already, speaking with a small white-haired man in a striped suit. He must be the new lawyer, and with that getup on, he's not a novice. That's good.

"Hey, you found him," Parrish says when he notices the three of us walking up. Grady and the lawyer also glance up, and I stop dead in my tracks, staring back at Grady. He slumps as his eyes dart away.

Then, before I know it, I'm being pushed into the row by both Kayley and Afton. Now I've got no choice but to sit next to Grady. I was planning to sit in the back row again.

At least any potential confrontation between the two of us gets sidelined by introductions with the new lawyer.

"Hello, Shun Juskecwiz. Nice to meet the three of you. I'm here to complete the trial, serving as the public defender for the rest of the trial. Actually, I'm a judge these days, but not to worry, we're all qualified to sit any position in the court. I'm here because, well, they couldn't get anyone else here in time."

"Mr. Juskecwiz, is it normal for a judge to do this?" I ask. "I mean, shouldn't there have been a postponement?"

"Well, if Jimmy...sorry, Judge Hamlin for you...if he thought that the defense had made enough of a convincing statement already, there might not be a need to. I know Janek Moreno well, and he is a talented lawyer. Honestly, if I were the presiding judge here, I might have done the same. The jury coming back quickly could also be a good sign. So"—he glances at Grady before coming back to us—"keep your spirits up. Luck may be on our side."

As if on cue, the court officer announces Judge Hamlin, and we all rise. He takes a long look across the mostly empty courtroom with a somber face, stopping on the defendant's box. He gives Grady's parents a nod as if to apologize to them.

"Be seated."

The courtroom goes from quiet to silent as the handful of people settle into their seats. The only sounds I hear are the soft hiss from the voice amplification system and the whir of the single vid cam in the back of the room. It's a far cry from the anarchy of less than an hour ago.

"Before we begin, I would like to say something about what just occurred." Judge Hamlin checks to make sure we're all paying attention before continuing. "Never, in the entirety of my career, have I ever witnessed something so heinous, so disturbing, and so vile. It is with the deepest regret that I must even discuss this with you.

"Dr. Sugiyama and Dr. O'Grady-Davies, I feel that I owe you an explanation as to why I have decided to continue this trial, despite the appalling thing that just happened here. I made that decision for two reasons. First, I believe that it is absolutely imperative that, as a judge, I must at all times maintain a safe environment for a trial to take place. If we were to postpone this case, we would risk endangering the lives of everyone involved, and I will not take that risk.

"Second, I have a lot of respect for Mr. Moreno...a great deal of respect for his abilities as counsel and a general like for his character. If I, for one second, believed that he had more to say on any point, I would grant a temporary stay of this trial. However—yes, young Mr. Sugiyama, I see the objection in your eyes. Let me finish, please. Mr. Moreno had achieved his objectives, and I personally believe he could not have done better for the defense.

"Now, before we call in the jury, are there any other comments?" Judge Hamlin once again surveys both sides, paying special attention to Grady. My bud stares at the railing in front of his face. He knows there's no putting this trial on hold. The jury has already made their decision, and there is no possibility of changing their minds.

I watch Grady for a moment, wondering if I should reach out to him. A hand on his shoulder, an arm around both? What happens if he rejects my support? Neither one of us wants to make a scene, even if it would only be like the snap of my fingers compared to the explosion that came before.

After a moment of silence, the judge calls the jury in. I watch their faces for some type of hint as to which way they voted, but it's like every one of them is wearing a death mask. Their faces are unmoving, untouched, and it scares me.

"Foreman, has the jury reached a verdict?"

"We have, Your Honor, on all counts." The foreman reaches forward and presses a button on the console in front of him. It must have sent something to the judge because he taps on his screen and reads it. His practiced court face betrays no emotions.

"Very well, you may read your verdict to the court."

"On the first count, unlawful appropriation of Imperial documents. Guilty.

"On the second count, intent to ensconce Imperial documents. Guilty.

"On the third count, transgression against a direct order from the Emperor. Guilty.

"On the fourth and final count, treason against the Empire—"

I feel Grady's shoulder press against mine, and I tense up. This is the most serious charge by far. If the jury found them guilty, they could be executed. Grady couldn't handle that. His suffering would be far too great—my friend would be getting a death sentence right along with his parents. My back gets hot, and my brow sweaty. I feel a sudden need to reach for Kayley's hand, and she's there, squeezing tight.

"Not guilty."

The collective gasp that comes is by far the loudest sound to permeate the courtroom since the near riot earlier. I look over at the prosecution's table to catch their reaction. My father's team nod solemnly to each other—celebrating a job well done without being boastful or disrespectful about it. They even seem a little relieved about that last charge. Perhaps Mr. Moreno had gotten to them, just a little.

My eyes fall on my father then, expecting to see a big grin on his face. I get nothing of the sort. He seems smaller than before, and he fidgets with a stylus with both hands. His focus is on how it winds in and out between his fingers—that's confusing to me. Is he not happy with the verdict? Did he want Grady's parents sentenced to death? Those thoughts fill me with a burning desire to run over to him and smash something heavy over his head. I can't believe I ever thought there was a possibility of getting him back.

"I will now render the sentence," says Judge Hamlin. "Would the defendants please rise?"

Grady's parents struggle to stand upright. His mom helps his father to grab the railing in front of him. Despite that, they each form a brave face and stiffen their backs. They knew this day would come, even when they were considering what to do before. But I know that doesn't make them any less afraid.

"Dr. Tadao Sugiyama and Dr. Elenora O'Grady-Davies, you have heard the verdicts. Each one of these is a very serious crime in and of itself. Despite that, I am not interested in forcing the harshest sentence on you. However, as the law gives a minimum sentence for each one of these crimes against the Empire, I have no choice but to sentence you to fifty years each, to be carried out on Exodus, effective immediately."

"No," Grady whimpers so softly I almost miss it. My heart sinks for my bud, and my need to comfort him beats out my worry over his reaction. I reach out to wrap an arm around him, and he instantly falls into it.

"Grady...I'm so sorry," I say, because I don't know what to say, and I don't expect words to work in a situation like this, anyway.

As I hold Grady in my arms, I glance over to the other side of the courtroom. My father is already on his way out. With no prompt, he turns our way and his eyes connect with mine. A second later, he turns his gaze away and walks out.

"Did you want to talk to him?" Kayley whispers in my ear, her voice hopeful.

"No," I reply. "I *never* want to talk to him again."

Thirty-Five

THE JUDGE WAS CONSIDERATE enough to let Grady talk to his parents before guards took them away. They agreed to let him visit, provided he maintains his grades, promotes his engine design, and takes care of the house. I'm not worried that he'll be up to the challenge. His buds won't let him fail, even if we have to hire a ship full of Teddys to pull it off.

Grady cried like I've never seen him cry before. It was like someone turned on a shower and left it washing over his face for a good twenty minutes. His parents cried, too. Everyone, including a few guards and members of the prosecution who stuck around, did.

But as we exited the courthouse, with no plan on where to go from there, I noticed something different about my best bud. He was walking strong, his shoulders straight, and his chin high. He was even laughing at some of Afton's worst jokes, and she gave him a raised eyebrow after one or two.

"Hey, guys," Grady says, "would you want to stay over tonight? I mean, we'll have the place all to ourselves."

"I'm already staying there." Afton pokes his shoulder. "Or did you already forget?"

"Hey, I could cook for everyone," Parrish suggests. "I've wanted to try out this new recipe for you guys…"

"I'll help," Kayley says, beaming up at him. "I think I need to start stealing recipes from you."

After such a hard day, I'm glad everyone is trying to keep each other's spirits up. We all need some wholesome buddy time tonight, and we'll be watching Grady for any sign of a frown or watery eye to make sure that he doesn't start sinking into the deep end of the pool of misery.

That doesn't explain why everyone is staring at me with eyes dipped deeply in expectation.

"What? I'm going to be there. Don't you—"

My Sergo buzzes, and I pull it from my pocket to see who it is. My mom probably wants to know how many for dinner tonight, or she might want to tell me I'm on my own this evening instead. She's been spending a lot of time with Kayley's mom lately, and Kayley and I are both highly suspicious this means there's some behind-the-scenes parental scheming going on.

When I see the message ID, it's unfamiliar. I flick open the messenger screen to delete it because it's likely just a wrong connection. But then I read the it and realize it's not wrong at all.

Rance He' — I've got something you're going to want to see. Meet me at the Emperor's fountain tonight at 22:00, alone. Make sure you're not followed, or I disappear.

"Is that Mom? I bet she's leaving you stranded tonight, right?" Kayley bounces over to me, all smiles. Then I show her the message. All signs of chipperness disappear from her face. She snatches the Sergo out of my hand and stares at the message again.

The others take notice and stop to watch Kayley as she scrutinizes the message word by word. I explain to Grady, Afton, and Parrish, and their foreheads all wrinkle in unison.

"You know," Parrish says, "I'd just say that was some prank, but we've been through way too much to just dismiss something like that."

"What are you going to do?" Afton asks.

"I'm—"

"Of course he's going to meet this person," Grady says, sounding decisive, "and we're going to back him up."

Four heads turn to stare at Grady. There's a long moment of silence as we try to figure out where this newfound brashness is coming from. Now, Grady can laser-snark like any of us, but he's never this straightforward with the decision-making. That's Kayley's territory, and he just totally invaded.

We look at each other, and there are shrugs all around.

"Well," Parrish says. "I guess I'd better get cooking."

***

The night is cool enough to see our breath in the moist air as we make our way to the park. I'm getting a chill down my back, and not just because of the cold. I was just here to speak with my father. I hadn't been to this park before, and now I've been here twice in a month. If I never have to come here again it'll be too soon.

"See anything?" Grady asks over Teddy comm. I'm glad we've got the Teddys involved in this one. It could be dangerous, or it could be a complete scam. All our lives just became more precious today, so nobody wants to take the risk of being wrong. We'll play it safe this time.

"Not yet." I stuff my hands in my pockets as I pass through the entrance to the park and make my way towards the fountain. As would be expected on a work night, there's only a handful of people enjoying an evening stroll at this hour. I see an old man who's likely retired, a young couple likely on their first date, but so far, no mysterious informer.

"We're not far away, so if you need us, we'll be there in a jiff." Kayley's on her motherly kick, which means she's more worried about this meeting than I am.

"Got it…Teddy, are you in place?"

"Location is acquired."

"Okay, I see someone on the far side of the fountain. I'm going quiet until this is over…or until there's trouble."

The mysterious informer is covered in a long dark cloak. The hood is up, but I can tell by the height it's a woman. Just my luck—mysterious women are bad for my health. Mental and physical. I could be wrong. It might just be a kid, but that I doubt. No kid would have the smarts to work a scam like this, and they definitely wouldn't have anything I want.

Long Dark Cloak turns as I approach—I was right. It's a woman, and I think I may have even seen her somewhere before. As I get closer, it becomes obvious. I know exactly who it is.

"Dr. Cooper-Wake." It's Grady's mom's associate, and she's not happy I just called her by name. She does a quick scan of the area before she grabs my arm and drags me to an isolated corner of the square.

"They could be listening…don't use my name," she hisses.

"We are listening," Grady jokes.

"Gratin is accurate," Original Teddy adds.

I have to bite down on my lip to stop myself from smirking. It helps to keep the sternness on my face, at least. I don't want to burn this connection now that I've made it.

"So, you're the one that sent the text? What is this about?"

"I have something that might help my colleague get released from jail."

"Wait." I feel my eyebrows twitch in confusion. "If you have evidence, why didn't you submit it to Mr. Moreno?"

"Because I didn't think anyone would believe me."

Okay, so if a scientist—who has mastered the scientific method, and could easily create a hypothesis and a means by which to prove it—has something that she thinks is not believable, then I'm all ears. I really hope this is going to be as juicy as I'm building it up to be.

"Well, you asked me here, so why don't you tell me?"

"This morning, while I was at the lab, two goons broke in and threatened me with violence if I didn't give them the engine designs. They also said that if I told anyone, I'd never work for the Empire again."

It *is* juicy! And because the good doctor here is a master of observation, I bet she knows exactly what those goons look like, and I have a feeling I do, too. But why would they do something so audacious like that? There's got to be cameras, security, even other witnesses. Why take the risk? Unless...

"They didn't tell you who they were or where they were from, did they? No identifying marks or tattoos? Anything like that?"

"What are you onto, Rance?" Kayley asks. "Oh! Do you think it could be them?"

"No." Dr. Cooper-Wake shakes her head. "I would have noticed that."

"Then how did they get in?"

"They had security badges and were in proper lab gear. No one would have looked at them twice."

As if she just reminded herself of something, she spins around and glances behind her. Not a second later, she turns back. Boy, she's in a real panic. I'll have to keep her calm, which will be a challenge. My own pulse is racing.

"Not too many people would have the connections, money, or greed to do that," Grady says—I agree. Our pretentious woman in yellow likely had something to do with this.

"Were both men rather muscular to a ridiculous extent? Like they stole their bodies from a bronze statue?"

"Yes, exactly like that!" Dr. Cooper-Wake blinks. "How did you—you mean, you may know who these men are?"

"I think we might have an idea, yes."

"Who? We've got to tell the military! Or some agency! Maybe the Anti-Sedition Action Ministry!"

"No!" I wave both my hands earnestly. "You don't want to talk to them!"

"Maybe we can get Captain Cortell to help us out," Kayley suggests. "I still owe him a call."

"Good idea," I reply and immediately realize my mistake. Dr. Cooper-Wake's eyes go wide, and she backs away, her hands rising to her face.

"Who are you talking to?"

"Nobody, I was just thinking out loud." I put my hands up, too, patting the air in a calming motion, but it doesn't get her to relax. She's already turning her head in a fury to glance at every possible spot some unknown lurker might be hiding.

"Are you with them? Is that why you know who they are?"

"No! Of course not! Grady, I mean, Mutsumaji is my best friend! We want to help his parents, not hurt them!"

"Who is *we*?"

"Oh, now you've done it, dunkelhead," Afton moans.

"Keep your trap shut, Surela!" Grady shouts, loud enough that I'm concerned our alarmed informer has heard it.

"Hey, that's my line!" Kayley complains.

Their little slap-happy back-and-forth distracts me long enough that I miss Dr. Cooper-Wake turning and running. Before she's gone for good, she turns back to throw a sharp finger at me.

"If you're really his friend, you'll get those plans back! Otherwise, I'm reporting this to the Chamberlain himself!"

And then she's gone.

"Well, isn't this an interesting turn of events?" Afton says.

"Yeah," I reply, "but Cecelia isn't going to get away with it, because we know her little secret."

"What's that?" Parrish asks.

"She's in love with my father."

Thirty-six

"WHAT'S YOUR FATHER GOT to do with any of this?" Kayley asks as she leans over the back of the sofa in our new headquarters. We didn't actually have a headquarters before, but Grady's house makes for one heck of a home base. It might be temporary, but it sure is swank.

"Think about it, KayKay. That night, when we went to go beg him for help, he was meeting with Cecelia then, right?"

"True." Kayley purses her lips in thought for a moment before she gets it. "So you're saying that it's not just one-sided. Your dad—"

"Father," I correct, and she rolls her eyes at my interruption.

"Your father also has feelings for her?"

"Exactly, so what if he knew what she was doing and was taking steps to protect her from trouble?"

"A little far-fetched, if you ask me," Doc Elizabeth says, lounging on the sofa across from Kayley. "After all, you said yourself that your father is a highly ambitious man. Surely that means that he wouldn't do anything to jeopardize his position."

Our team is at full strength for this meeting: six humans, three Teddys, and a whole lot of gumption to take down bad guys and free Grady's parents. While we may not achieve that second part, we are full-on determined to accomplish the first. I think the way we do that is to knock my father out of the picture so that Cecelia is an easy target. I know he's got to be protecting her.

"You'd be surprised what love will make you do." I glance at Kayley, and she blows a kiss at me. The rest of the room's humans are likely vomiting in response, but it's been far too long since I've shown her how grateful I am for the blessings in my life.

"I wouldn't be surprised at all," Doc Elizabeth counters, "but what I think you're jumping to conclusions on is if he truly is in love with her. Get that assumption wrong, and you'll find you're in a place difficult to swim back from. If you get my meaning."

I acknowledge her warning, and it's fair enough. But as I think about my last conversation with him, there are a lot of signs that make me think he is. Kayley caught one when my father called her Cecelia. That is a sure sign they're on very familiar terms. Like "I've got a cabinet for your clothes at my place" kind of terms. He walked away from a family he loved. There's no telling what he could be capable of.

"Let's just make that assumption for now," Kayley says, backing me up. "Meaning that Rance's dad—"

"Father."

"Darling, enough already." Kayley sighs. "I understand you want to make the distinction, but could we just get on with this, please?"

"Sure, honey bun." I grin.

"Oh Goddesses, I really think I'm going to lose that great salad that Parrish just made." Afton drops her head back onto the sofa from her position on the floor and feigns illness. She adds to her melodrama by piling her set of jewels onto her face.

"Not in my living room, you don't!" Grady cries, pointing at her.

"Are we all done?" Mother Kayley eyes the gang.

"That is not accurate," Original Teddy comments. "Discussion is not complete."

Kayley presses her lips together and glances up as if she's praying to the Goddess of patience. There isn't one of those, specifically, but I guess you could say that Sophia, Goddess of wisdom, would have a good amount of that. Then again, Kwanon, Goddess of compassion, might be a better pick.

"So," she continues, "as I was saying before our meeting was just taken over by the preschoolers, we should assume that Mr. Cavalcante is protecting her. Why? Because it's less risky to assume that than it is to not. We don't want to be caught unprepared when we go after them."

"And how exactly are we going to do that?" Parrish asks.

We share glances all around—no ideas yet. We need to figure it out quick, though, or else we're going to miss out on any initiative we might have. I put my brain into overdrive to come up with something, but I'm drawing zero octane at the moment.

That is, until Original Teddy speaks up.

"Pictures are invaluable."

"Pictures, Teddy?" Grady frowns and turns to him. "What kind of pictures? Like of those guys robbing Dr. Tipiwai?"

"Dr. who?"

"Oh." Grady blushes a little. "Dr. Cooper-Wake. She's been working with my mom for so long that I always remember her by how she was introduced to me when I was little. My mom always called her by her first name."

"So, yes," Kayley says. "And no. I don't think that photos of the robbery are going to cut it. We need something much more...effective."

"Effective, how?" I ask.

"Effective in that it can push your father out of the way."

I think I just fell in love again. Kayley read my mind and went in the exact direction that I hoped this conversation would go. They say that couples that get so close often take up each other's habits and sayings. In this case, Kayley's got my thinking down as her own...or is it the other way around?

Speaking of falling in love.

"Guys, think about it—what might be a scandal big enough to scare him? Something that he'd just have to walk away from, or risk losing everything he's worked for?" I ask.

"That's easy," Afton replies. "A key witness in a romantic relationship with the head prosecutor in the trial of the century? The gossip shows on Angel-6 would throw a year-long festival with that kind of dirt."

"Got it in one, Surela!" I grin while Afton pouts at my backhanded compliment. "We just get some sharp images of the two of them locking lips...yuck...and we've got him!"

Parrish snaps his fingers the way he used to do when he finished calling a play, and Doc Elizabeth nods, impressed.

"Sounds reasonable," she says. "But how do you plan to get those photos? Surely their romantic escapades are kept well out of the public eye?"

I ponder for a moment. "No way we're getting back into Cecelia's house again, and my father probably has so much security around his apartment building that we'd have to resort to some seriously destructive practices. Wall smashing won't get us the subtlety that we need for a mission like this."

"We need to catch them somewhere that's at least somewhat public, so we could get in, but private enough that they would feel relaxed enough to"—Kayley glances at me, her cheeks reddening—"want to get intimate with each other."

"What if there was a party that the two of them were at?" Grady asks, tapping on his laptop.

"What kind of a party?"

"Like the kind that the mayor is going to throw tomorrow night?"

We all jump to surround Grady's tiny terminal, crunching ourselves together so we can get a peep at his screen. It's a good thing the Teddys are short. They act more like leg warmers than impediments to our vision.

As I read the invite—amazing how my bud just pulled that up—I see that it's some kind of fundraiser for the city. Only the top elite of the city is invited. Which either means my father is Cecelia's guest, or he's making a lot more money than I thought he was.

"Even with a fake invite, it won't be easy to crash that party," I say. "No journalists allowed, and even in a nice suit, I won't look anything like the part."

"I could try to sneak in as a chef," Parrish suggests.

"You could *be* the chef," Kayley says.

"But then you'd be stuck in the kitchen all night," Doc Elizabeth says. "No, you'll need to be a guest."

I fold my arms and pace around the room while the others slump back into their former positions on the sofas. We're onto something here. If only we could figure out how to get in and stay in long enough to get those images.

"We're going to need a distraction," Afton says. I stop to watch her as she dangles her jeweled headpiece above her mouth as if it's a bunch of grapes and she's the crown princess.

Wait a second!

"That's it!" I shout. Everyone snaps their heads towards me, save for Afton, who just glances sideways at me while the biggest jewel of her headpiece rests in between her teeth. "You still have that costume thing? The thing your mom told you to take and then we snuck into your bag?"

"It's not a costume. It's a saree, an ancient and very traditional bit of clothing. I—" Afton frowns and stares at me, the elements of my idea coming together in her brain. The moment it hits her, she waggles a finger at me. "No...no, no, no, no...and no. I am *not* doing that!"

"Yes! That would be perfect!" Parrish's eyes are alight with the idea.

"You might like it, but I don't."

"Afton, let's discuss this," Kayley says, attempting to be the adult in the room. "If you want to take a moment to think about it, that's fine. I can wait."

"Well, you'll be waiting until the next eon, and I'd still say no!"

"Interval is not acceptable," Original Teddy says. "Curtailment is recommended."

I can understand how she doesn't want to wear something that connects her directly to her mother. I wouldn't wear my father's jacket either, even if it fit me. My father's jacket won't get us into this ultra-exclusive party, however. Only Afton, dressed like some wealthy landowner from one of the more exotic planets, is going to be convincing enough to pass muster. All we have to do is persuade her that she's our only hope.

"Afton, be reasonable," Kayley says. "You could be our only hope."

Crackers, she did it again. We're so connected, my girl and I.

"Listen, Afton, if there was another way, we would take it. I swear." I get a little closer, sitting down on the table in front of her.

Afton huffs and rolls her eyes. That's a good sign we're getting to her. Just a bit more gentle prodding will get us there.

I think. Her glare in my direction is not promising.

She says, "You, of all people, should know what it means for me to do what you're asking."

"I do." I nod with as much sincerity as I can—it's not difficult. I really mean what I say. "And I know it won't easy for you, but think of it this way: if we get Grady's parents free, that's how we get back at my dad, and if you use the..."

"Saree."

"Yeah, that...if you use your saree thing to crash a party of the ultra-elite, your mother won't approve, right?"

A small smile appears on Afton's face. "She would totally *not* approve." The smile gets wider.

"So then, this would be how you get back at her, right? But this would be more than that. I know you don't want to call it a costume, but for one night, it would be. It'd be a costume you get to wear, and be whoever you want to be. Your mother's got no say in that. You get to decide. Have some fun, even. Then we get the images we need and you become the hero!"

My heart beats a little faster when she doesn't answer right away. Afton stares for a moment, then glances around, her eyes landing on Grady. There's a small twitch of her lips, and she sighs as she runs a hand through her hair.

"You really think it'll work?" She holds the headpiece up to the light and stares into its sparkling splendor.

"Hey, do you think we'd do this if we weren't sure?" I hold up a hand. "No, never mind, don't answer that."

"We're going to make this work." Kayley comes over to kneel in front of Afton, taking her hand. "You're going to be our beautiful secret weapon. You'll be turning all the heads at the party."

"Hopefully not all of the heads," Afton replies. "I don't want to blow this by getting recognized."

"Don't worry." Doc Elizabeth smiles as she crouches down next to Kayley. "We've got that covered."

I take a quick glance around. We're all nodding and grinning. Even Original Teddy makes a respectable attempt, showing only the non-pointy parts of his teeth.

I'm a bit reluctant to get full-throttle excited about this plan. We still need to be careful, but I'm going to stay positive about the outcome. All we need is a few pictures and we'll be well positioned to make a deal.

Watch out, Dad. Your son is coming for you!

Thirty-seven

I SUCK IN A sharp breath as I pass through the massive carved wood doors leading into the governor's mansion. The building, cut from massive stone blocks, is covered in decorative crystal. The balance between refined and spectacular has been achieved in such a way that I can't help but want to gawk, yet I keep my mouth from falling open. We're on a mission, so the sightseeing will have to wait.

Parrish and I trail the even more refined and spectacular Afton in her maroon and gold-trimmed saree. It starts as a long skirt, pleated in the front, which wraps around and covers across the front of her body to fall over her shoulder. The excess is folded neatly and draped over her arm to create a stunning visage. What really makes the entire outfit is the headpiece—the Matha Patti, as she called it. It tops her head in a net of gold chain. Decorative beads trace her hairline, culminating in one gorgeous ruby in a setting of smaller jewels. I have to keep reminding myself that Afton was attempting to eat that delicate adornment, or I might just get lost in its splendor.

"Do you think anyone's recognized me?" Afton whispers to Parrish and me. We're acting as her two attendants. "Everyone keeps staring."

"That's because you look amazing," Parrish says. "Elizabeth and Kayley really outdid themselves with the makeup."

I'm more concerned that someone, such as my father, will recognize *me*. To counter that, we're donned ancient-looking helms we picked up at a costume shop. They're completely ridiculous, but they complement the phenomenon that is Afton. They're also doing a good job covering our faces enough so we won't get spotted outright. We will get a ton of strange stares, though. Hopefully, our plan has that covered, too.

"I never liked this top," Afton grumbles. "It's too tight, and it's itching my back."

"Stay sharp, you guys, you're about to be announced," Kayley says over Teddy comm. The Teddys brought down a bunch of tech from their ship and set it up in Grady's living room. Now we've got as much ability to see and hear as we did on the ship and then some. Apparently, the nanobots that they injected can tap into my visual cortex as well, so the others can see through my eyes. I was a bit shocked to learn that.

A pair of white-gloved attendants hold up hands and ask for Afton's invitation. She produces her Sergo—which we bedazzled with fake gold leaf—and waves it over a hand terminal that the attendant holds. He observes the unit for a moment and then bows. The other attendant taps a few keys on a wall panel, and a synthetic female voice emanates from the ceiling, gently echoing through the ballroom.

"The Lady Surela Chawla Kalpana of Magnarapax, heiress to the Rama Corporation Trust, bearing her gift of ten million jorin for the Bradbury Children's Association."

A polite round of applause fills the room with quiet respect. As I glance around, I see responses ranging from sincere appreciation to outright sneers. So, that's how it is at a fundraiser like this.

"Afton, don't forget to show gratitude," Kayley orders.

"Oh, right." Afton presses her hands together, fingers up, and bows. At least she's got that part down. I catch a few people try to imitate her motions and fail miserably at it. As long as they believe Afton is the real thing, I could care less what they do.

"Rance, do you see your father yet?"

I scan the room as we make our way to our table—thank goodness it's out of the way. A second later, I spot him next to Cecelia. She's giving Afton the evil eye as she adjusts her trademark canary-colored evening gown. It's a far cry from the outright style and flair of Afton's outfit, which could be why envy is written all over Cecelia's face.

"Got him," I say and pause just long enough so that Kayley and Grady can spot him, too.

"Four bodyguards," Grady says.

"Yeah, and two of them are those goons from the other day. Likely the same two that robbed Dr. Cooper-Wake." As I consider the likely firepower they've got with them, I wonder if we're going to get anywhere near close enough to my father and Cecelia without becoming crispy. The other two have got to be government agents, and without a doubt, they're packing the latest in plasma weaponry.

"Shoot," Afton hisses. "Cecelia's coming over!"

I go all Teddy-popsicle-like as Ms. Nilsson-Lim approaches, along with my father. They've put on the fakest smiles I've ever seen. So, they're not so ready to welcome the young Lady Surela into their elite fold. This should be interesting.

"Lady Kalpana." My father bows with a hand crossed over his chest. Cecelia just stands there and pretends to smile. "As chairman of the Bradbury Children's Association, I wanted to personally thank you for your generous gift."

"I thank *you*, kind sir." Afton's voice is melodious and light. She sounds like one of those cines where two people fall in love while everyone dances and sings around them. It's unexpected, but I'm impressed—I had no idea that Afton had it in her.

My father introduces Cecelia, and she steps forward, a snide smile on her lips. She looks Afton up and down while Afton pretends to be happy to meet her. I guess being an elite is all about how much you can pretend to be nice to someone.

"So this is the little Rama brat," Cecelia says. "How's Daddy?"

I catch my father lose control of his pleasant expression. He does a great job of recovering, but the damage is done. I've got no idea how Afton's going to reply.

"Madam," Afton says, maintaining her sweet tone, "if you know my father, then you must know his light left us last season. I hope you had a chance to pray for his soul's happy journey to its next life. Perhaps you would do us the kindness of an offering in his honor?"

"I'll take credit for that," Grady says. "I did the research so Afton would have some background in her persona. The actual heiress is only twelve years old."

"You may have found the information, but she's the one that memorized it," Kayley adds.

"Maybe." Cecelia turns and waves a hand behind her. "Try not to make a fool of yourself tonight, little Rama."

My father makes a sloppy attempt to cover up for Cecelia. He forces a smile and does an awkward bow before he spins to follow, making a few fast steps to catch up to her as if he was her sidekick.

But then my father does something more in character for him: he grabs Cecelia by the arm and directs her off to the side. Startled, she glances up at him. From what I can see, my father has a strong need to explain something to her. They head towards a set of glass doors that lead out to the balcony.

"Hey, this could be our chance!" I try to keep my voice low. "I don't think anyone else is out there!"

"Parrish, you have the camera?" Kayley asks.

"Yep, I can sneak out after them."

"No, I'll do it!" Afton says.

"You're not sneaking anywhere in that getup," I counter.

"Let Rance do it," Kayley says, overruling the others. "He knows his father best, so he'll be keyed into anything unusual happening. Afton, you and Parrish do what you said we needed...be the distraction. Flirt a little if you want."

"Okay." Afton grins. "Flirting with the rich people. I can do that. Especially if it ruins their evening."

"I'm so glad we made a plan before doing this," I mutter, retrieving the camera from Parrish. He pats me on the shoulder and follows Afton, who's already choosing her first target.

It's tricky getting through the glass doors without being spotted. I check and double-check that no one is watching while still attempting to appear like I'm going out to get a breath of air.

Cecelia and my father are off to one side of the lengthy balcony, so I head in the opposite direction once I'm out. There's enough shadow here for me to keep hidden while I try to capture the incriminating evidence.

As I watch, they gesture wildly at each other, but then after a moment, he turns to her and takes her by her arms. She looks up at him, gazing into his eyes. This is it! I ready the camera and lift the visor to my eyes, zooming in with the lens to get the perfect close-up of their scandalous moment.

They press closer, their arms wrapping around each other's bodies. I try not to consider the fact that I'm about to get a pervert's close-up view of their smooch. Worse than that, I'm going to see my father kiss a woman who isn't my mother. Since my parents are officially divorced, he can, technically. That doesn't mean I have to like it.

"Rance, start taking pictures!" Kayley's voice wakes me from my daymare, and my finger finds the shutter button. The camera vibrates gently, signaling that it's taken an image. I keep my finger on the shutter, taking as many images as the camera has memory for.

"Okay, I think I got it."

"Good, now get Afton and Parrish and get out of there."

I glance one more time at my father and Cecelia making out like a pair of schoolkids out on their first date. I swallow hard as a chill runs down my back. There's no way I ever want to see that again. I despise my father enough as it is. Yet, somewhere deep down, I still want to reconnect with him. Family ties are brutal.

"Parrish." I sidle up to him as he stands stiff as a buttress, like he's holding up the wall he's leaning on. He turns to glance at me and shakes his head. I'm taking that as a message to keep quiet, so I take a spot next to him and press my hands on the wall, leaning against them.

"Where's Afton?"

"Dancing."

"What?" Grady, Kayley, and I say simultaneously.

"Well, you told her to be a diversion, so that's what she's doing."

My eyes slide to the small dance floor, and I catch a handful of the Empire's most powerful, making absolute fools of themselves as a group of musicians perform a light and peppy dance piece. There, in the center of them, spins Afton, arms raised in the air, grinning the largest grin I've seen on her face since she beat me in an arm wrestle. A rotund man with a shiny head adorned with wisps of gray hair attempts to match her athlete's grace while she—literally—dances circles around him.

"Who is that with her?" Kayley asks, seeing through my eyes.

"Uh, I think that's the mayor."

I would be able to hear Kayley and Grady's sighs even without Teddy comm. Of all the people she could have toyed with, the mayor is certainly not the person I would have asked her to choose. Still, she is doing exactly what we asked of her...and having a lifetime of fun doing it.

From the corner of my eye, I notice my father and Cecelia returning to the party. That's just another layer of complication we don't need. The way they were kissing, I would have expected them to stay out there the rest of the evening.

"Hey Afton, party's over. Let's go," I say, taking another worried look in their direction. Her response is to stick her tongue out at me and continue dancing.

Goddesses! Why, at this moment, does she decide that dancing is more important than our mission?

"Kayley..."

"No worries, I'm on it." Kayley clears her throat and prepares to call the retreat. But Afton takes the hint and makes a graceful exit off the dance floor. She beelines right towards me, her eyes intent.

"Wow, that was fun!" Afton exhales contentedly and points a finger at me. "You need to take that lady of yours dancing sometime, buddy boy. I bet she's dying to."

"Uh, sure?"

"Forget that for now," Kayley orders. "Get out of there."

"You got what you need?"

"Yes," I reply as we step into line behind Afton and walk towards the exit.

"Why do you sound so disappointed, then? I totally got back at my mom tonight. She's going to hate the sweat stains I just put on this rag. Didn't you get what you needed to get back at your dad?"

"Yeah, I guess I did."

We're going to free Grady's parents. I wonder why I'm not more excited about that.

Thirty-eight

We make a quick exit and head down the block towards where the Teddys have our chariot awaiting. They tried to rapid prototype a flying car so they could just pick us up at the front door of the mansion. We nixed that idea with little hesitation. Better to stick with what is already working. Luckily, there was a landing pad not far away.

We were very lucky not to get found out. If Cecelia knew more about the Rama family than she did, it would have been over instantly. I'm a little surprised that it wasn't more of a problem getting into the party. I guess the rich and popular don't think the little nobodys that they step on to stay in power can crash their fundraiser.

A police cruiser with its lights on passes us by. I give it a suspicious eye because it's moving slower than it should. It's only when it picks up speed and heads off that I let my breath go. I don't think anyone made us out at the party. All we need right now is to get stopped by the local constabulary, only to be called out by some guest on their way home.

I'm still not sure how we're going to use these images. We never got specific on this small but important detail when we came up with this plan. That's something to work on for future missions, for certain. I see now how impulsive we are about getting things done.

"You three! Stop where you are!" a voice over a loudspeaker roars out behind us. Afton whirls around to look. When she sees whatever's behind us, she spins back around again, eyes wide.

"Imperial agents!" she cries and doubles her pace.

Parrish boosts his own speed to keep up, and the two of them tear down the sidewalk towards our escape. I pound my feet to the pavement, but our athletes extraordinaire are just too quick. Even in heels and a wrap designed to trip her up, Afton's still half a block ahead of me.

To make matters worse, the cruiser has turned around and is making to block our getaway. Parrish hurdles the hood of the vehicle, followed by Afton. She clears it but lands badly, dropping into a tumble.

An officer pops out of the cruiser as I approach. He raises his weapon, aiming right at me. I skid to a stop, spinning on my heel to flee the other way. But I can't. There are three agents behind me, and I'm trapped—again.

I really need to get better at this evading thing.

"Guys, keep running!" I say as quietly as Teddy comm will allow. "They won't touch me if I tell them who I am."

"He's got the camera!" Parrish cries. "And the pictures!"

That's a good point—I do have the camera. I try to think positive, though. Maybe this is just a case of mistaken identity, and even if it's not, I'm the son of the Imperial prosecutor. That's the one good thing my father leaving has brought me.

"Just stay calm, Rance," Kayley says, her own voice betraying her lack of calm. "We'll figure a way to get you free. Just don't do anything dumb."

I raise my hands above my head even before they order me to. One agent comes up with a small device and raises it up to my eye—a bio scanner. Well, they're sure to learn who I am that way. I hope my data still shows I'm Ransom Quigley Cavalcante like it says on my ID.

I really need to get that updated at some point. But right now, I'm glad I didn't.

"Ransom Cavalcante, you're under arrest for trespass and destruction of Imperial property," the one female agent says. "We'll be taking you in for questioning about your friends who just ran away."

"Wait a second, I didn't destroy anything!"

"You want to make it attempted murder?"

I roll my eyes and sigh. These government types are all the same. They always want to show off the leverage they have over you because the law allows it.

"So now you know my name, so you should know that I'm the son of the head prosecutor in this district. That should be enough to let me alone."

The female agent smirks and steps closer as the constable behind me grabs both my arms and swings them back to cuff me.

"Oh, yeah, we know who you are," she says. "Your father is looking forward to speaking with you."

Oh, shoot.

When we arrive at the agents' office, I'm brought up into a room containing a metal table, two chairs and a lot of intimidation. The walls are all metal, and, surprisingly, there's no two-way mirror like I had last time. I wonder if that means they're not planning to record or observe me.

I am glad that the local fuzz is gentler than the Imperial brutes that caught me on the *Mursilis*. Those guys weren't at all appreciative of my high-level governmental connection. Then again, I didn't bring it up to them, either. Not that they would have cared much. They were more than happy to take a few bits out of me.

Even my pat-down wasn't too bad, save for the fact that they took the camera and my Sergo. If they check the images that are on there, I could be in for an awful night.

A few minutes after I'm seated and cuffed to the cold metal chair, my father steps in, still in his ballroom attire. He pauses at the door and glares at me before coming in, slamming the door behind him. He doesn't bother to take the chair on the opposite side of the table. Instead, he steps up beside me and folds his arms.

"I'm only asking you this once, Rance. What were you doing at the governor's mansion tonight?"

"What makes you think I was at the governor's mansion? I don't even know the governor."

"Don't play games, Rance!" His face reddens. "We have your bio scan at the door. You and that girl pretending to be some heiress! What were you there for?"

It crosses my mind to point out to him that he just asked the same question twice when he said he wasn't going to. My father is more heated than I've ever seen him before. There must be some serious stakes at hand if we're getting to him like this.

Which means we were right on target.

"Were you trying to go after Ms. Nilsson-Lim? Is that it? Are you blaming her for the trial?"

"What makes you think that?"

"I know you were at her house, Rance." He jabs a finger at me. "You broke into her house, and then you tried to get yourself out of trouble by trying to set me against her. Why?"

"I didn't do anything like that."

"Do you really think I forgot about our conversation? The one where you crashed your..."

"Glider."

"Yes, that." He paces to the other side of the table, then turns to face me. "You disrupted my meeting and damaged public property, and for what?

To get me to think she was trying to push the Sugiyamas out of the picture. How's that for motive?"

I stare back at him, keeping my face as neutral as possible. But I know there's still plenty of fury on my face, which helps to hide the fact that I'm more than a little scared. My father has never been this angry with me. If I'm putting him in jeopardy, then he may just choose to put me away to protect his own status.

A uniformed officer comes in—with the camera. His face is troubled, and I can guess why that might be. Shoot. Now I've got a problem.

"Sir, you should see this," the officer says as he holds the camera out to my father. His eyes dart over to the officer, and then, with a bit of reluctance, he takes the camera. I hold my breath as he scrolls through the images, looking more and more enraged with every image.

"Thank you, I'll take it from here," my father says, his voice just barely under control. He waits until the officer leaves, then spins on me. "Well, now I know what you were doing at the fundraiser. What do you think you were going to do with this, huh? Do you know what kind of trouble you would cause me if this got out? *Do you?* Or were you so hell-bent to take Ms. Nilsson—*Cecelia* down that you forgot you'd be hurting your father in the process?"

"Rance," Kayley says softly over Teddy comm. "Don't react. That's what he wants. Right now, you're not in legal trouble. Stay calm...I believe in you, darling."

I rescind any thought I had before that filling my body with nanobots was a bad idea. My connection to Kayley is the only thing keeping me from exploding on my father and telling him exactly what we were going to do with those photos. Blackmailing him was a great idea. He'd dump Cecelia in a second if he thought his romance with her would affect his rise to greatness.

"You can count your blessings that I'm the one who has these images and not some minister who thinks they're the moral compass for the Empire." My father shakes his head. "People would kill you for these images, son. Kill you. Without a second thought about it. Do you even understand that?"

I just stare back at him.

"Answer me!" He shouts, and I wince.

"I understand more than you think I do," I say.

"No!" My father hurls the camera into the wall, sending broken bits of plastic rebounding across the room. "No, I don't think you do!"

He shakes his head again and paces around the room.

"You know, when I saw you at the trial that first day, I had some hope that we could become close again. I would have you come work for me, and one day, we could become partners, just like we had agreed to do. But I see your mother's influence has ruined you. You've chosen to go the wrong way, forever erasing any chance for you to become what you should have."

"Stay quiet, Rance!" Kayley hisses.

The last time we met, I was ready to let him go. It would have broken my heart for a long time—my father no longer existing to me as someone I could aspire to. He's gone way beyond that now, and I realize he hasn't been that man that I loved so dearly for a very long time. I could never shed a tear over the man that stands before me.

"Mom hasn't ruined me. She's given me the sense to realize that you're nothing but a selfish bastard. I hate you for leaving us!"

My father presses his lips together and narrows his eyes. Perhaps that means I scored a point or two. Good. He deserves to be hurt for insulting my mother. He deserves much worse than that.

"I'm going to let you go because you're going to promise me you will keep your distance from Cecelia...and yes, I am dating her. Not that I have to explain that to you." He stops in front of me and glares downward. "I am warning you, Rance, if I so much as find you in the same city as her, I'm going to lock you up for the rest of your life on any charge that I see fit, and I will make it stick. Do you hear me?"

I don't even bother to look at him. I don't want his face as it is now burned into my memory. If I can just remember the good times I had with him when I was young, then that's enough for me. He might as well have offed himself the day he walked out because he's definitely dead to me now.

"I need to hear an answer before I let you go."

"You can go to hell."

"I'll take that as a confirmation that you understand." He walks to the door and pauses, but doesn't turn around. "I wish we could have worked together. A shame we won't. Not ever. Goodbye, son."

Thirty-nine

I LEAN MY HEAD back, resting it on the soft cushion of the Teddy shuttle's seat. The cool Teddy-temp air wafting down through the duct onto my face is calming, but try as I might, I can't get comfortable. When I close my eyes and try to relax, I'm confronted by a visage of my father's angry face. Afton and Parrish staring at me and frowning isn't helping, either.

"Guys, I'm sorry, there was nothing I could do. The camera was gone the moment he saw those photos."

"The camera being gone isn't what's bothering us," Parrish says. "Are *you* okay?"

"He's not," Afton replies for me. "But he will be."

I give them both a half smile, hoping to reassure them I'm not about to fall apart, but their frowns remain. They likely know the same thing I do. That the weight of what just happened hasn't really hit me yet. I know it's coming, and when it does, I hope to be somewhere near them. In the meantime, I'll try to hold it off as long as I can. I have a friend who needs more support than I do right now.

"Grady's going to be disappointed," I say. "I hope he understands."

"Grady can hear you," Grady says—right, I forgot. Teddy comm is still on. "And of course I'm disappointed, dude, but not in you. You've been through enough for me already."

"You've been through worse," I reply.

"It's not a contest, Rance," Kayley says. "Even if it was, nobody is trying to win it."

I can't argue with that. Even if she was wrong—which she's not—I couldn't muster the strength to try. I'm desperate to close my eyes, but I don't want to see my father's face again. I've also got Grady's parents digging into the other side of my head, and I know I can't rest until they're free. Not until they're back home.

Then I can pull the sheets over my head and close my eyes for as long as I can stand.

Grady's Sergo chimes, bringing me out of my melancholy. He excuses himself to pick it up, and I hear his footsteps pad away at a brisk pace.

"Hey guys, it's Mr. Moreno," Kayley whispers.

We spend the next few minutes attempting to eavesdrop on his call. Grady must have taken out his Teddy comm earpiece and left it wherever he was sitting. From what we can hear, it sounds like he's moved into the kitchen. He's going to be embarrassed when he realizes he didn't need to do that. It's just his polite upbringing that makes him not want to disturb others with his conversation.

But we're dying to know what's being said.

"Don't worry, I'm moving closer," Kayley whispers, reading our minds. Not like that was hard.

"Yes...yes...I'm sure they will. How—yes, I understand."

We all share anxious glances as we listen in. Grady's voice is shaky, and he's stuttering even more than usual. I lean forward, dipping my head just like Afton and Parrish. It's a reflexive action—it's not like we're going to hear any better doing it. That doesn't stop us from trying.

"Okay...no...no, that's unnecessary, Mr. Moreno. Please, just take care of yourself...yes...yes...thank you. You too."

There's a moment's pause as Grady disconnects. He must have caught Kayley approaching him, and I'm sure he can tell from her face she wants to know what the call was about. Heck, we all do.

"That was Mr. Moreno," Grady says, putting his earpiece back in. "He's doing okay, just a few stitches. His doctor said—"

"Grady," Kayley says in her softest mom's voice. "That's really great that he's healing well. We're all happy about that. Did he say anything else? About your parents, perhaps?"

Grady's "Yeah" is one of the saddest confirmations I've ever heard.

"Dude, what is it?" I get the words out before anyone else does, but I'm sure we're all thinking the same thing.

"Dad's in the prison hospital with some kind of respiratory infection. They don't think it's that serious."

"*That* serious?" I shout. "Grady! That doesn't sound good at all!"

I'm no doctor, but Grady's dad is at the age where stuff like a respiratory infection can get out of control in a matter of hours. Especially one of those new veloxaviruses that I've heard about. If they don't get the antiviral into the patient in a day, that's it.

"Can we visit?" Kayley asks.

"I don't know."

"How could you not know?" Afton's voice is winding up, just like all our nerves. This is a bad development. If Dr. Sugiyama is already getting sick at this early stage of his internment, then the longer he's in there, the higher his chances are of getting deathly ill. Besides that, who knows what else could go wrong?

"Easy, Afton." I reach out to touch her arm, trying to hide my own worry. "We're all on the same page."

"Guys, let's not read too much into this," Kayley warns. "It could just be from the stress of the trial."

"No," Grady corrects, not happily. "My dad has a chronic lung problem. Dirty air irritates it."

"The polluted air of the prison" is what Grady doesn't say. His voice is overloaded with a heavy sense of dread, so I know what he means. He also doesn't add what we're all thinking, that there's now a serious chance that his father could die in prison.

"We've got to get him out of there. We've got to get them both out of there!" Parrish says. It might be obvious, but it spurs us into action.

"Grady, call Mr. Moreno back," Kayley says. "See if the judge will grant a temporary transfer off Exodus to a hospital down planet. He'll get better care there. That's first. It'll give us a chance to come up with a new plan."

"I know what we can do," I say. "We can go get new pictures of my father and his mistress. Then we get Grady's parents out of there for good."

Afton and Parrish look at me, a slight lift to their eyebrows. I return their gaze, trying to have more confidence than I feel. It would solve our problem, even if that means I'm putting myself at severe risk. I'd prefer to find another way, of course, but if we can get it done, that could save Grady's dad.

If only I'd given the camera back to Parrish.

"Let's put that idea aside for now," Kayley says. "Better to not try that again when they'll be looking for it. How about some other ideas, first?"

The three of us share a blank look. I'm not sure I have the brainpower to come up with something new right now. A pillow with my head on it for many hours is what I feel capable of. Even if I wasn't close to collapse, I would still think that getting those photos would be our best bet.

"Guys, I'm okay with sleeping on this and discussing in the morning," Grady says.

"They've still got twenty minutes before they get here," Kayley replies. "We can at least try for that long."

Teddy comm gets quiet, and I imagine Grady's staring blankly at Kayley right now. I'm a bit jealous, actually. What I wouldn't give to just wrap my arms about her and rest my head on her shoulder at this very moment. All of my worries would disappear, if only until I let go. Not that I would want to.

"How about this?" Kayley says. "Let's call Captain Cortell and get his people on it. They'd be willing to spy on Cecelia Nilsson-Lim, I bet. Especially if we tell him we think she's trying to steal from the government."

"Yeah, that's a great idea, but do we really have time for that?" I ask, rubbing the back of my neck. "Let's just get new pictures."

"Rance, no! Are you that excited to get locked up?"

Now I get why she's so against it. Still, that seemed to come out of nowhere. What's Kayley got on her mind?

"Of course not! But we could be short on time!"

"Might not want to put it like that," Afton comments quietly.

"Rance, we mess this up, and not only will Grady's parents be locked up in prison for life, you'll be too!" Kayley's voice breaks. "And I don't want to think about that. You and I are just getting started, Rance. This is just the beginning of *us*, and I want a future with you! I want a future for all of us! Stop trying to throw that away!"

Oh! So *that's* why she's against it. What an idiot I am. I'm trying to look out for my bud and his parents, and I failed to receive Kayley's real message. I'd chalk this up to how tired I am, save for the fact that I always seem to miss stuff like this.

"I'm not—I don't want to throw away what we have. Never!"

But then I realize something. I always want to do so much, end up letting others down because I'm too busy doing something else. I really need to be a perfect partner to Kayley and a best friend to all my buds. I'm burning myself out trying to have a team that can save the people of Angelcanis, the Empire, the Teddys...everyone. I'm drowning in my self-expectation, and no one can throw me a lifeline until I can learn how to swim on my own.

Until just an hour ago, there was still a hope that my father would be a partner in some of that. That dream is gone, now. Not only has he disassociated himself from it, but now he's an obstacle blocking my way. As committed as I am to saving people, I'm realizing that I may need to do the opposite to make it happen. And that conflict, on top of everything else, is what's knocking me down.

My expression must be making Afton and Parrish uncomfortable. They've retreated into their seats, Afton turning sideways and curling up while Parrish slides down, his arms flopping into his lap.

"I don't want to throw away what we have," I repeat, quieter this time. "But what we have is not just each other, KayKay. We've got Grady, Parrish, Afton, my mom, your parents...and Grady's parents. I know you want them free just as much as I do, and—" I catch my breath with a heavy sigh.

"It's okay, Rance...it's okay." My amazing girlfriend suddenly transforms from lost kitten to angel of mercy. "I know it's a lot. We'll talk when you're here. We'll all talk and figure this out. Okay? I just want you to know how much I love you, that's all, and I hope—"

"I do, Kayley. I love you more than anything."

Forty

"Rance," Kayley says softly. I feel her hand touch my shoulder, then caress my cheek. I lean into it, then open my eyes, blinking a few times to get the blurriness out. As I stare up at the ceiling, my vision adjusts and I see ornate decorations in the canopy above me—I'm not home, for sure. Even if my bed had a canopy, I'd never pick white marble-patterned curtains to hang over my head.

That repulsive pattern also reminds me of where I am: back at Grady's house. And it reminds me of the almost-fight that Kayley and I had last night. Neither of us wanted a confrontation, but everyone's emotions were running high, and our talk blew up again. It was worse because we were face to face, rather than on comm. We wound up talking it out, and then I must have crashed, bringing me to where I am now.

I turn towards Kayley. She's smiling down at me, already dressed. Her smile dissipates once our eyes connect. I gulp, trying to keep my nerves down. I hope she's not about to call me out on some dumb thing I said last night.

"Mr. Moreno called," she says. "The judge won't grant a transfer."

I close my eyes again, wishing that she didn't just deliver that unfortunate bit of news. Grady's dad might be in real trouble now. I'll still try to stay optimistic, even so. We might be worrying over nothing. His dad could just have a minor infection, like the doctor said.

"Okay." I sit up and run a hand through my hair. "Let's go figure this out."

"Hey, easy," Kayley says. "We're not in that big of a rush. Mr. Moreno is already going to a higher court for an appeal to the judge's decision. He's on it."

"Still, we've got work to do." I throw the covers off and start to get out of bed, but Kayley blocks me by sitting on my legs. She turns to face me, sliding her hands to my shoulders.

"We will, but first—" She leans in and touches her lips to mine, brushing them ever so gently across until they find the perfect spot. She presses them closer, holding them there as her hands come around to embrace me. As she pulls me to her, my own hands come up to hold her.

It feels like so long since we've had a superb kiss. I close my eyes, feeling her warm exhale as she does it again. I remember just how truly thankful I am to have her.

"What was that for?" I ask.

"Do I need a reason?" She smiles and pecks me on the lips before sliding down off the bed and offering me her hand. "Come on, breakfast is waiting."

The morning sun is just beginning to peek around the corner of the large bay window in the front of Grady's house. Its beam is a fine sliver of light that slices through the living room and strikes a photo of Grady's parents hanging from the wall. It's a scene from when they were young. They're standing behind one of their first large-scale design successes, an early star cruiser with Dr. Sugiyama's first try at an FTL engine. I smile, seeing them so full of pride as they are in that image.

I'm glad for the moment of respite because soon we're digging deep into the problem at hand. Even if Grady's dad is okay, we've still got to get them out. My father threw a bolt into our circuit board of success, so we're back to square one. After a good night's sleep, we're all energized and ready to take down our enemy. Only one problem—the current number of ideas we have is zero.

After our talk last night, I think I've given up on trying to get new photos. Kayley is right. Even after seven years, my father still knows me better than I think he does. They'll be better prepared for us if we try again. I still feel like I messed our best chance up by getting captured. Now whatever we choose is just going to be like old tech. It might work, or it might not. Either way, it won't be fast.

"We can kidnap Cecelia and hold her for ransom," Afton suggests, swinging her legs as she sits on the dining table.

"Um, no," Grady replies. "How is that going to help my parents?"

"No idea." Afton shrugs. "Just thought it would be fun."

"We can have fun later. Let's focus on ideas that will work." Kayley gets up from the table and paces around to the living room and back. I watch her as she folds her arms and bows her head, getting lost in thought. Some days when I look at her, it's like I'm seeing her for the first time, and the air goes out of me. I hope I can do that for the rest of my life. If only I—

"Rance!" Grady shouts. I spin to see him glaring at me. "Back on this planet, please?"

"Yeah." I shake my head to get the daydreams out. "Yeah, I'm here."

"Well, what do you think?"

"Think of?"

"Parrish's idea."

"Which is?"

Grady, Afton, and Parrish all moan. I look at the three of them, wondering what I missed and hoping it was good enough to repeat.

"Sorry, tell me again?"

"Alright." Parrish leans forward, elbows on knees. "So you know how Grady's parents said they did what they did for the good of the Empire?"

"Yeah?"

"So, what if we petitioned the Emperor for a pardon? I mean, we'd have to get some heavy influencers on our side, but his parents are bound to have supporters who believe they were unfairly convicted, right? People in the military, heads of planetary governments? Wouldn't those people that benefited from their work want to see them free?"

I consider his idea as I scratch the back of my neck. It's good, but when I get an itch like this, I know I'm missing something. He's right on all his points. Gather up a powerful group of people, and petition the Emperor to release them...the Emperor...

Oh, that's it.

"Sorry, dude." I sigh. "It's a great idea, save for one important point."

"What's that?" Parrish asks, blinking.

"It was the Emperor who commanded my father to take charge of the case."

Parrish's head drops. I feel bad for busting his bubble, but we wouldn't want to get halfway through a plan like that only to remember that small but critical detail. Plus, it would take a really long time to find, speak to, convince, and then organize whoever we find. And there it is. Old tech.

The doorbell chimes, and we all look in that direction. I raise an eyebrow at Grady. He shrugs and gets up to answer it.

"Well, we know it's not agents," I comment. "They'd be using the windows instead."

It's not agents at all. It's Doc Elizabeth with Original Teddy, BB1, and BB2. At least that's which blue buddies I think it is. We haven't spent enough time with them to know their quirks yet. Likely, thanks to Teddynet, the opposite is not true.

"Everyone well? Or as well as we can be?" Doc Elizabeth asks, giving greetings and hugs as she enters. The Teddys follow but stop in front of me.

"Healthy, yes," Parrish says. "Happy, no."

"Understandable." Doc Elizabeth pats him on the shoulder and takes a seat at the dining table next to him.

"Of course we're happy to see you all," Kayley says. "But you should have let us know you were coming. We could have at least prepared something. Water at the least."

Parrish and Afton take that as a hint to go get some glasses and a pitcher. We already cleared the table after breakfast, so other than Grady's laptop terminal, it's clean.

"Really?" Doc Elizabeth frowns. "The Teddys said you knew."

"Rancid is aware," Original Teddy says, and everyone turns to me.

"Yeah, I knew. I guess it just slipped my mind." I give a sheepish smile and shrug. But, wait a minute—it didn't slip my mind. I didn't know earlier. I'm certain of that. Yet, I also know that I knew they were coming. "No, wait...that can't be right."

"Information is accurate, Rancid. Recollection has been conveyed."

I blink at my fuzzy friend. His Common is getting better, but his collection of words isn't in an order that makes sense to me.

"Teddy," Kayley says, stepping up next to him. "Do you mean you told Rance over Teddy comm?"

"That is not accurate. Rancid is Teddy. Vocalization system is unrequired."

"Yeah, that's true." I nod.

"How do you know that?" Kayley looks at me, her forehead wrinkling.

"Don't we all know that?"

"No..." everyone replies at once.

"Oh, yeah," I say, nodding once again, but it's like I'm not in control of my body. "That's because I'm hooked into Teddynet."

"What did you just say?" Afton asks.

"What did I just say?"

"That you're connected to Teddynet," Kayley replies, watching me with a worried stare.

"That is accurate," Original Teddy says. He turns to click and whirr to his buddies, and they wave their arms in a motion that I've learned means agreement.

"Well, that makes sense," Doc Elizabeth says, and we all turn to her. "The nanobots that I put in him are capable of more than just aural communications. I just didn't think they'd work in a human."

"Wait, you used Rance as a test subject?" Kayley's eyes flash fire at the doc.

"He asked me to. For his leg, if you remember."

Kayley puts her palms to her temples and exhales slowly. It's a moment before she regains her calm.

"So let me get this straight. You put nanobots in Rance to fix his leg, but they also connected him to Teddynet? So he's connected to Teddynet from now on?"

"That is accurate," says Original Teddy.

Of course it is. I knew that...no. Hold on, I didn't know that! Is this how Teddynet works? Does that mean that if I can know stuff from the Teddys, they can know stuff from me? I start to ask, but then I answer the question in my head. Yes, they can. And there are only a few embarrassing things there. I can be thankful that the Teddys don't have the same sense of modesty as Angelicans. Then they'd be embarrassed for me. I bet they just learned what getting embarrassed is. No way to tell. Teddys don't blush.

"Hey." Afton taps me with her toe. "Finish your thoughts out loud, please. The rest of us humans would like to hear too."

"Sorry, it's like I'm having a conversation with someone else, only it's just my own internal voice."

"Does it hurt?" Kayley asks.

"No, but I'm wondering how long I've had this capability."

"Likely since the injection," Doc Elizabeth explains. "That's how it is for Teddys. But they get theirs just after birth."

My eyes go wide. I get a thought, and it's answered in a microsecond. I glance at Original Teddy, and I realize that's why they're here. They wanted to help me realize what was going on. I know it. I know that's what Original Teddy wanted to do.

"Holy Goddesses!" I jump up, my chair falling over from the force of my ascent.

"Rance? What is it? Are you okay?" Kayley rushes to me, fear in her eyes. She takes me by the shoulders and stares.

"Oh, yeah, I'm good." I grin at her and squeeze her tightly. "Fantastic, actually."

I wrap an arm around Kayley's shoulders and face the rest of the team with a big grin.

"Guys, we don't have to think of another plan anymore. We're going to stick with the original plan."

They just stare at me.

"Why?" Kayley asks.

"Because we still have the images...sort of. They're in Teddynet. Everything I experienced that night is. And Kayley's and my little run-in with Cecelia is there too."

"Will people believe them?" Parrish asks. "Like, won't they say we just faked them?"

"We don't care what people think," I reply with a smirk. "We only care what Cecelia and my father think, and they already know what they did. We show them proof, and we win."

"Rancid." Original Teddy drops a tentacle on my shoulder. "That is accurate."

Forty-one

"RANCE, CUT IT OUT." Kayley puts her hand on mine and stops the umbrella from shaking as we walk along the avenue that leads to my father's office.

I don't know why we even bothered with a rain cover. The misty vapor that floats in the air avoids the umbrella, landing on my face as if I'm not holding anything over our heads. We should have just stuck with water-repellant jerseys. Of course, that would require us having some. Our town doesn't get much rain, so when it does, we usually just let ourselves get soaked. But Kayley insisted we look presentable in front of my father when we blackmail him, so here we are.

I wonder how Original Teddy and his blue buddies are handling this, but I think rain doesn't bother them. Correction, I *know* rain doesn't bother them. I also *know* that there's rain on their home planet, and that just blows my mind. If I wanted to, I could know everything about them.

"Rance, pay attention. We're almost there. I'd prefer it if you weren't sliding through Teddynet when your father shows up."

"Okay, okay. I'm here. Not that I want to be."

Kayley slides her arm around mine. She pulls me closer, our bodies connecting. I'm glad Kayley is here to keep me in the moment. Otherwise, I'd just take the deep dive into Teddynet and likely not come out for a while. Between that and facing my father again, I'd much prefer the former.

I decide that taking in the surrounding sights is a good way to stay in the here and now. The avenue we stroll down is a lot more scenic than I had realized. The elm trees that line the opposite side of the street hang over the walkway and provide a bit of shelter for pedestrians. Their oval leaves are shiny, giving off an emerald glow along the avenue. If it weren't for the fact that I'm about to do something I would never, ever dream of doing, I might enjoy it.

Before I'm ready for it to happen, we arrive at the main entrance of my father's office building. I lean my head back and look all the way up. On the top floor is where my father is getting ready to put on his overcoat, and just like us, face the weather.

"Let's wait across the street," I say, grabbing at the collar of my shirt. "Maybe it's not a good idea to surprise him so quickly."

"Rance." She turns and faces me with a gentle smile. "We're doing the right thing. Think of Grady's parents. That should stop you freaking out so much."

Kayley doesn't need Teddynet to know what I'm thinking or feeling. She can just look at me and know it. That's because of how long we've known each other—it's like our own form of mind reading, and I'm glad for it.

"Hey, there he is." I spin her around to face her in his direction. He's distracted with some call on his Sergo as he steps over to the taxi stand. "Shoot, we've got to get him before he gets a taxi!"

Kayley and I forget about the rain and rush over to the taxi stand, intercepting him just in time. My father notices us, and he pauses mid-step.

"Rance." My father blinks and gets lost for words. That's better than him calling for us to be arrested.

"Dad, I need to talk to you."

"Of course." An air of hopeful expectation forms around him. "Did you want to go up to my office?"

"No," Kayley interjects. "We have a place."

My father frowns and stares at her. When he sees Kayley's firm look, his body goes rigid, and his hands come out of his pockets.

"What is this about?" he asks, his voice louder.

"Come with us, and you'll see." I lean forward, daring him with my glare. He takes a step back, glancing between the two of us.

"Rance, you're still my son, and I'm willing to speak with you any time, but I warn you. If you're planning something..."

The rain picks up, filling the street with a wash of sound. I lock eyes with my father, calculating the likelihood of him running. I bet that chance is pretty high at the moment. His eyes flicker between Kayley and me again, then he glances to the taxi stand and back to the building's entrance. There's a pair of armed guards there. All he would need to do is call out to them, and they'd be on Kayley and me before we could run. We thought of that, which is why the Teddys are just around the corner. That would only bring us to a stand-off, however.

I've got to do something that'll make him agree to come with us. Should I plead, or should I try a more aggressive tactic? As I look into my father's eyes, I'm reminded that the time for negotiation is long past. I reach into my jacket pocket and pull out my Sergo.

"You need to take a walk with us." I flick my Sergo open and display the first picture the Teddys pulled from my memory. "Or we're going to have to report this."

My father's jaw goes slack. His wide eyes dart between mine and the Sergo screen.

"How did—okay! Put that away, I'll talk with you. Just tell me where."

"Follow us."

Our spot is a secluded underpass not far away. A major thoroughfare crosses over one of the many canals in Bradbury, creating a scenic space that's part of a stroll path that runs along the canal. Although we're still in the capitol building district, this area is deserted, save for a few health-obsessed joggers who don't let a little water stop their marathon training.

The rain turns into a downpour just as we find a spot off the stroll path. The beating rhythm creates a mask of sound, just perfect for a conversation like this. Kayley and I stop and turn to face him, my father now looking more like a wounded animal than an apex predator.

"So, you followed us again, did you?" He shakes his head and sighs hard. "Rance, I warned you what would happen if you did that."

My father must think that the best defense is always a strong attack. He's never had to do anything but prosecute, so he's falling back on what he knows. If he's trying to intimidate me, it's not going to work this time.

"Nope, look again." I pull out my Sergo and show him the image once more. This time he gets a better look at it.

"That can't be real." He pulls back, stuffing his hands back into his pockets. Then he turns to Kayley. "Is this your doing? Did you put him up to this?"

Kayley throws a quick look at me and smirks. "Not at all."

"So then, what is this all about? You plan to ruin me? Is that it?" He seethes and turns away. "You won't. It's your word versus mine. Who will they believe?"

There's a flash of lightning, followed quickly by an oppressive rumble just beyond the ring of buildings that surrounds us. The wind blows the rain under the overpass and sprays us with a fine mist. We made it here just in time. I hope that goes for this conversation with my father, too.

"Depends upon who you mean by they." But before he can throw out another denial, I hold up a hand to stop him. "I don't want to ruin your life or your career. We only want one thing."

"And what is that?"

"Freedom for Tadao Sugiyama and Elenora O'Grady-Davies."

My father snorts.

"Impossible! They were tried and convicted. Fairly! The evidence was against them, and now they, like every other criminal, are serving their term in prison. If you think a few photos are going to get them free, you're even more naïve than I thought you were."

I tighten my jaw. I don't really know what I thought he would do when I came to face him. Just the thought of looking him in the eye again made me shaky. Maybe I was naïve to hope that once he saw the photos, he'd just be willing to do whatever we told him to.

He might be bluffing. It could very well be possible that he's got the power to do something here. Maybe not free them, but talk to someone who might.

"So is that all, then? Now that you've made your attempt, and failed because you didn't think things through, I expect that you'll be destroying those images and any copies. If you don't, I'm coming after both of you. I don't know how you've become such a failure, Rance, but I don't think I going to waste any more of my time with you."

He sighs through his teeth and turns to go. Kayley throws me a panicked glance, and my breathing gets tighter and faster. If we let him walk away, that's the end, for sure. I've got to do this.

"Not just yet...Dad."

He pivots on his heel and looks at me with narrowed eyes. His stare burns through the cold and wet, but I'm unaffected. My desire to get Grady's parents free is far stronger than any fear of judgment from my father.

"There's another person in these images, and I bet she won't be as reluctant to agree to do what we ask."

"Cecelia can't get them free, even if she wanted to!"

"That's right, she doesn't want them to go free because she plans to take over all military manufacture for the Empire. She needs them out of the way so her own people can take their place. One she's got that, then she's got control."

"A bit far-fetched, son. I bet you don't even have evidence of that." My father looks up at the concrete structure above us as if it's more interesting than what I have to say. He better listen to what I'm about to tell him because pretty soon, he'll be regretting all of it.

"Actually, we do," Kayley says.

That gets his attention. I smile at Kayley in thanks.

"We have evidence, and we have a video recording of her trying to cover it up," I add.

"Where did you get it from?"

"My own two eyes."

"I don't know what that means, but it whatever it is, it won't be accepted as evidence in court."

"We don't need a judge to accept it." Kayley starts tag-teaming with me.

"That's right. We only need Cecelia to believe it. And then she'll do whatever we ask," I add with a grin.

My father's mouth hangs open. Now he's taking us seriously. He presses his lips back into a more serious expression.

"So then, what are you asking?"

"Walk away from Cecelia," I say. "Let us investigate her and uncover evidence that will hold up in court. Then we'll appeal for Grady's parents' release."

"And if I don't?"

"Then Cecelia gets the same choice you have right now," Kayley says.

My father looks down, rubbing his chin. That's it—we've made our threat clear. If he doesn't go for it, it'll be a race to get to Cecelia first. Good thing we can win that one too. Though, if we have to take this to court, this could turn into a drawn-out slugfest, and Grady's parents could stay in prison while we set up appeal after appeal on limited evidence. I need to try my own appeal here.

"Dad, remember, all we really want is for the innocent to be free. Isn't that what you and I always dreamed about doing?"

He looks up at me, one side of his mouth curling upward. I even sense a bit of respect or pride coming from him. But the silence that hangs between us while I wait for his reply is even louder than the thunderstorm above our heads. He could easily tell us to go jump in the canal, and we'd have to scramble for a new way to approach him. Either that, or we make good on our threat, and ruin his life. That would be as good as drowning my father with my own hands. I'm not sure I'm ready to do that.

"Okay, fine," he says. "Cecelia's all yours. I didn't like her all that much, anyway. I'll walk away from her, then you can gather whatever evidence you think you're going to get. If it's legitimate, then I'll accept it into the record." He points a finger at me. "That doesn't mean they go free. Only the system gets to decide that. If you believe otherwise, then that's on you. Deal?"

I nod, clenching down on my teeth to stop myself from screaming elation into his face.

"Perhaps I misjudged you, Rance. Looks like you have what it takes, after all. Now, that doesn't mean I'm going to hire you. I'd be naïve to think that would be a good thing to do. Still, I'm impressed."

He turns away and raises a hand to wave at us. As he walks from under the overpass, he glances up at the sky. That's when I notice the rain has slowed—far from over, but getting lighter little by little.

"See you around, son."

<h1 style="text-align:center">Forty-two</h1>

"I THOUGHT WE WEREN'T coming here again?" Afton snorts and crouches down in front of the gate to Cecelia's house.

"That must have just been you dreaming," I reply. "You're welcome to go take a nap on the shuttle, and relive it if you want."

"And miss all the fun? Never."

The sky is nearing that wonderful moment when there's still just enough light to turn it a gorgeous shade of midnight blue, except it's still a few hours until midnight. It's my favorite time of day, where everything settles in for the night yet there's still motion about.

"Everyone ready?" Kayley asks.

"Remind me what we're doing here first," Afton replies.

"Are you kidding?"

I put a hand on Kayley's shoulder to stop her from ripping Afton's eyes out. Afton is likely just being her usual snarky self and doesn't need a reminder. For the sake of keeping the peace, I give her the benefit of the doubt—with a little snark of my own.

"The plan is twofold, oh Great Chu-nu. We sneak in, grab whatever we can from the basement stash, and then head upstairs to see if we can get Cecelia herself."

Grady snickers over Teddy comm. I'm glad someone else besides me has access to a handful of ancient words. I'm not sure if it came from my memory or something off Teddynet, but I'm glad I can tease Afton with something more than her first name.

"What makes you think we're going to capture her here? And what did you just call me?"

Grady and I both chuckle. I have no idea if Afton is really a virgin or not, but it was the first word that popped into my head that worked. That she has no idea of the word's meaning is even better than telling her.

"Grady, I will strangle you when we get back if you don't tell me now!"

"Drop it. We're on a mission." Kayley resumes control, and I'm happy to acquiesce. I've won the battle. Me, ten points. Surela, zip. "Parrish, you and the Teddys ready?"

"Yes, just say the word."

To create a bit of diversion, in case my father has already warned Cecelia that we were coming, we're going to cross over the gate in two different places. That will hopefully confuse the guards enough that at least one of our teams gets through. We've got Original Teddy, and Parrish has got the four blue buddies. So we're covered in case we need to popsicle a guard or two.

Kayley looks at me, her eyes full of serious intent. I acknowledge it with a nod. Message received—no fooling around. Cecelia won't be going easy on us this time. It's her company, her career, and her life on the line. She's not likely to give any of those up easily.

"Let's go."

We move fast, silently this time, and overwhelm the guards at each entrance before they even know what hit them. Their frozen stances might make the guards in the main office think their vid's busted. We're not waiting for that—this is a frontal assault. We'll popsicle everyone in the house if we have to.

Afton leads our team, sprinting towards the glass door at the back of the living room. We're just a few seconds behind, but she doesn't wait. A few strategically placed hits—as determined by Grady—and the glass crumbles to the ground. Afton checks to see where we are and then hops in.

I'm through next, followed by Kayley. Original Teddy wraps his tentacles around the door frame and flies through, avoiding the glass on his bare feet.

"Elevator!" Kayley hisses, and we head in that direction.

Good thing we've been here before. There's no concern about where to go. We just move as one, intent on our singular direction and our solitary purpose. We will get what we came for.

"We got the security office," Parrish says. "Only two guards there, but the alarm was tripped. Be careful."

"You too. Get to the basement. We're headed up," Kayley responds, nearly breathless. After Grady, she's the least active of the five of us. If we keep doing this kind of thing, that will change.

We're near the elevator when a guard jumps out with a shout. His weapon comes around but never makes it. One zap from Original Teddy, and he becomes a life-sized action figure.

"Grab his card!" Kayley orders, and Afton rifles through his pockets until she finds what she needs.

"Ugh, nasty." Afton hands me the card, pinched between her thumb and forefinger. When I grab it, I get the reason for her comment. It's warm, moist, and a little sticky. I use the nearest curtain to wipe it off, and I follow the others.

A quick swipe of the card at the elevator, and we're granted access. The four of us rush in…only to stand and wait for the elevator to lift us to the penthouse.

"Excursion has lost excitement," Original Teddy comments.

"Agreed, Teddy," I reply. "This part of the mission is lame."

That's only until the elevator chimes, and we all tense, not knowing what to expect on the other side. We tripped the alarm and they know we're here. Let's hope we're not about to walk into a hailstorm of gunfire.

The door opens and we drop to the floor, ready for anything. When nothing happens, we glance at each other and slide through into the hallway. No one confronts us out here, either.

"Teddy, come on!" I hiss. He's glancing around the elevator when the door chimes again. I dive and hold the door on one side, Afton on the other. It still takes him a moment to stroll through while the three humans are prone on the floor like three sneaky thieves in a cine.

Know what? We kinda are.

"Go slowly," Kayley whispers. "The elevator chime might have tipped her off."

"Or she could be asleep," Afton counters.

I peer ahead of us—the door to her office bedroom is closed, and there's no light from under the door. She could be asleep. Or…

It occurs to me we might just be three fools, sliding around on the carpet of Cecelia's hallway for no reason. Cecelia might not be here at all. That was the one piece of critical information we were missing. With limited time to beat my father to her, we had to choose where to go quickly.

"Try the door handle," Kayley whispers. Afton reaches up and pulls down on it. The door slides open with almost no sound. I'm impressed—only really expensive ones do that. Though, if I were the CEO of a multi-world corporation that built weapons, I might want noisier doors.

We slide into the near dark of the office and pause. The only light comes from a single blue dot, the status indicator of the air system.

Original Teddy takes the lead and continues into the bedroom, his eyes and ears much more capable with this lack of light and sound.

He waddles out of sight, and the three of us huddle close, awaiting his confirmation. It's so quiet that I can hear the air move. Kayley takes a breath, while Afton slowly exhales one. The air system wafts a newly cooled breeze down on us—it's very calming. If I weren't so edgy, I might close my eyes for a bit.

"Where is he?" Afton says into my ear. I'm wondering the same thing. It feels like he's been gone for ten minutes already. In this sensory-deficient environment, there's no way to tell just how long it's been. We left our Sergos in the shuttle so no one could track us here, but I wouldn't check it right now anyway for fear that the spotlight-bright screen would wake Cecelia up.

It's not warm in here, but I feel sweat forming on my brow. This is taking too long. I desperately want to call out to Original Teddy, but even a small bit of noise could alert Cecelia to our presence. I can only imagine what kind of defensive weaponry she might have tucked under her pillow.

Suddenly, the lights go on. I cry out as I'm blinded, and I throw my arms up across my face for protection. All I can think of as I brace myself for the attack is that we were idiots to think we could pull this off. Sorry, Grady.

No strike comes, and as my eyes adjust to the brightness, I see Original Teddy saunter out of the bedroom.

"Cecelia is unavailable," he says.

Afton, Kayley, and I slump into each other, our individual moans coming together to form a harmony of relief.

"Teddy! Why didn't you warn us you were about to turn the lights on?"

Original Teddy just makes a series of clicks that end in a whistle.

"You didn't think our eyes needed time to adjust?" I ask, though I already know the answer. He just uploaded it to Teddynet. One of these days, I'm going to learn how to do that.

"Parrish, you copy?" Kayley asks as she pushes herself up on one arm.

"I'm here. Did you get her?"

"No, she's not here. Tell me you're luckier than we are."

"Maybe. You guys should come down once you're done."

"Yeah, it's looking like we just might be."

"Wait," Afton says, leaning over the desk. "We should check her terminal. Maybe it's got her schedule or travel info on it."

I'm the first to scramble up next to her as she powers on the terminal. We stare at it as the unit runs through its boot routine. It takes longer than I expect, and I notice the unit is an older model. Even so, it's still better than anything I've ever put my hands on, much less owned.

A prompt comes up for a password. I expected that. Now we just have to get lucky, or we'll have to bring it back with us to get Grady to hack it for us.

Speaking of Grady.

"Hey, dude, any suggestions on what the password might be?"

"Try Benicio," Grady suggests in a casual tone.

"Not funny, dude. And I doubt that's it."

Afton tries it anyway.

"Big fat nope," Afton says, but then bites her lower lip and tilts her head. "But maybe not so far off. Let's try 'I love Benicio.'"

"You've got to be kidding."

As much as I want to get into this machine, I'm glad that's also not it.

"Try 'Benicio and Cecelia forever,'" Kayley suggests. I turn to her, my mouth open. She shrugs in a "it couldn't hurt" kind of way. I think it's going to scar me for life if that's it.

The terminal beeps, and a menu opens up, displaying a rather ordinary list of choices. What isn't ordinary is the flowery design that flows around the menu buttons, ending in a single yellow rose.

"Wow, that was it," Afton says and digs into the schedule. We lean in and watch as she scrolls through the timeline to get to the current dates.

"There!" Kayley points. "She's attending a conference on Littus."

"Great, I always wanted to go there." Afton turns to me, eyebrows raised. "Your mom made it look so fun."

I stare back at her, wondering if she even remembers that my mom was being held hostage when she was there. Sure, she *looked* like she was having a good time, but that's really not the point! Afton shouldn't be using my formerly kidnapped mother as a gauge to decide what's fun.

"Parrish, meet us at the gate, and bring whatever you found. We're going on holiday."

"Got it, I'm on my—wait, what?"

Forty-three

THE BLISTERING SUN, THE ocean breeze cooling down the sweaty bodies recreating on the beach, the salty smell of the water—we won't be enjoying any of these things. Our focus is our mission, and even though I look longingly at the soft white sand, I know that's not what we're here for.

Our target is a woman, and her name is Cecelia Nilsson-Lim.

We pad down the boardwalk, headed towards the only tall building in the vicinity. The Imperial Dusit Resort and Spa is a six-floor multi-acre facility built by the current Emperor, originally intended to entertain guests when he's on-planet. Since the Emperor is seldom on-planet, they opened it up for public use. It's extremely popular with the top brass, and I'm guessing that's why Cecelia is doing her presentation here. At least that's what Grady's net-diving came up with.

"Dude, do you see what you're missing?" I ask Grady.

"Sitting around on tiny bits of pulverized rock and shell is not my idea of a good time," Grady replies. "Besides, you don't get to enjoy it, either."

"No problem. I'm going to enjoy taking down this yellow floozy instead."

Afton bursts out laughing. I stop and turn around. Her face is turning red as she tries to control her laughter, though I don't think she's trying too hard.

"Oh, Rance," she says in between giggles. "You watch way too much cine!"

"What's wrong with that?"

"Do you really need me to explain just how corny that was?"

"Never mind." Kayley grabs me by the arm and tugs me along. "Mission focus, please."

As I get dragged, I throw Afton a side-eye glare. She's still holding her stomach and smiling to herself—so glad that I get to entertain her. I sometimes wonder what she would do for fun if I wasn't around. Perhaps pick on some other poor soul who couldn't retaliate in full because their girlfriend would wind up ripping their head off.

But Kayley's right. We're about to step into a major conference hall where there will be not a few security people. Which reminds me…

"Parrish, you and the Teddys in place?"

"Yeah. Good to go."

I feel a little bad about putting him with the Teddys again. He doesn't seem to mind, but even if he did, he'd never complain about it. Parrish has always been about what the team needs, which makes him so valuable. It doesn't matter if it's powerball or taking down the bad dudes. He does what the team needs him to do.

"Okay," Kayley says, "remember, passes clipped on, and move straight into the conference. We wait until she's done with her presentation, and then we grab her."

The conference hall is filled. Everyone from engineers to the military to a few members of Parliament are here. That's no surprise, and it even helps us remain anonymous. We're lucky we put on our best duds. They may not match the shine and polish of what the top dogs are wearing, but those people aren't about to get physical.

"Ladies and gentlemen, honored members of Parliament, please welcome the CEO of Jinse Shaloo Technology, the esteemed Cecelia Nilsson-Lim!"

The audience breaks into a vigorous round of applause as the lady in yellow herself strolls onto the stage, waving her hands. Once she arrives at the podium, the applause dies down. Cecelia places both hands on the podium and scans the room before she speaks.

"This better not take too long," Afton grumbles. "Teddy and I have a rematch planned."

The speech drags on, and after an hour of Cecelia spewing what sounds to me like utter nonsense, the three of us are ready to crash. I yawn and blink, glancing around the room. Half of the audience is right there with us, and I wonder if this was her plan all along.

"Heads up, guys," Parrish calls. "The stage manager just called for the next speaker."

"Okay, let's move up." Kayley presses on my lower back, moving me forward.

As we get to the edge of the stage and try to find an inconspicuous spot to launch our snatch 'n' grab, Cecelia finishes up to roaring applause.

It's strange to me she'd get that much of a response, but hey, I'm not here to judge her presentation skills. Maybe the audience is just happy her presentation's over.

"Here she comes," Afton whispers.

We tuck in behind a few autograph hopefuls as Cecelia walks towards the edge of the stage, getting ready to follow her backstage, where we'll make the grab. Safely behind secure lines, she'll be relaxed and unguarded. Parrish and his Teddy team will take care of any security.

Cecelia comes down the steps on the side of the stage, smiling widely as she greets her would-be fans. She shakes a few hands and signs a few tablets and souvenirs, all while attempting to make her way behind the stage.

"Get in behind this lieutenant," Kayley says, and we slip through the throng of people towards her. "And keep a watch on where she's looking."

It's a good thing that Cecelia's either had her head down or has been meeting the eyes of the people in front of her. That's allowed us to get within snatching distance. I keep my eyes trained on her face as Afton, and fiery-haired Kayley especially, keep hidden behind the backs of others.

I get an itch on the back of my neck as we slide closer. There are only two bodies between us and our target, and I grin. We made an excellent decision intercepting her here. She's completely oblivious to our presence.

Until she's not.

"You!" Cecelia's eyes open wide, and she backs away, shoving bodies between her and me.

"Shoot, she's spotted us!" I hiss and push after her as she dives through the backstage curtain. We break through the crowd and are hot on her tail.

A security guard spots us and holds up his hand—no way that's going to stop us. He remains in that position as we pass him by. Perfect. No one should notice for a little while.

"Thanks, Teddy," I say.

"Roger dodger," replies Original Teddy.

We rocket into the backstage area, pausing only to spot our prey. She's easy to find in her canary costume. Too bad for her she wore a color that contrasts strongly with backstage black.

Cecelia yelps as she spots us gaining on her. She darts down a side corridor that slopes down, her arms flailing about as she tries to keep her balance.

"Give it up! No one's gonna save you!" I shout after her.

Her face is full of panic as she rounds a bend and jets back towards the stage. She's headed under it, for what reason, I don't know. She's making our task easier by trapping herself.

"Parrish, block the stage-right stairs. She's headed down!" Kayley yells.

"Okay! Which side is stage right?"

"The one you're on!"

We hit the bottom of the ramp and enter the darkness beneath the stage. As my eyes adjust, my sense of smell takes over. I catch a whiff of old solvents and the scent of new electronics. Somebody must have moved something down here recently.

Kayley raises an arm and holds us up. We've lost her for the moment, but no way she's getting past us.

"Spread out," Kayley whispers.

Afton goes left and I go right, my senses hyperactive, searching for any sound or hint of movement. I spot a collection of backdrops leaning on each other. I'll bet that's where she is.

I get up on the tips of my boots and advance towards the side of the backdrops. There's a small, dark space behind the last one where it leans against the wall. I wish I had a light, but my presence might just be enough to spook her out.

If she were there, but she's not.

There are two more spaces that look like obvious places to hide. I check those but find nothing.

I glance back towards Kayley and Afton, making them out by the sliver of light that comes down the ramp and the stairwell on the other side. They've nearly covered their areas, and soon we'll be coming up short, with Cecelia nowhere to be found.

The sudden whine of machinery catches me off guard, and I spin towards the sound. Light radiates out of a cubby space I didn't see before. I charge towards it, knowing it's got to be her.

The light is coming from a tall rectangular object, but it's strange. It ripples, with the crest of the wave radiating with specular intensity. The rest is a translucent sheet, but there's illumination on the other side. It's like I can see farther inside of it than should be possible—as if there's a tunnel or a corridor there. It's beautiful and mysterious, and for a moment I forget why I charged over here.

Cecelia bursts out from behind the object, plowing into me and knocking me back into a stack of cardboard boxes. Idiot! Why did I let myself get hypnotized by a bunch of pretty lights?

"Hey! She's here!"

She turns a panicked glance towards me and grasps for the railing, but she misses. Her foot slips on the edge of the stairs and she drops to her knees. Cecelia spins around to face me, her arms pressed behind her. Afton and Kayley join me as I confront her. Kayley makes a quick call to Parrish to let him know the good news and make sure nobody comes down. Afton has other, more aggressive things on her mind.

"You better not try to hurt me! You remember what happened last time!" Cecelia cries.

"Oh, we most certainly do," I say, smirking. "We'll never forget that."

"But we won't hurt you," Kayley adds, her steely eyes narrowing. "Not if you give us what we want."

"What?" Cecelia tries to push herself up, but her shoe comes off, and she falls back again. "What is it you want?"

"Justice," I reply. "And with it, we're going to free Grady's parents."

"Sorry, who?"

I sigh. Why can't everyone just know him as Grady?

"You know exactly who we're talking about," Afton snarls. "Don't make me beat it out of you!"

Cecelia flinches and throws an arm across her face. When no pummeling comes, she lowers it slightly, peering over her forearm.

"What makes you think I can get them free?"

"Because you're holding the one bit of evidence we need to prove their innocence," Kayley says, placing her hands on her hips. "The design files. You're going to tell us where they are, and you're going to tell us now."

"Or else!" Afton jumps at her, and Cecelia cries out.

"Okay, okay! Just don't hurt me! Please!" She sits up and dusts herself off, throwing me a hurt look. "You've already ruined my personal life, did you know that? Isn't that enough for you?"

"You've hurt us and people we care about, so no."

"Fine." Cecelia sighs and reaches her hand out. "Help me up, and I'll tell you where they are. Not that I think they'll help you. The Emperor has already decided he doesn't like Tadao and Elenora anymore."

Yes! We're nearly there! Of course, we didn't mention we're also going to use those files and the vid from the lab to get her accused of treason. I feel a little bad about that, so I step forward and take her hand to pull her up.

Cecelia flies up and shoves me into Kayley. I knock her down, and we both land hard on the floor.

"Ha! Sucker!" Cecelia barks a cry of joy and sprints towards the cubby with the light coming from it. Afton tries to give chase, but she's got to climb over me to do it. It delays her, and she shouts out a curse.

Kayley and I scramble up and dash towards the source of the light. Cecelia is nowhere in sight. We search every nook and cranny, but it's like she just disappeared.

Maybe she did.

Forty-four

I LOOK AT THE box with the rippling light, and I feel a tightness form in my stomach. That device—it's got to be a device—has something to do with her instant disappearance. I approach it, giving it a thorough examination from all angles so Grady can have a solid idea of what it looks like.

"Hey, Grady, what do you think it is?"

"Not sure, but I'm intrigued."

"I bet I know," Kayley says. "It's a quantum portal, and Cecelia just went through it."

Afton and I whirl around to see her sporting a huge grin. She's so confident she's right that even Grady is amazed.

"How in the universe do you know that?" he asks.

"Because." Kayley raises a flirtatious eyebrow and points at the device behind us. "She lost her other shoe right before she went through."

Sure enough, there's Cecelia's yellow pump, propped up against the bottom of the device. With that piece of evidence, there's no doubt in my mind now that she went through it. Somehow.

"Parry, get down here. Cecelia's escaped the building," Kayley says. "We think she's gone through this device, but we're—"

"Already behind you."

Kayley's eyes widen, and she turns. Parrish gives her a small smile, and I wish I could see her reaction. Instead, I get surrounded by Teddys as they move past me and head towards the device. As they surround it, they click and whirr between themselves at a level of excitement that I've never heard from them before.

"Hey, careful, we don't know how that thing operates!" I say.

"Nonsense," Original Teddy says and steps right through the light. I jolt towards him as a cry of disbelief gets caught in my throat. For a second, his pink fuzz is still visible behind the sheet of light, then he's gone.

One by one, the blue buddies follow until all of them have disappeared. My mouth hangs open. I'm struggling to find words or even questions.

"Afton, don't!" Kayley cries.

"What?" Afton glances back at us, with one foot already through the portal. "The Teddys did it."

And she's gone.

"Well, I guess we're doing this," Parrish says, jogging up to the device. "Here we go!"

I turn to Kayley. Her stunned face stares back at me. Again, we share the same thought—are we really going to do this? Everyone else did, but that's not a reason for us to follow. Who knows what, if anything, is on the other side? What if Cecelia tricked us and didn't go through at all?

With a tight grip on Kayley's hand, I go through.

Whatever happens is instantaneous. One moment we were underneath a stage on the planet Littus, and the next, we're standing in an enormous warehouse. The trussed roof must be ten stories high, and the walls stretch out around us at stadium-sized distances. None of that, however, is as impressive as the many rows of black, rectangular devices lined up before us. Some are operational, while others appear to be in the process of construction.

"What the heck is this?" I ask.

"Forget it for now. Let's find the others," Kayley responds.

Despite the size of the place, we find someone quickly. Only it's not one of our friends. An armed guard stalks down the next aisle, hunting someone or something. His weapon is aimed and ready for action. Nope. We're not going that way.

Kayley spins me, and we slip down another aisle.

"Rance, there she is!" Kayley hisses. It's easy to see Cecelia's canary suit against a backdrop of dark gray machines. She's turned sideways to us, peering through to another aisle. "Let's get her!"

We break into a flat-out charge, hoping that we get to her before she notices us.

It's a terrible choice.

She spots us as we're about to pounce. But we didn't spot her gun. She turns and takes aim. It's only though fast thinking that I grab Kayley and we dive through the nearest device.

We land hard on the other side—back under the stage on Littus. At least I think it is. Everything seems the same. It even smells the same.

But I don't have any more time than that to confirm. Not far away from us stands a pair of Cecelia's burly men. They're as startled as we are, except they recover faster.

"You!" one shouts. He doesn't look happy. "I'm gonna mangle you so good you ain't never gonna walk again!"

It's Kayley's turn to give me a shove. Her feet find my hips, and she thrusts hard. I fly backward, straight through the portal, and land on my butt back on the other side. I only have a second to react as Kayley dives head-first into me. I catch her as she lands on me, knocking me flat on my back

A gasp comes from my right, and I spin my head. Cecelia's standing here, mouth open. It's not the best position for someone to catch us in, much less someone who wants to burn plasma through our skulls.

I take advantage of the moment, grab Kayley's wrist and tug her through to the next aisle. We rocket down it, trying to put as much distance as possible between us and them before we find a hiding spot.

"They went that way!" Cecelia cries as we escape. Those two muscle-heads must have come through the device after us. Great. Now there's three of them chasing us. What happened to us capturing her?

I glance back to make sure they're not behind us, and it's a mistake. Afton jumps out of a device right in front of us and we all collide. I flip over and land on my back, the air blowing out of my lungs.

"Rance!" Kayley cries, her hands running over me, looking for some kind of wound. I try my best to signal that I can't breathe, but she's not getting it.

A flurry of plasma flies over our heads. Kayley looks up, her eyes going wide. So much for hiding.

"Grab him, let's go!" Afton shouts, tugging Kayley after her. Kayley reaches out to me, and I her. But our grasp breaks when the two of them disappear into a device.

Shoot, now I'm on my own.

I push myself over, my breath returning. Cecelia and her bodyguards are racing towards me, guns out. They fire, and I bury my face in the ground. Their shots get closer, impacting a device just behind me and blowing sparks over my head. I'm glad that they're not good shots at a run.

I need to get up, or one of their shots is going to get lucky. With a weapon like that, they only need to hit me once.

"All aboard!" A voice like a Teddy shouts.

It's Original Teddy and Parrish! They break through a portal and snatch me up, and then we're all moving through to the next aisle and into another device.

Cold hits my face, and suddenly the three of us are skidding. Parrish cries out and falls, digging his feet into the snow and ice underneath us. I'm still moving forward—I look down, and the ground disappears beneath my feet. I cry out as I feel myself falling. My arms flail for a handhold. There's nothing, and I wonder if this is my end.

Tentacles wrap around my ankles, and Parrish's hands grab my waist. They rip me backwards, and a second later I'm back on snowy ground.

"Who the hell programmed this one in?" I shout into the foggy mist. Still, I'm happy not to be plummeting to my death right now.

"Exactly. Let's get back. It's freezing here!" Parrish says, helping me to my feet.

As we exit the portal, we drop and check our surroundings. Original Teddy waddles over to the side of the device and stares at it.

"Teddy, what are you looking at?"

His answer is to indicate a small screen on the side of the device. It lists coordinates, but then there's a named location, planet, and city underneath it. As we check the others around us, we see that most read a single planet—Magnarapax.

"So, we're in one of her factories. I wonder if the Emperor knows she's got operational portals."

A plasma round flies past my head, cutting off any more conversation. Another hits a device to my right. We take cover, but those shots weren't aimed at us. That's when I hear it. A full-on firefight is happening a few rows over.

"Break a leg," Original Teddy says and takes off, cutting in between the rows to head right towards the battle. At least I know why. Teddynet is online now, and I understand he's going to help his buddies.

"Come on," I say to Parrish. "The other Teddys are over there. They need help!"

"And what are we going to do?"

We follow Original Teddy as best we can, careful not to get our feet caught in the cable troughs that run behind the rows of devices. I let Parrish go first. He's faster and more agile.

"How many are there?" Parrish asks as we duck down behind a unit.

"Five, I think. Including those two tough guys. That's what Teddynet is telling me."

I peek my head into the row to get a better idea of where everyone is. The four blue buddies are swinging and bouncing off the devices to get closer to their attackers, but the rapid pulses of the plasma rifles are keeping them at bay. Cecelia's men are hiding behind the devices in the row and trying to knock off the Teddys one by one as they make their attempt to cut the distance between them.

Suddenly there's a squeal, and one of the blue buddies crashes to the ground, lifeless. My brain goes blank. I'm not sure if it's Teddynet causing my shock or if it's really me reacting to what I just saw. I feel a welling up in my throat, and tears come to my eyes.

"Is...is he dead?" Parish asks.

"Yeah." I can't believe it myself. I never expected one of them to be killed. They're Teddys. They don't die, right? Don't be naïve, Rance. I swallow hard and steel my emotions. "We're not letting any others die!"

Rifle fire rails into a nearby device, sending sparks everywhere. We duck and cover our heads, but I feel something hot land on my back, and I squirm to get it off. Smoke is filling our area as the struck device catches fire.

"What can we do?" Parrish says, glancing at the burning device. The acrid smell it gives off stings our eyes and noses. Carbon structural material—strong, but not all that heavy. As I put a hand on a device, I get an idea.

"Try to better the odds."

I instruct Parrish to follow my lead. We put our feet up on the side of a device and our backs low on the one next to it. We press on the device, lifting the edge up with our feet, then releasing to rock it back and forth.

The attackers gain confidence and increase their fire. One of them throws a hand bomb. It explodes across the way. Carbon splinters and small dagger-like bits impale themselves into the surrounding devices. Parrish and I flatten ourselves to the ground, avoiding most, but a few pieces get us.

"Ready?" Our destabilized device rocks towards us at such an angle, it almost touches the one next to it. I wait until it swings back the other way, and then I yell out, "Now!"

With all our might, we shove, toppling the device. It tips and hits the next one, which tips into the next, creating a chain reaction that picks up speed down the row. A pair of cries mix with the rumble of the device train. Not enough to kill, but enough to take them out of the fight.

The shooting stops, and I slide my head into the aisle again. One guard lies facedown in the aisle, his legs trapped under the toppled devices. The two burly men sling their weapons and lift the units to free their companion while the other guard keeps watch on the aisle.

"Hey, we're going to create a quick diversion," I whisper to Parrish, who nods. "After I go, wait a few seconds and follow."

I take a breath, realizing I'm about to make myself a moving target. Let's hope that guy down there can't aim well. With as much speed as I've got in me, I jump out and run across to the other side, sliding behind a portal unit.

"Haha!" I cry. "Missed me!"

Parrish flies across, using his athletic skill to find an off moment to move. The plasma burst that follows after him is late by almost a full second.

"You totally suck!" I yell. "I hope Cecelia fires you for being such a loser!"

"Haha yourself!" the guard calls back. "I killed your blue friend, and I'm going to kill you, too! You've got no weapons, or you would have fired back already. Now watch out, because here I come to finish the job!"

Well, he's right about that. Took him a while to figure it out, though. He comes out of his hiding spot and walks down the aisle, a heavy sneer on his face. He'll be on us in a second and have us to point-blank rights.

That's when the Teddys strike.

He gets popsicled mid-step and tips over, crashing to the floor like an antique statue. The two burly men freeze in the middle of lifting a device. They tip forward, weighed down by the unit, and smash their faces into the side of it.

A high-pitched whirring sound comes from the Teddys—their war cry of sorts, if Teddys have a war cry. I sigh deeply and get up, walking towards the deceased Teddy. We've won, but not without cost. I didn't know this Teddy all that well, but his memories are all in Teddynet for me to view someday.

As I watch the Teddys circle around their lost buddy, I begin to wonder about how much they've sacrificed for us. Them, an alien race, full of more compassion and empathy for us than most of our own race has for itself.

I'm so deep in thought, I miss the gun that fires off until I'm lying on my back, propped up against the side of a portal unit. My shoulder burns something fierce, as if a red-hot metal spear has run it through.

Cecelia grins down at me. She must have exited a nearby device and spotted me. Shoot. I can't believe I was stupid enough to let my guard down like that. Now this is real trouble.

"All of you, back off! Unless you want to see me put a big hole in his head!" Cecelia waves her pistol back and forth. "And stay where I can see you."

"Do as she says, Teddy. You too, Parrish. I'll be alright," I say, which is hardly true.

"Alright? I doubt that," Cecelia says with a smirk. "You've lost, kid...but, I'll make you a deal. You and your friends agree to keep your mouths shut about everything, including this little warehouse space, and I'll agree not to kill you."

"You mean, the Emperor doesn't know about these devices?"

"The Emperor is a looney bird! He couldn't rule a puddle of mud! The Chamberlin runs the Empire, and he wants *me* to be the sole supplier to the military. So that's the—"

Cecelia frowns and peers at me as I feel the side of my mouth curl up.

"What the hell do you have to smile at?"

"Cecelia, I feel sorry for you."

"What? Why?"

"Because you don't have amazing friends like I do," I say, and point behind her.

Cecelia reels around to find Kayley and Afton there. Afton's fist is so fast, Cecelia doesn't have time to react. A second later, she's on the ground, weaponless. Afton squats down next to her, her face a solid mask.

"That was for Rance." Afton rubs her fist in her hand. "And this is for Grady and his parents."

Cecelia yelps before Afton knocks her out. Although the woman shot me, I hope she didn't get hurt badly. Her life sentence is going to be punishment enough.

I catch Kayley's worried look and smile to lessen her concern. It's a bit of a lie. The wound in my shoulder is agonizing. It's hard to keep my eyes open, but as she rushes past the unconscious Cecelia to me, I realize I don't need to anymore.

Everything is going to be alright.

Forty-five

As I RECOVER IN the hospital, Kayley keeps me updated on how the appeal is going for Grady's parents. Everyone does, really. My father even sent me a get-well bouquet, though I had the nurse throw it out when I found out it was from him. I kept the card he sent with it...for evidence.

It said:

Here's to your speedy recovery. See you on the battlefield.

—Dad

On the day of my release, everyone, including the Teddys, comes to pick me up. My mom was going to come too, but she decided to let my buds on their own. The last time she came to visit, we had a long talk about my father. It was then that she told me she had no worries about my future. I had become the person she always thought I could be.

Mom scolded me for putting myself in harm's way, though. I guess she wouldn't be a mom if she didn't do that.

"Thank you, Mr. Moreno," Grady says on his Sergo as we head out the door. "Yes...yes, sir...and really, thank you. You have done an awesome job for my parents and me....Of course I understand. It's the best we could hope for, right?"

"What happened, dude?" I ask as Parrish pushes me in a hoverchair—I don't need it, but apparently, it's standard procedure. "What did he say?"

"Give him a chance," Kayley says, putting a hand on my arm. "He hasn't even signed off yet."

We all stare expectantly at him. Once Grady pockets his Sergo, he notices and glances around with his forehead in wrinkles.

"Well?" Afton says. "You keeping it a secret for some reason?"

"No..." Grady frowns deeper and his shoulders slump. "Yeah, so Mr. Moreno said, no way to get a full pardon unless the Emperor gives it, and he's not likely to do that…something about 'keeping his image untarnished.' Like I care about that."

"Was there more?" I ask. "There had to be more, right?"

"Yeah, the prosecution agreed to the evidence that we supplied—the lab videos, the files that were marked with headers from Jinse Shaloo, and even that Cecelia attacked you—but they wouldn't accept the Teddy stuff that had her confession on it. Even though it sounded exactly like her."

"So? Does she go to jail?" Parrish asks.

"Forget her!" Afton shoots back. "What about your parents?"

"Their sentence was reduced to three years, and my father was granted a temporary stay at an outside hospital until he's better. We can see him there."

"Dude! That's great!" I say. "Why are you still looking so bummed out?"

Grady shrugs and looks down.

"Is it because you've got another three years before they're home?" Kayley asks.

"Dude," I say. "You can see them anytime. Sure, they're not home, but when were they ever home that much?"

"Yeah, I know. It's not so much that. I can manage on my own."

"Look at that!" Afton says. "Grady's growing up!"

Grady curls the side of his mouth up at Afton's tease. It's a small happiness for him, and I agree with Afton. Grady has grown up a bit. But something deeper is bothering him. I can see it in his face.

"But?" I tilt my head at him. Then shake his arm when he doesn't respond. "Come on, dude, don't make us rip it out of you."

"Well, now that the trial and stuff is all over, you guys are going to be going back to your own homes, right?"

So that's it. He's sad that we're not all going to be there anymore, which is far from the truth, of course. Yes, I'll be sleeping in my own bed from here on out. I've been neglecting my house and my mom. She's totally capable of doing everything, of course, but it's my responsibility too. Not that I won't miss all of us crashing together at Grady's place.

Parrish answers first. "I have to. I've got to look after my mom. She hasn't been feeling well lately. But I'll come stop by as much as possible, you know?"

"I do, dude," Grady nods. "Thanks for cooking for me all the time."

"Anything for you, dude."

So that's two of us. I glance at Kayley. She's watching Grady with a bit of regret in her eyes. Kayley is torn, wanting to help Grady, but also wanting to take care of me. At least, that's what I'm hoping she wants to do. Still, if she decided to look after him for a while, I wouldn't object. My shoulder still needs to heal. But once I'm back to full functionality, I might just choose to be a little selfish for once. Kayley and I haven't had all that much alone time lately. It would be great for our relationship if we could steal some.

"Hey dude," I begin. "You know you're always welcome at my place for as long as you want. You know my mom adores you, right?"

"Yeah." That gets his mouth curving up even more. Grady has always had a surrogate mom in my mother. I can see him dreaming about freshly made congee every morning. It's more than that, obviously. A big house like his isn't a good place for one person to spend much time by themselves. I'm sure he'll dig back into designing as his main time-suck and forget about the world for a while, but he's going to miss us in those quiet moments.

"Sorry, Grady," Kayley says, looking at me. "I'm going to have my hands full for a bit, going back and forth between houses."

Yes! I'm trying to hold my excitement in as best as I can, as I don't want to make him feel worse, but I am over the moon that Kayley's going to be taking care of me. I could try to drag out my recovery for a while, though I expect she'll catch on, eventually.

We arrive at the shuttle. Doc Elizabeth and Original Teddy are waiting at the bottom of the ramp. The doc wants to make sure that the hacks at the hospital didn't make my shoulder worse and plans to check me out personally. With Kayley overseeing the entire examination, in case Doc Elizabeth tries to inject me with more nanobots.

I've wanted to share my condolences with the Teddys, but when I reach out to Teddynet, I don't get any sense of sorrow or loss. Perhaps it's because so much of Blue Buddy Three is there. I found out that he was originally in navigation, and he was really curious about Grady and me right from the start—he was there when we first arrived on board. I also found out that he was born on the Teddy homeworld and that, despite Teddynet, he missed being there. I guess we all give up something to live our dreams.

"How you feeling, Rance?" Doc Elizabeth asks.

"Good as original!" Original Teddy says, interpreting my thoughts. I've got to remember to ask him not to do that. Though, I wonder if remembering to ask him is as good as telling him.

"I think you mean 'good as new,' Teddy," she says.

"That is accurate."

"Mmm, well." Doc Elizabeth chews on her lower lip. "I think I might just check you out to be sure, anyway, yeah?"

I look at Kayley for help. The idea of any more needles, medicines, or procedures on my body is not a pleasant thought at all. But instead of giving the doc some kind of warning, she just pats my hand and smiles. Now I'm completely confused. Is there some kind of conspiracy going on here?

"So, Mr. Grady, all's well with you, too?" Doc Elizabeth folds her arms and watches him. "No more nightmares?"

"Not at all," Grady replies. "I'm good."

"Then why the sad face?"

Kayley explains what we've been chatting about, and the doc nods with understanding.

"Well, you could always stay on the ship. You've got your own berth, just like everyone else. Don't forget how special that is. Teddys don't have their own."

I could correct the doc by saying their society doesn't have the concept of personal ownership. But they do understand it, of course. That's how the humans got their own quarters, though we fuzzyless animals have special needs, anyway.

"Thanks, but I've got a house I need to look after," Grady says and takes a deep breath. It's got to kill him to say that. Honestly, I'm really impressed by his new level of maturity. The old Grady would have gone in an instant with that kind of invitation.

"I'll stay," Afton says. I turn to her, realizing that she's the only one who hadn't confirmed anything yet. I also realize that she's been quiet since we started talking about it. Has she been considering what she'd do this whole time?

"Really?" Grady looks at her, hopeful but likely also preparing for an Afton tease, should it come.

"Well, if you don't mind, that is." Afton drops her gaze, and I suddenly understand why she's offering. When Afton told her mother that she was leaving, she meant for good.

"Mind?" Grady blinks at her.

"I mean, I'd be staying there kinda long-term." It's not often we get to see Afton in full-on modest mode, and it's sincere. "So I don't want to...you know..."

Grady charges at her like a child who just got the best gift ever—in some ways, he just did. His arms go flying under hers and around her back, squeezing Afton into a gigantic hug.

"Hey! No, wait!" Her arms fly up, and her eyes get big as she tries to maneuver with her new Grady attachment. "Not so tight!"

But Grady doesn't let go. If anything, he redoubles his embrace of her until she gives in and wraps her own arms around him.

"Okay, okay," Afton says in a gentle voice, stroking Grady's mop-top as they hug each other. I chuckle a little, even though it hurts a little to do so. I'm glad they've both found a solution to their needs. And while the two of them sharing a house is likely going to be more awkward than when I asked Parrish for permission to date Kayley, it's also going to be good for both of them.

At least, until Grady's parents find out.

About the Author

Marc B. DeGeorge has made every attempt in his adult life to maintain a balance between how much science and how much art he dabbles in. Sometimes, he's even successful. When he was young, he wanted to be an astronaut, and then an aeronautical engineer—he even went to Space Camp! But then he learned how to play guitar and his space dreams took a back seat. He spent a decade playing professionally in bands and studying music in college (university only took five years). These days, things have come round full circle, and Marc envisions the future by writing books that imagine what challenges humanity may face, and what we might accomplish together.

When Marc isn't writing, he performs traditional Japanese music on shamisen and writes, shoots, and edits performing arts photos and documentaries under the MuseMarc Studio name.